"Hello, anyone here?"

"Yes, I'm here." Grayson heard the voice at the same time he saw the woman standing there, facing the door he had just entered, holding a pair of scissors threateningly toward him. "But you can go now."

He aimed the light toward her eyes, hoping to blind her enough to stop menacing him. And then he blinked at the same time she did—but for a different reason.

He recognized her.

At least he thought he did. It was Savannah Oliver— but if so, this Savannah didn't exactly look like the woman he'd seen at the various parties and fund-raisers he'd been dragged to by his Colton siblings, silently kicking and screaming, though he'd gone along anyway because...well, they were his brothers and sisters.

And now he had a good idea who had disappeared from the back of the prison van: the woman before him, still aiming scissor blades at him.

* * *

Book 4 of The Coltons of Mustang Valley

* * *

**If you're on Twitter, tell us what you think of Harlequin Romantic Suspense!
#harlequinromsuspense**

Dear Reader,

Here is my second book in the wonderful, long-running Colton series.

Colton First Responder is book number four in the new twelve-book Coltons of Mustang Valley miniseries, which involves a large family in which a secret is brought to light.

Colton First Responder features Grayson Colton, the third child of patriarch Payne Colton; he chooses not to get too close to his family members. Instead of working for Colton Oil or spending much time at Rattlesnake Ridge Ranch, he began his own company of first responders who help in emergencies. When a major earthquake occurs in Cactus Creek, Grayson tries to find survivors—which is how he meets Savannah Oliver. The earthquake allowed her to escape from the van returning her to prison after a court appearance gone bad, since she's accused of murdering her husband. She asserts her innocence and Grayson believes her... but should he? Still, together, they search for the truth.

I hope you enjoy *Colton First Responder*. Please come visit me at my website, lindaojohnston.com, and at my weekly blog, killerhobbies.Blogspot.com. And, yes, I'm on Facebook, too.

Linda O. Johnston

COLTON FIRST RESPONDER

Linda O. Johnston

HARLEQUIN
ROMANTIC
SUSPENSE

Special thanks and acknowledgment are given to
Linda O. Johnston for her contribution to
The Coltons of Mustang Valley miniseries.

Recycling programs
for this product may
not exist in your area.

ISBN-13: 978-1-335-62641-7

Colton First Responder

Copyright © 2020 by Harlequin Books S.A.

For questions and comments about the quality of this book, please contact us at CustomerService@Harlequin.com.

Harlequin Enterprises ULC
22 Adelaide St. West, 40th Floor
Toronto, Ontario M5H 4E3, Canada
www.Harlequin.com

Printed in U.S.A.

Linda O. Johnston loves to write. While honing her writing skills, she worked in advertising and public relations, then became a lawyer...and enjoyed writing contracts. Linda's first published fiction appeared in *Ellery Queen's Mystery Magazine* and won a Robert L. Fish Memorial Award for Best First Mystery Short Story of the Year. Linda now spends most of her time creating memorable tales of paranormal romance, romantic suspense and mystery. Visit her on the web at www.lindaojohnston.com.

Books by Linda O. Johnston

Harlequin Romantic Suspense

The Coltons of Mustang Valley
Colton First Responder

Colton 911
Colton 911: Caught in the Crossfire

K-9 Ranch Rescue
Second Chance Soldier
Trained to Protect

Undercover Soldier
Covert Attraction

Harlequin Nocturne

Alpha Force
Alpha Wolf
Alaskan Wolf
Guardian Wolf
Undercover Wolf
Loyal Wolf
Canadian Wolf
Protector Wolf

Back to Life

Visit the Author Profile page at Harlequin.com for more titles.

And yes, again and as always, this story is dedicated to my dear husband, Fred. I also want to thank all the other authors in this enjoyable series, as well as Carly Silver, our wonderful editor for the Colton books.

Chapter 1

No.

The word kept reverberating through Savannah Oliver's mind, and not only now. It had done so for days. Even longer.

That wasn't surprising. This couldn't be happening.

But of course she knew it was.

She looked around the bland—yet terrifying—enclosed back area of the ugly transport van that was returning her to the Arizona Prison Complex in Phoenix. From where she sat strapped onto a bench—not particularly for her safety—with her back against the partition leading to the driver's area, she glanced up toward the high, wire-meshed rear windows of the van. No way could she get out of the vehicle through those and onto the rural road, in the middle of nowhere, that they now traversed. The windows were too small—and besides, cuffs kept her hands shackled together behind her.

She couldn't brush any of her hair away from her face. It was shoulder length and blond—and disheveled, she assumed, as it so often was these days. She couldn't even secure it with one of the pretty hair clips she loved.

She couldn't brush away any tears, either, but fortunately those had nearly stopped—though they threatened to begin again any moment.

Without meaning to, she looked down at her legs as she sat there—and nearly smiled in irony. At least she had been allowed to dress in brown slacks and a beige shirt for this outing, instead of the bright orange prison jumpsuit that was her usual attire these days. Her shoes were the same ones she wore every day now—casual black slip-ons.

She had just been in court. Not only had she been arraigned, but she had been denied bail. She would remain in prison—and not just the local jail because of the severity of her alleged crime—until her trial, and who knew when that would be?

But did it matter? Her lawyer, Ian Wright, had promised he'd try for bail, but he had warned her in advance that it was unlikely. She had already been labeled a flight risk, and the charges against her were serious. Very serious.

He had also told her that, notwithstanding the solid defense he would mount for her, she was likely to be convicted.

Now she sat on one of the few seats in this area of the van as it continued forward, attempting futilely once more to pull her hands out of the cuffs.

Wishing she had some way to get out of there, even

if it involved somehow shoving open one of those windows and squeezing through. Better yet, if she could open one of the doors where the windows were located, and leap down onto the road.

Of course, she'd get badly injured, or worse.

But what could be worse than being incarcerated, possibly forever, for a crime she didn't commit?

A crime that might not have been committed at all, since no body had been found.

She was accused of murdering her ex-husband, Zane Oliver. Good old Zane.

Horrible, disgusting, appalling Zane.

His body hadn't been found, and she felt certain he wasn't really dead.

No, more likely he was hanging out somewhere, laughing at setting her up this way. He'd learn about this hearing, confirm that she wasn't permitted bail. And he'd smile and smile…

She needed to get her mind off this somehow. She needed a shoulder to cry on, but for the moment, at least, she was all alone.

Except for the driver in the cab of the van. He'd been the same one who'd driven her to court.

His name was Ari. They'd been introduced as she was led into the van at the prison and strapped in before heading to the courthouse. Not that he'd said a word to her then. He was young and skinny, with dark hair and a constant frown, dressed in a police uniform.

Of course they'd send a cop to ensure that vicious, murderous Savannah wouldn't harm anyone else.

She cringed at the irony her own mind presented.

Outside the courthouse, all Ari had done was to open the back door and unhook her when they'd arrived. Then he'd handed her over to another uniformed cop, who had led her inside to the courtroom where her attorney waited, as did the District Attorney, Karly Fitzpatrick. She'd been shown where to sit—as if that was a surprise. Right up front, facing the judge. The procedure had gone forward, with its terrible result, not even any bail, and she had been led back outside, handcuffed again and strapped once more into this van.

Ari had acknowledged her only with a nod of his head.

But now—well, she could at least try to get his attention. She turned as much as she could to face the closed window that led into the van's cab.

"Ari?" she called. "Ari, I know we're still a distance from the prison, and…well, I have a bit of an emergency back here."

She had many emergencies, but she was making up the one she would tell him about.

He didn't respond, or at least she didn't hear him.

"Ari, could we please stop at a gas station or something? I really need to use the restroom."

She concentrated to hear beyond the vehicle's rumble and the road noise beneath it in case Ari was mumbling, but she heard nothing.

Not that she was surprised. Even if she did have that kind of emergency, he probably wouldn't care. She'd either have to tough it out or just go—

Bam!

The van shook horribly at the same time Savannah experienced a shocking, deafening sound that lasted several seconds, maybe the loudest noise she had ever heard. She screamed, wishing yet again that her hands were free, this time so she could cover her ears.

Better yet, she wished she could use them to brace herself, since the van was careening from side to side. She hurtled back and forth despite being strapped in. She had to protect herself.

What had happened? What was that noise? Why hadn't the van stopped? Had it hit something? Had something hit it?

But no. The vehicle skidded and finally stopped with Savannah still attached to the seat, and even then the ground continued to shake beneath it.

Noises of other kinds abounded, too—as if trees were thudding to the ground. Savannah added to the noise, calling for help, unsure what to do.

She hadn't wanted to return to prison—but was she instead going to die?

She finally realized the likely source of the shaking, the bumping and the sounds.

An earthquake.

No time to think about it—though she'd been in a few smaller quakes and tremors here in Arizona. She hadn't had her life endangered then.

And now—what could she do?

Before any ideas came to her, the worst noise and movement of all occurred—a smashing metallic sound, abrupt. The van had hit something…hard. Or been hit. Something must have crashed down onto the front of the stopped van, behind where Savannah now lay sideways on the bench, her back sore from where it had hit the partition.

She screamed for help again. But she realized in a moment that one good thing—maybe—had come out of it. Her seat belt had loosened.

The van finally stopped moving. Whatever had happened, it remained upright. And Savannah tried to stand, wondering if the vehicle would begin shifting again.

Slowly, crouching, ignoring her soreness, which was fortunately not too bad, she made her way to the door. She had to go backward. The only way she had a chance of opening that door would be to use her hands, and they remained cuffed behind her.

At least the van wasn't moving any longer. She thought about calling out to Ari again but decided to wait, to try to get outside and find him, and maybe they could get to safety together.

Better yet, maybe she could somehow sneak away.

She wished she could see better. But the fact that the evening was already growing darker didn't help. Even so, she managed to find the door with her bound hands behind her, as well as the handle on one side that opened it. Was it locked from the outside? She hoped not.

She pushed down the handle—and the door opened! She felt like shouting in triumph, but this was only a small step in the right direction.

Speaking of steps, could she find the ones at the back of the van and get down without falling? She wouldn't be able to hold on with her hands behind her.

She shoved the door open as well as she could, still moving backward, then very slowly lowered her right leg till her foot touched a step. She glanced down but could see very little in the darkness. She carefully allowed her left foot to join the right one, and then remained on that step for a few seconds, half expecting the ground to roll again beneath her—or for Ari to show up and shove her back inside.

Neither happened. And after a short while she went down to the next step. The one below that was the ground, and she soon stood there, outside the van, breathing fast and allowing herself to smile, if only a little.

She had beaten one hurdle but there could be plenty more to follow.

She turned and looked at the road behind her. It was narrow, and there was some light shining on it from a few dim electric streetlights spaced long distances apart, probably put there for safety since the road was so rural.

Yikes. It seemed amazing that any of the light poles had survived. Most of the trees around there hadn't. Uprooted, they splayed onto the concrete, and one even blocked part of the road.

Had it been one of them that hit the van? Savannah assumed so, so she started walking carefully around the vehicle on the driver's side.

Sure enough, a large tree had obliterated that part of the cab, crushing the car from the hood all the way to the passenger area. Savannah swallowed hard as she drew closer, looking at the smashed area where Ari had sat to drive.

How amazing that the tree had only crushed the front of the van, and not where she had been sitting. Despite all that had been happening to her, she had actually experienced a little bit of luck.

But what about Ari? Had he been hit by the tree?

She hoped he'd had time to slide over to the other side, assuming it was less destroyed.

As she got closer, she even called out his name. "Ari? Ari, are you okay?"

She heard nothing—and as she got to the huge tree branch that stuck out past the crumpled van door, she managed to look inside.

And backed up fast.

Ari was there…what was left of him. She couldn't see everything with those branches there, but she did see part of his body. What she could make out was covered with blood.

She gasped. "Ari?" she said again. No response. No movement. Since the window was broken, she made herself turn and carefully reach inside, her hands still behind her, and managed to touch Ari's neck. No indication of a pulse—and considering what he looked like, she knew he was dead.

She felt tears stream down her face. Okay, she hadn't liked the guy, and he clearly had felt no compassion toward her. It wasn't his job to give a damn about her. But no matter who he was, she didn't wish this on anyone.

She moved away—but what could she do now? She had only the slightest idea where they were, since she really didn't know the route from the courthouse to the prison, and this was way off in the middle of nowhere.

And even if she wasn't hit by a falling tree, how long could she survive out here in the elements, after an awful earthquake—and unable to free or use her hands?

Ari had secured her in the back of the van, remembering to check her handcuffs before they'd left. Was there any possibility he'd kept the keys?

Surely so. He'd need to unlock the cuffs when they reached the prison. Of course there might be a separate set there, but just in case he had one, she moved toward the passenger side of the van's front cab, going around the back of the truck since the tree blocked her from the front.

As she walked, she listened. No more loud sounds like those caused by the quake but there were plenty of calls of animals and birds in the surrounding area. No sound of other vehicles—or people—that she could hear.

Nothing else suggesting further tremors—or worse. At least not at the moment.

Reaching the passenger door, she turned around and used her bound hands to try to open it.

Success!

And amazingly, there was a key ring attached to the console between the two seats. Not only that, but there was a small leather suitcase on the floor—and it had her name on it. She'd seen it before. It contained some of her personal possessions that the cops had seized upon her arrest and kept at the prison—and would have been given back to her in the event she was released from court that day.

Well, that hadn't happened, but those were still her things.

She tried not to look at Ari any more than she had to as she entered the van—although she did see his bleeding arm and grasped his wrist, again hoping for some sign of life, but there was none. She then turned so she could grab the keys. She got out and laid the keys on the seat. Contorting with a lot of effort, she tried to unlock the cuffs.

No luck, damn it. Not at first, at least. But somehow she managed to succeed after five minutes of trying over and over.

There! She shook her hands free and dropped the cuffs on the ground. She wouldn't need them and didn't want to see them ever again. Next, she grabbed her bag from the floor.

She couldn't help glancing once more at Ari. He hadn't moved. No surprise.

"I'm so sorry, Ari," she said, meaning it. He'd just been doing his job—and that probably included ignoring requests and pleas from suspects he was transporting.

She looked around at what she could see of the road, the surrounding forest, the downed trees and more. She still had no idea where she was—but she nevertheless got moving, running for her life.

She was free! At least for now. And somehow, she needed to use this opportunity to clear her name, though she'd no idea how yet.

She only knew she had to find her rat of an ex. Unless he'd actually stayed around this area and had been killed in the quake.

Under other circumstances, she would cheer at that idea—but she had to find him, to make him confess to his lies, so she would be able to show the world that she was no murderer, no matter how much she detested the creep.

So now she ran into the vaguely illuminated night, carrying her bag, having no idea where she was going— but hoping she would find some kind of shelter...and somehow survive.

After the initial earthquake more than an hour ago, Grayson Colton had foreseen that the drive along this rural yet usually well-traveled road leading out of Mustang Valley, Arizona, would be a battle against nature. But after his initial assistance and communications, he had chosen this part of town and beyond to search for people who needed help after the highly disturbing tremors the area had experienced.

And was still experiencing to some extent, since the ground continued to rock now and then with aftershocks.

Grayson slowly drove his specially equipped company SUV along what was left of the road as well as he could, avoiding, where possible, the cracks and cavities in the formerly well-paved surface—as well as some downed trees. It was dark out, so his headlights helped him see what he was coming up against. So did the few but helpful lights on remaining poles along the roadside.

That moderate quake, reported so far as 5.9 in magnitude, had been centered around here, so he had taken it upon himself to head this way. He knew what he was doing—although his staff members did, too, or they wouldn't be working for him.

Right now, he had to traverse what was left of this minor highway as best he could. It was who he was, his responsibility, his calling.

And more. He had founded, and continued to run, First Hand First Responders. His small but significant agency employed dedicated first responders who assisted official responders in the police and fire departments, hospitals and other formal emergency organizations in Mustang Valley. And FHFR members helped out often, since the authorized organizations were understaffed in this area.

Grayson had been at his company headquarters when the quake struck that evening. Not much damage had been done to the three-story building he owned in town, fortunately, although the walls had swayed around him and some items on top of desks and shelves had been thrown to the floor.

Calls and police radio communications had immediately started coming in to the office from the Mustang Valley Police Department, including its primary 911 dispatcher and other agencies.

Apparently the structures housing the police and fire departments and even the local hospital hadn't been damaged significantly, a good thing. Same thing with local schools, from what he'd heard. But quite a few buildings in town had suffered damage, sometimes significant, particularly in older areas. As had a bunch of homes,

And who knew what people were out and about and might be in danger?

That took first responders to find out. And the authorities who called had requested their help—extensively and immediately.

Grayson's staff included an emergency medical technician, EMT—Norah Fellini—as well as Pedro Perez, a former firefighter, and Chad Eilbert, a former K-9 cop. Eilbert also had an emergency responder background, and just happened to still have his well-trained search and rescue dog Winchell as his partner.

They'd all been in the FHFR offices, too, when the help requests had started coming in. He'd given them their assignments based on what he'd heard from the official departments' representatives regarding suspicions of where injuries, missing persons and fires were most threatening, primarily in city areas that were not close to downtown, and therefore most in need of attention from extra first responders.

They had all driven off in their vehicles similar to his, containing special equipment such as defibrillators to help to save people's lives. Pedro had a portable fire hose with a pump system in his vehicle. And Chad also had special safety equipment for Winchell.

Then Grayson had made some calls himself. Fortunately, the exclusive, upscale Colton property, Rattlesnake Ridge Ranch—where he still lived most of the time with his large family, including parents and siblings—had been spared any damage.

He'd thrown on his bright neon green first responder vest over his long-sleeved T-shirt and heavily pocketed black pants.

Then he had dashed out, entered his vehicle and spent some time checking on some of the hardest hit areas outside downtown, where he had helped several people out of buildings destroyed by the quake. Fortunately, other firefighters had also shown up there.

That allowed him to head briefly toward one of his favorite spots, an abandoned bunker he had adopted as his own when he was a kid trying to find some privacy from his family. It wasn't far from the family ranch, and like many similar places in this area, it was also an abandoned mineshaft. No one else seemed to know about it, and he'd been able to fix it up over time to be less of a mine and more of a livable hideout. He had headed there now because it was important to him and he wanted to check on its condition. And fortunately, it had completely survived the quake.

Next, he had chosen to head to this area far out of town. He'd begun his career as a wilderness guide. He would be much more skilled in locating and helping people injured out here by the quake than the rest of his staff.

So here he was in his vehicle, glad he'd continued throughout his life to work out intensely and often. With all the potential for disasters way out here, he might need even more strength today to follow his chosen path.

Leaving town along the main streets of Mustang Valley had been interesting. Lots of people out on the sidewalks. Lots of damage visible to some downtown buildings, though, fortunately, none seemed to have been destroyed. The pavement there appeared more wrecked than anything else. No deaths around there, fortunately, and no fires in this area, either.

Grayson had stopped once to help a mother holding her young child cross a damaged street to EMTs and an ambulance. He stopped another time to help a teen catch his fleeing dog.

After that, Grayson kept going out of town, avoiding cracks in the road as best he could.

So far, on this rural road, he hadn't seen much of interest except many downed trees, which sometimes meant he had to ignore what was left of the pavement and drive on the leaf-strewn ground as well as he could. He had seen no recent indication of anyone, either on the road or the roadside, requiring a first responder's assistance.

He decided to proceed for another ten minutes, and if no situation he needed to deal with materialized, he'd check in then with his employees to determine where he should go next to be of the most help.

The road turned to the right a bit, so he did, too. And then he saw what he'd been after but had hoped not to see: a van crushed by a large tree that had fallen on its front. At least that was what it appeared to be as he approached it from behind. In fact, the road was effectively blocked by the black van and the felled tree.

"Okay, what's happened here?" Grayson said out loud, pulling his SUV to the side and parking. He got out quickly, grabbing the medical bag he kept on the floor. He had earned his EMT certification, so he knew how to conduct more than the basics of on-site medical care that could be necessary to save a life.

He also grabbed his large flashlight and used it first to check the ground as he approached the driver's door of the van. He saw, as he got close, that the vehicle's markings labeled it as belonging to the Arizona State Department of Corrections, the kind of van used to transport prisoners from one place to another.

If so—well, first things first. He needed to make sure everyone had gotten out of the vehicle's cab safely.

Only…that wasn't the case. In the bright glow of his flashlight, he immediately saw a man in what was left of the driver's seat, covered in blood.

Grayson's EMT training immediately kicked into gear. He opened the door carefully and checked to see if he could remove the injured person from where he lay after disconnecting his seat belt, without having to get the tree off the van.

Fortunately, he was able to.

Unfortunately, after he gently laid the victim on the ground and began checking for vital signs, he found none. He nevertheless ran into his van and got the defibrillator, but still no response.

Even so, he yanked his phone from his pocket.

"911," said a female voice nearly immediately. "What's your emergency?"

Grayson identified himself and quickly explained the situation, including the fact that he believed the person he'd found to be dead.

"But in case I'm wrong—"

"We'll get someone there as fast as we can under the circumstances, Grayson," the operator, Betty, said. "I promise."

"Fast" turned out to be about half an hour. Grayson couldn't complain, particularly given the fact that there were likely to be a huge number of 911 calls that evening. Meanwhile, he attempted further CPR on the van driver—to no avail.

An ambulance eventually appeared. The EMTs in it—two guys he'd met before—took over for Grayson, but their conclusion was the same as his.

"We'll take him to Mustang Valley General," Sid said, while the other guy, Kurt, hooked the victim up to an IV. Necessary? Grayson doubted it, but hoped the man really was still alive.

"Thanks," Grayson said. "Keep me informed about how things go." Or not. Did he really want to hear that he was right, that the falling tree had killed the man?

Might as well, he figured.

He took a few photos on his phone of the fallen tree and ruined van. And as the ambulance took off, he looked around further.

He had already checked out the back of the van earlier, as he waited. The door was open, and there was no one inside.

Did the open door mean someone had been incarcerated inside? Maybe.

He'd walked around before the ambulance arrived and hadn't seen any sign of someone else injured—or worse. But he felt obligated to check a bit farther now, just in case.

At least he knew that ambulances were currently available, if necessary. But had there been someone inside the van's rear area? Someone this now-deceased driver had been transporting? If so, was he or she okay?

Grayson was not a cop. If whoever it was needed to be captured again, that wasn't his job, although he could notify the Mustang Valley PD if he found him or her—most likely his sort-of best buddy there, Detective PJ Doherty; his brother Rafe's fiancée, Detective Kerry Wilder; or even his cousin, Sergeant Spencer Colton. Though all were undoubtedly swamped right now.

But if anyone had been inside the van and was now hurt and out there somewhere in the forest, injured and needing help—well, that was something Grayson intended to find out. He would remain careful, though. Anyone who had been in the back of that van was most likely a criminal and could be dangerous.

Chapter 2

Sitting on a wooden kitchen chair in the remote and damaged cabin she had somehow found here in the middle of nowhere, Savannah breathed slowly, carefully—pensively, for that was what she was doing: thinking, while staring at her hands clasped in her lap.

Her unshackled hands.

Where was she? She didn't know. For the moment, at least, it didn't matter.

So far, the earthquake had somehow brought her good luck. There'd been a couple of aftershocks from the quake, but they'd been mild.

Oh, she certainly hadn't wished Ari the kind of harm he had suffered, notwithstanding the way he'd essentially ignored her. But at least she was free, for now and hopefully forever.

Especially if she could find her louse of an ex and prove she hadn't murdered him.

But first things first. Tonight, she had at least located someplace to sleep, to bide her time till she decided what to do next. To ponder how to fulfill her promise to herself: find Zane, reveal his lies and treachery to the world, and return to as normal a life as she could.

A cabin. She'd never have imagined there could be one way out here in the woods. She had hardly been able to see anything once she'd left the place where the van had been smashed. Frightened, yet determined to survive, she'd needed to figure out what came next.

She'd heard a lot of animal noises around her and had nearly stumbled into a nearby lake before she'd found the cabin.

Eventually, the moon—only a half moon—had appeared overhead and provided at least a small amount of light.

And somehow, miraculously, it had helped her find this cabin. Lots of miracles, in fact, despite the fact that a portion of the cabin had crumbled because of the earthquake. But what was left seemed at least somewhat habitable.

In the undamaged area, the door was locked, but she had pushed open a window and climbed inside. None of the switches turned on any light, so she found herself in near total darkness, with no electricity, evidently. That was thanks to the quake, or thanks to the owner's turning it off before leaving. But she had nevertheless located a flashlight someone had left on one of the counters.

Who and where was the owner? Were they coming back soon? That appeared unlikely, considering the location and the earthquake, but who knew?

Fortunately, she had at least found no indication that anyone was living here now. Looking around with the flashlight's illumination, she had seen some dust here and there, but some of it could have been caused by the quake.

However, it seemed a nice enough cabin. There was even some furniture—a kitchen table surrounded by other chairs like the one she now sat on. A bed at the far side of the room with sheets on it. If she removed the sheets and turned them over, they should be clean enough for her to sleep on.

Assuming she found herself eventually calm enough to fall sleep. Exhaustion wouldn't help her accomplish what she needed to do tomorrow.

But she also couldn't forget that she was a fugitive. Once the van was found without her, she had no doubt that the authorities would be searching for her. She would have to remain careful.

For a better idea of her current environment, she unlocked the door and walked outside, using the flashlight to look around. She aimed it carefully, mostly toward the ground, although she had no reason to believe any other people were close enough to see the light. A narrow dirt road that ended at this house hadn't been affected by the caving in of part of the cabin.

Where did it lead? Maybe she would find out tomorrow.

She also looked at the area at the back of the house that was crumbled. Fortunately, it still provided a wall of sorts, a barrier, so no person or wild animal would be able to enter that way.

For now, she went back inside. One thing she had to do was to find some water and food. Was there anything like that in this deserted cabin? If she found anything, would she dare to eat or drink it, or might it make her sick?

Well, first things first. She would at least look around a bit more. She stood up again and, using the flashlight, walked along the wooden floor, making as little noise as possible—not that she anticipated anyone was close enough to hear her footsteps. She first looked at the inside of the partially caved-in wall and the part of the cabin that had suffered some damage. She wasn't certain what had been there—a storage area, maybe. But the rest of the place seemed fairly livable.

Next, she headed toward a kitchen with a sink and cabinets.

The door of the first cabinet creaked a bit as she opened it. All that was inside were some light green plastic plates and bowls.

She closed that door and tried another. A little better. There were some cans in it, of soup and corn and black beans. Yeah! Assuming she could find a can opener, she might be able to get both sustenance and a bit of liquid in her from one of those. She pulled out the vegetable soup, figuring it would potentially be the most nutritious. Since beggars couldn't be choosers, she considered not even checking the expiration date stamped on the bottom of the can—but it probably would be better for her to know, if it was out of date, by how much.

Making herself ill after her escape wouldn't be a good idea.

Still standing there by the cabinet above the sink, she moved the flashlight to examine the bottom of the can more closely.

And smiled. It had plenty of time left before its expiration date. That suggested people had used this cabin recently, but she remained glad they weren't there now.

Okay. Now she needed to find that can opener, plus a spoon. She aimed the flashlight toward the areas on both sides of the sink, seeing drawers there.

The first drawer she opened had some gadgets in it, including a spatula, whisk—and, yes, a can opener and scissors.

Scissors. One of the things she could do to change her appearance was to cut her hair, make it a lot shorter than its current shoulder length. People who didn't know her might not recognize her—since she was now on the run.

She had already gone inside the bathroom after her arrival and had noticed a mirror over the sink there. Now, scissors in hand, she hurried back across the wooden floor in that direction.

Was this too impulsive, especially in the darkness? The flashlight helped, but it wasn't very bright. Sure, it might be a dumb thing to do, but achieving anything to alter her appearance even a little couldn't hurt.

And so, after regarding herself and her current hairstyle in the mirror, she started snipping. Then snipped some more, creating short bangs, cutting her hair everywhere she could see, everywhere she could reach.

When she was done a few minutes later, she shook her head and laughed, just a little. Who was that waif with a chin-length haircut staring at her in the mirror?

Surely that couldn't be Savannah Oliver, right?

And actually, she wasn't an Oliver anymore. Zane and she were recently divorced, but, partly thanks to his disappearance and its consequences, she hadn't yet legally returned to using her maiden name, Murphy. First on her list of places to go would be the DMV, where she could get a new driver's license.

Someday.

For now, she used her hands to gather as much of her hair from the sink and floor as she could and placed it in a small pile on the floor near the wall. Once it was light out again, she would need to find a plastic bag or wastebasket to dump it in and hide it. No need to leave evidence of her changed looks if anyone searching for her found this place.

Okay, now she was finally ready to eat, and to drink what she could from the can she chose. She exited the bathroom and returned to the kitchen.

Before opening the soup, though, she went looking for bottled water. The refrigerator was turned off, but she found a few bottles of water inside.

Yes! Savannah took one out and closed the door.

She opened the can of soup while standing near the sink, pulled a spoon out of another drawer after looking around again and sat down at the kitchen table.

Even cold, the vegetable soup tasted good. She ate it slowly, savoring it, continuing to see in the near darkness thanks to the glow of the flashlight, and keeping the scissors with her, too, in case she felt compelled to cut even more hair off. She'd check in the mirror again once daylight arrived, to see if additional trimming was necessary to even it out.

And as much as she hated to think about it, the scissors could also become a weapon if she was attacked by anyone looking for her, or even a looter or wild animal, out here in the middle of nowhere.

As she ate, she felt exhaustion closing in. And no wonder. It had been one heck of a difficult yet promising day. She'd go to sleep after this. What would tomorrow bring?

She finished soon and stood, waving the flashlight again toward where she presumed the garbage can would be. And—

What was that? A sound from outside—a scraping, maybe, from the front yard.

Had she imagined it? It could just be something moving after the quake....

She moved slightly to face a window near the front door—and saw light. Not moonlight, but a glow that could have come from a flashlight, only more heavy-duty than hers, since the light was really bright.

Had the cabin owners come back here now, in the middle of the night after an earthquake?

Or—might the van have been found, and any authorities sent out to find her?

Savannah looked hurriedly around, attempting to find something to use as cover but wound up staying where she was.

Had she locked the door behind her when she had ventured outside? Damn. She didn't believe she had, since she had intended to peek out again.

She clasped the handle of the scissors tightly. If necessary, she could—and would—defend herself.

His search had actually led to someone.

Grayson hadn't really believed he would find anyone out here in the middle of the night and this far out from town. It was his mission to continue to seek people in trouble after the earthquake, including whoever had left the back of the van, if anyone. Whether or not a criminal, any person in that position could have been injured.

Still, if someone had been inside that vehicle and got-ten out—well, it was a van from the prison department, so Grayson did not forget his promise to himself to be careful. He didn't want to lose his own life attempting to save someone else, especially someone who was dan-gerous and didn't want to be found.

After the EMTs had taken away the deceased driver, he'd continued to look, finding no one else on the road or in the woods on his way here. He had reached a cabin, one of his last potential locations to scout before heading home. He had figured this cabin or another one nearby would be a logical place for anyone in trouble to seek out. It was a fishing cabin owned by one of the fami-lies in Mustang Valley. There was a small lake nearby, fed by a stream.

At first glance there seemed to be no one present, but he'd stopped to check. Especially when he thought he had seen a moving light through a window.

Using his own bright light to look around, he noticed that one side of the cabin, maybe a quarter of the whole structure, looked nearly destroyed. Would anyone re-ally have gone inside?

Maybe, if they were injured or desperate. He had to find out.

Slowly, carefully, still using his own light to be sure he saw anything, he approached.

First, though, he knocked on the front door before testing to see if it was unlocked. It was. He pushed it and called as he walked inside, "Hello, anyone here?"

"Yes, I'm here." He heard the voice at the same time he saw a woman standing there, facing the door he had just entered, holding a pair of scissors threateningly. "But you can go now."

He aimed the light toward her eyes, hoping to blind her enough to stop menacing him. And then he blinked at the same time she did—but for a different reason.

He recognized her.

At least he thought he did. She was Savannah Oliver—but if so, this Savannah didn't look exactly like the woman he'd seen at the various parties and fund-raisers he'd been dragged to by his Colton siblings, silently kicking and screaming, though he'd gone along anyway because...well, they were his brothers and sisters.

And now he had a good idea who had disappeared from the back of the prison van: she stood before him, still aiming scissor blades toward him.

Her hair was a lot shorter than he'd seen it before. Even so, or maybe even because of it, she was one beautiful, sexy woman.

A woman he'd avoided feeling attracted to. After all, she was married—no, she had been married—to one of the biggest investment bankers in Arizona, Zane Oliver.

The husband she'd recently been accused of murdering.

"Hello, Savannah," he said calmly. He wasn't armed, had no weapon with him—and wouldn't have used it on her even if he had.

For one thing, he had heard about her arrest, the charges against her, in the news. But he hadn't believed them.

"Hello, Grayson," she said without moving the scissors—except that her slender arm, in its long-sleeved beige shirt, was trembling a bit. "What are you doing here?"

"I could ask you the same thing, although I can guess. You're running away, right?"

She didn't answer directly but said, "And I assume you're doing your first responder thing out here after the quake. Well, if you're looking for people to help, you don't need to worry about me."

"That's good, but—"

"But what? Should I make you stay here?" She waved the scissors toward him, but the expression on her face appeared more desperate than threatening.

Under other circumstances, he might have liked the idea of staying overnight in a deserted cabin with a woman as lovely as Savannah. But she was a fugitive, accused of murdering her ex-husband. And at the moment, another earthquake could hit at any time.

"No thanks," he said.

"But—I don't think I'd better let you leave. I mean, well—you own that first responder company, right?"

"First Hand First Responders," he said. "That's right."

"So if I let you leave here—you'll just go tell your cop friends or associates that you found me. Or—you're not going to try to bring me with you now, are you?" She suddenly appeared panicked.

And why not? She didn't know, no matter what he'd said, that he wasn't carrying a gun or other weapon.

He glanced around what he could see of the cabin in the light he carried. It looked like—well, a regular fishing cabin, except for the area destroyed by the earthquake.

And Savannah? She wasn't in any kind of jail garb, but everyday clothes of a light-colored shirt over darker slacks. Maybe he was wrong about her.

And maybe not.

"Look, Savannah," he said. "If what I've heard about you is true, then I can understand why you feel threatened by my being here."

"I assume you heard the worst about me," she said. "And—well, I didn't kill my ex-husband." Looking at him for a reaction, she raised her hand with the scissors even more. He just stayed calm, nodding his head. "I can't let you arrest me."

Grayson shook his head. "Let me tell you right now that I'm only the kind of first responder who tries to help people in trouble, both medically and otherwise. I don't attempt to arrest anyone, or anything like that."

"But you can get in touch with those who do," she retorted.

"But I won't," he said. "Look, why don't we sit down over there." He gestured toward the kitchen table across the room where she had apparently been sitting and eating. "I'll tell you what I've heard about you—and how much of it I believe. Which isn't much."

"Really?" Her eyes widened. And even in the light he carried, he could see their lovely greenness glowing, even as her blond eyebrows narrowed in apparent disbelief.

Yeah, she was definitely good-looking—and he'd better be careful. He didn't want to get too interested in her.

He might not intend to turn her in, but neither did he intend to try helping an accused murderer escape justice.

Did he?

"Really," he said. But she still didn't appear convinced. And why should she? "Hey, I see you have a bottle of water over there. I assume a place like this doesn't have anything stronger, so is there any more?"

"Yes, in the refrigerator, though it's not cold." She still looked and sounded wary.

"That's fine. I'll go get a bottle for me, then sit down over there." He gestured toward the table. "Then we'll talk, okay?"

"Do I have a choice?" Her voice sounded hoarse and he wished he could say something more to reassure her. But what?

"Not really," he said with a grin. "Only, I'm really not such a bad guy. Honest."

"Honest?" she repeated. "Hah." But when he looked at her, still standing not far from him, her posture seemed at least a little more relaxed. "Okay, let's give this a try," she said.

"Great. I'll go get my water." And Grayson headed to the refrigerator.

Oh, yes, he intended to talk with her. Maybe get her side of the story, since she had asserted her innocence.

And he didn't think it was just their unusual circumstances at the moment that made him want to believe in her.

Chapter 3

Savannah lowered the scissors as she watched Grayson get water from the refrigerator, then sit down. He placed the bottle in front of him beside his large flashlight.

What should she do? What could she do? She hoped he was telling the truth, that even as a first responder he wasn't here to arrest her again, or call those in authority at the police station who'd bring her in. But even if he lied, she wasn't really going to stab him. The best she could do would be to run out the door when he wasn't looking, then continue running—in the near darkness. But where?

For now she would just remain alert and wary and hold a conversation. If he'd been telling the truth before, maybe it would be okay to talk with him.

But even then, when he was ready to go—well, would

she be able to trust him not to turn her in, no matter what he said?

She would just have to see how things went.

Not that she could control them anyway. At least not entirely.

"So tell me what happened," Grayson said as she sat down facing him, gently placing the scissors on the table before her but within reach. "Tell me how the van was struck and how you got out of it. I assume you're aware the driver was killed."

Savannah nodded solemnly. "Yes. His name was Ari. I... I didn't know him well, but I did check on him when I finally got out of the van and...and...well, I'm not an expert like a first responder, but I tried to help him and didn't see any sign of life." She felt herself tear up. Well, she truly was sad about the situation.

Grayson. She had seen him at parties and social events now and then. They were from similar backgrounds, since their families were both among the Mustang Valley elite. She had enjoyed those kinds of festivities, even after she married Zane.

But Savannah hadn't paid much attention to Grayson—except to notice his good looks. His body tall and slim, yet muscular, beneath the high-end clothing he generally wore at parties, his well-styled dark brown hair and gorgeous blue eyes. He wore his current outfit well, too—a long-sleeved black T-shirt with a neon emergency vest over it. His stubble was trimmed short and added to his sexiness. Of course, she hadn't been interested in how attractive a man he might have been when she believed she had most recently seen him, although she couldn't recall exactly when it had been. But she believed now that she had still been married, and though her marriage was ending she certainly wasn't interested in flirting with someone else. And with Grayson—well, she had gotten the impression he wasn't thrilled about being at most of those parties, that his family had twisted his arm to come. She knew he wasn't part of the family business, Colton Oil.

"I assume you found Ari's... Ari," she continued, choosing not to use the term "body."

He nodded. "I wasn't able to get a response, though, and neither did the EMTs that Mustang Valley General Hospital sent after my 911 call."

"I'm sorry," Savannah said.

"You were in the back of his van, right? Was he moving you from the state prison somewhere?"

She felt her eyes grow huge as she reached slowly for her bottle of water and stared at it—but she shouldn't have been surprised at Grayson's spot-on guess. She'd been in the news, as much as she hated that. As much as she hated all of this.

"Yes," she said quietly. That was close enough. Ari had been moving her from court back to prison, but she didn't choose to elaborate.

"So you were able to escape unharmed," Grayson stated. He took a swig from his bottle, but his eyes didn't leave hers. "That's a good thing, especially since you already told me you didn't kill your husband. And I assume that's the truth."

"It is." She kept her voice low but wanted to scream it out—the truth. Instead, she glanced toward the door. Should she run now?

Would Grayson grab her?

But when she looked back toward him, he hadn't

moved. He was watching her, though, with an expression on that handsome face of his that suggested amusement.

Amusement? When her entire life had been turned upside down, and he now was in a position to possibly ruin her tiny, precarious opportunity for freedom that resulted from an unpredicted earthquake?

"Got it," he said. "Now, want to tell me about it?"

Grayson was used to finding people in difficult positions and not only helping them physically but mentally, too. To doing all he could to assure their survival in all ways.

This beautiful woman he had met several times before appeared totally fragile now—and frightened. Of him.

Which he understood. But he didn't like it. And he wanted to help her in all ways.

And there was something he'd recalled about her, how well she had treated someone at one of the parties they'd both attended, that told him she was the kind of person who helped people, too—and didn't kill them. In fact, she had helped to save the life of a woman who had just been extremely nasty to her.

"I really don't like talking about the situation with Zane," she said now. "And there's really not much to tell. What's out there is all lies."

Well, she could be lying, too, of course. But he wanted to hear her side of it, since the media often liked to take things out of context and exaggerate them, even stress the nastiest facts—anything for a good story, although they also did base it on truth most of the time. Or so he believed.

So even though Grayson could in fact bring Savannah back to the appropriate authorities, no matter what he'd told her, or could just leave her here to do whatever she wanted, he still would rather hear her side of the story before deciding.

"Convince me," he said with a smile he hoped she would interpret as friendly.

For now, at least, it was.

"Okay. Let's start with the fact I don't believe Zane is dead."

That startled him a bit. With all the news and hype, he'd considered that a given. "Really?"

"Really," she replied. "My ex is missing. I'll admit that's true. But I didn't kill him and hide his body somewhere, and don't believe anyone else did, either. We'd stopped caring about each other quite a while ago but our divorce was only final about a month ago. He blamed it on me, made some pretty nasty allegations that were totally untrue, that I'd been unfaithful when he was the one having affairs…and he was furious with me for wanting a divorce. And—well, I can't prove it yet, but I believe he even got one of his friends to help him and frame me, while he's off somewhere, maybe even someplace as remote as Bali. He used to talk about going there someday. Wherever he is, I'm sure he's checking what's going on from his computer and otherwise—and laughing his head off. He's undoubtedly considering his revenge against me sweet. And this way, he might even be able to keep my part of the divorce settlement."

She really appeared steamed now, looking down toward the table and shaking her head so her short hair rubbed at her shirt collar.

He couldn't help it. He needed to know more about this allegation that her ex wasn't even dead, let alone murdered—and Zane might have plotted the entire thing. He put his elbows on the table and leaned toward her.

"So Zane is really alive? Do you have any proof?"

"No, but there's no real proof he's dead, either. He's missing, yes. He and I argued, privately and in public. And when he went missing, the cops found a knife in the guesthouse on his property, where I was living temporarily till I decided where to move. They found it in my closet, of all places. There was blood on it—Zane's, according to the official analysis. There were no fingerprints on the knife, though, and his body wasn't found."

"But—"

"Sure, that doesn't look good for me. The district attorney apparently took it seriously, though my lawyer assured me all the evidence was circumstantial, clearly not proof that I did anything." She was clutching her water bottle as if it was the DA's throat and she wanted to strangle her. Or maybe Grayson was just imagining that from the anger and frustration on her face. "I admit it looks pretty bad that the bloody knife was in my closet. But someone clearly sneaked in and hid it there—Zane himself, probably."

"I understand," Grayson said. "Not sure if I know all the claims or evidence supposedly against you, but I did hear a lot a week or so ago, when they said you'd just been arrested."

He'd been surprised to learn that this woman he knew remotely and met occasionally, a mere acquaintance who'd seemed nice enough, was a murder suspect. But what had been blared out on TV, newspapers, online and radio news was that Zane Oliver had disappeared and was believed dead, partly thanks to that bloody knife.

Suspicions had immediately landed on his ex-wife.

They'd divorced not long ago, and the media more than hinted that the reason for it was that Zane's wife, Savannah, had been having a torrid affair with a local real estate developer.

"I can't tell you how thrilled I am to be the main, maybe only, suspect when Zane disappeared that way," Savannah went on, her tone dripping with sarcasm. "Oh, and you want to hear more of that circumstantial evidence that's all false?" She didn't wait for his reply before continuing. "There were—are—some horrible false rumors about me. It seems I was having a hot and heavy romance during the end of my marriage to Zane with Schuyler Wells, of all people." She glared at Grayson as if daring him to say something.

Which he did, though nothing accusatory. "Right. I read about that."

"Didn't you hear his interviews in the media? Zane must have paid him well, since he claimed we had something and planned to run away together as soon as my divorce from Zane was final. Not!" She practically screamed the last word and stood, grabbing the scissors as if she was going to use them on him—or someone. Fortunately, she quickly realized what she was doing and, tears running down her lovely cheeks, collapsed back into the chair, gently pushing the scissors, handle first, toward him. "Here."

He pulled them closer on the table but didn't hide them, as if showing he believed her.

"And," she continued, her voice rasping, "what a surprise. Schuyler has a solid, impeccable alibi, on a business trip during the crucial time of the supposed murder, with people who don't even work for him vouching for him. But, gee, he does admit to having had a really steamy affair with me." Her head shook back and forth in utter denial. "No way. I've met the guy, even got some real estate advice from him, but I never liked him. And as I said, one of the reasons Zane and I got divorced was because he was having affairs. I wasn't."

"I get it." Grayson reached across the table and grasped Savannah's hand, where it now rested beside her water bottle. And he did get it. He didn't believe she'd made her side of it up.

Besides, what he'd recalled before gave him a clue as to Savannah's underlying personality, someone who helped to save lives rather than taking them. That situation had occurred at a fund-raiser his siblings had thrown for First Hand First Responders when he was just starting up the business. As he recalled, Savannah was not only there, but she was arguing with another socialite type who seemed very malicious. As a few other attendees started hollering at them to be quiet, they'd gone out onto the balcony of the two-story, swanky restaurant in downtown Mustang Valley.

Grayson, somewhat amused at the time, had watched through a window near one of his family's tables as they continued to argue. He'd been shocked when the other woman took a swing at Savannah and missed her—but the woman had been close enough to the railing that the movement made her nearly fall over it.

And Savannah, acting fast, had leaned over the balcony to grab that woman's wrists, hanging partly over the side herself for a while till a couple of guys ran out and pulled them both safely and completely onto the balcony.

Though he barely knew her then, Grayson had been impressed that Savannah had immediately endangered her own life to help someone who'd just been mean to her. That was distinctly not the behavior of a cold-blooded killer.

And no matter how difficult her relationship with her ex had turned out, he just couldn't see her as a murderer.

He didn't mention that to Savannah. But he did say, "I assume you won't be going back to town tonight, maybe not for a long time. In case you're wondering, this place is a fishing cabin, and the owners never come here until late in the spring—and this is only April. You can hang out here for now, if you'd like."

"Oh yes, I'd like that." She sounded relieved and her expression as she looked at him across the table seemed—well, grateful.

There was nothing she needed to be grateful to him for. Not yet, at least, if ever. Did he really want to put his own freedom into jeopardy by helping her? Maybe. He would have to think about it.

What about bringing her back to town, then attempting to help her by finding her ex?

He doubted she would go along with that, and he wasn't about to take any steps to get her back into custody. Not now, at least.

Well, he figured this place was a good potential hideout for her, at least temporarily. Despite being a walkable distance from the destroyed van, it wasn't that close to where she had escaped from it, although the cops might wind up looking around here.

In any case, he wasn't about to help her find someplace else. But he figured he would help her a bit by bringing her some supplies, since he doubted this place held much in the way of food and other necessities at this time of the year.

He would have to be careful, though. He was buying into her story, but was it true? Was she innocent?

He would assume so…for now. But he would also stay alert for anything that told him otherwise.

"Let's take a look at the damaged part of the cabin, though," he said, waving toward the far side where the wooden walls were somewhat smashed.

They both stood and walked in that direction. Grayson had an urge to take Savannah's hand and hold it encouragingly, but he decided that would be a bad idea.

They stopped beside each other and looked at the damaged wall from this angle. Some panels had even fallen down and left gaps, and the windows at that part of the room no longer existed.

But fortunately, most of the broken glass and wooden boards, insulation, shelves and other building materials must have landed outside, and somehow the remaining walls had fallen into a sideways slant so there wasn't even much in the way of an opening.

The rest of the place certainly looked habitable.

"It's not so bad," Savannah, at his side, whispered.

"I agree," Grayson said more loudly. "I've got a couple of phone calls to make now to ensure that my team doesn't head this way looking for me or for any injured people, then I'll head downtown. I'll bring you some supplies tomorrow, okay?"

"Definitely okay," she said, smiling at him. He couldn't help smiling back. "And—"

She stopped, so he prodded, "And what?"

"Well, I no longer have my phone, as you can imagine. Is there some way you could get one for me? I'll be glad to repay you for all this whenever…whenever it's all over and I get my life and my money back."

He laughed. "Sure thing," he said. "I know where I can get you a burner phone with internet access, so you'll be able to stay in touch with what's going on."

"Thanks."

He moved away then and called Norah Fellini, the EMT on his team.

"Hi, Grayson," she said immediately. "Where are you? Is everything okay? Do you need help with any other victims?" Of course she knew about his finding the van driver who didn't make it, since he kept his team apprised.

"No, I don't need any help now, thanks. That deceased driver was picked up by an ambulance, and then I headed toward some of the fishing cabins just to make sure no one was hurt or trapped inside. So far, I've checked the cabin on Rural Route 2 and haven't found anything I need to deal with, so I'm going to the next one that's about five miles away before driving back to town. I'd appreciate it if you'd let the rest of our team know, okay?"

"Sure," she said. She filled him in on what she and the other two team members had been up to. They'd had to find a couple of missing kids and give medical attention to them and a few other people, but they hadn't dealt with any major emergencies. "We did report in to our local PD and other contacts and all, so we should get paid—although that's not the main thing, of course."

"Of course. Just glad no one appeared badly hurt. See you tomorrow." He said good-night and hung up.

He walked to the table once more since Savannah sat there, looking exhausted. Well, he was, too, but he'd do as he had told Norah, then head back to town. At least he should be able to drive there, although it would take a while since he had left his vehicle near the crushed van.

"I'll be back tomorrow with some supplies," he told Savannah as he got ready to go.

"That's so nice of you." She stood up again. "Oh— and, well, maybe I shouldn't mention it, but I wanted to let you know I'd heard that someone shot your dad. I'm so sorry. How is he?"

Grayson's father was Payne Colton, chairman of the board of Colton Oil and owner of Rattlesnake Ridge Ranch—where Grayson lived with his siblings.

He felt himself cringe at Savannah's question. His dad wasn't doing well at all. Recently shot by an unknown person, Payne had gone into a coma—and hadn't come out of it yet.

There were more family things going on, too. They had just recently learned, thanks to a strange email, that his oldest brother, Ace, might have been switched at birth with another baby.

But to Savannah he simply said, "We think he's improving. Thanks for asking." He reached out to take Savannah's hand, but she pulled him closer, giving him a brief hug.

A hug that somehow made him want to get even closer, though he didn't. "Glad to hear that. So—see you tomorrow?"

"Yes," he said. "See you tomorrow."

He hoped. Oh, yes, he would return. But would she still be here? Would she be okay?

He would find out when he got here.

Chapter 4

Savannah held open the cabin's door and watched Grayson walk away along the uneven ground and through the trees in the glow of his large flashlight, heading essentially the direction from which she had come. Soon, she didn't see any more signs of him.

She had a sudden urge to dive back inside, grab the small flashlight she'd found and leave this cabin, too.

To dash after Grayson? Only if she could feel certain he was genuine, that he was as nice as he'd seemed—and that he really believed in her innocence.

She had no reason to doubt him, except that this situation was so horrendous that she simply couldn't—and didn't—trust anyone.

Sure, he could have dragged her along with him now, called authorities who could take her into custody and been done with the situation, but he hadn't.

That didn't mean she didn't need to worry about what came next. Would he really just turn up here tomorrow with supplies and a phone for her? Allow her to remain loose while the cops looked for her, potentially gathering more false evidence of her guilt? Assuming, of course, that an escaped fugitive remained high on their radar at the moment, despite the earthquake.

In any case, would Grayson help her as he'd promised?

She wasn't stupid, though her marriage to Zane didn't exactly show her to be a good judge of character—notwithstanding the fact that she'd had impetus from her dad, who had been impressed with Zane's wealth, to be in that relationship. Partly thanks to him, she had convinced herself that she loved Zane, but in retrospect she wasn't sure how much she had really cared.

But what was her best alternative for staying here? Running from the cabin and going the opposite direction to Grayson? With that small flashlight being nearly her only illumination, and damage to the ground and any other buildings she might come across, plus the possibility of more aftershocks? There'd be a lot of potential danger in that, at least if she didn't wait till daylight.

"Okay," she finally whispered to herself, backing into the cabin once more and closing the door. Locking it this time, at least—so maybe she would hear if someone showed up and attempted to get inside.

Meanwhile, she felt exhausted. She decided to go lie down on that inviting bed, allow herself to sleep—and hope that her subconscious would awaken her if anything happened or someone else showed up.

And tomorrow? Well, she really wanted to believe in Grayson and his honesty. He was one heck of a guy, sure, but she'd had enough of men. She genuinely believed that Zane had set up his supposed murder to ruin the rest of her life.

But Grayson? He was a first responder, so he at least cared about people, even strangers, on some level.

Turning, she picked up the flashlight, walked to the bed and sat down.

Grayson. Would she decide in the morning to wait here for him, see if he was as kind as he appeared to be? Whether he responded to her needs rather than the reality of who and what she currently was—an escaped prison inmate?

She would see how she felt. She hadn't harmed anyone to allow herself to escape, though she was certainly happy for her freedom.

But what would she do next? How could she possibly look for Zane or any clues that would prove she was right, that he'd framed her and that he was still alive?

It might help if she had that burner phone Grayson and she had discussed.

And if he did turn up here tomorrow with the supplies he'd promised, including that phone, she would feel a lot more comfortable trusting him.

For now? She didn't want to wear out the flashlight batteries, so after she turned the sheets over and lay down on the bed—not particularly comfortable, but at least it had a pillow with a case she turned inside out—she shut the light off, then closed her eyes.

"Good night, Grayson," she whispered with a small smile, recognizing the irony in her words and current attitude. "I'll see you tomorrow, when all my worrying about your truthfulness will be over."

She hoped.

* * *

The next morning, Grayson awoke at the family ranch.

Now he sat at his wing's kitchen table, more decorative and undoubtedly more expensive than the plain wood one at the cabin last night. He grabbed toast and coffee for breakfast, getting ready to meet the new day and learn more about how his employees had done yesterday. From what he'd grasped when he spoke with Norah, everyone had been out there helping people successfully. But he hadn't spoken with any of them again afterward. He wanted confirmation today, as well as more details.

He also planned to check out what downtown Mustang Valley looked like after the quake, and do a shopping expedition there, as well.

Then—well, then, he would have the pleasure of going to see Savannah again. Lovely Savannah, who claimed she had been set up by her ex and falsely accused of murder. Very falsely.

He had thought about Savannah a lot last night after leaving her. Maybe he should just stay out of the whole thing, neither help her nor rat on her to the authorities. But—well, he liked her.

And he hated the idea that she was being framed by her ex, if that was true.

He'd gotten out of a bad relationship recently, too. But they'd both just walked away. His ex hadn't plotted any revenge against him, and he hadn't against her, either. That sounded so absurd in Savannah's situation. But it could of course, be true.

Hell, he was a first responder. He helped people who needed it. Who deserved it. And he truly believed, at least for now, that included Savannah.

He would find out soon, he figured, if he had been duped by her, and she actually was a killer.

He took a sip of coffee from his mug with the FHFR logo and phone number on it.

That mind of his unsurprisingly kept going back to yesterday and the quake and its aftermath.

Once he'd left Savannah the previous night, he had returned to the place where he'd earlier found the damaged van and its dead occupant. All was gone now—except his own useful SUV.

Then he carefully drove along a couple of the mangled dirt roads to check out other fishing cabins besides the one Savannah was occupying, but they were empty, a good thing. And he'd seen no other evidence of people needing help, though quake damage was still evident.

He had considered stopping again on his way home to check on Savannah but had decided against it, since he was sure she was asleep by then. He doubted anyone else knew she was out here, and he intended to see her tomorrow anyway, while bringing the supplies he had promised her.

And tomorrow had arrived. Now that he was awake and preparing to start his day, he kept thinking about her. A fugitive. One he couldn't get out of his mind. Was he nuts?

Maybe.

"Okay," he muttered. Today was going to be undoubtedly interesting. He stood and put his empty plate in the metal kitchen sink but carried his remaining half mug of coffee.

He headed down the stairs after closing the door of his bedroom behind him and locking it.

He drove to the First Hand office.

When he arrived in the greeting area, he rapped once on each of their doors in order from the bottom of the steps—Pedro's first, then Norah's and Chad's. He heard a low woof after that last knock and just smiled. Winchell, Chad's K-9 companion, knew better than to bark here, even when on duty, but he was always alert.

In moments, the gang had joined him in the reception area. They were all present here at the office, so apparently no additional calls had come in after the ones he had heard about last night, and they'd already accomplished the searches they had needed to do immediately after the earthquake, depending on their individual expertise.

His employees greeted him with handshakes and pats on his back, as he did with them. "Good to see you all," he said. "And I'm looking forward to your reports."

"We want to hear yours, too, boss," Pedro said.

There was a reception desk for greeting people who walked in off the street seeking help, against the far wall from the entry door. Plate glass windows circled the room—all intact, fortunately, after the quake, Grayson had noticed last night. The floor was laminate, and the walls beige drywall decorated with photos of successful rescue operations and waving people they had saved. Half a dozen blue upholstered Parsons chairs were arranged with their backs toward the windows, so the room's occupants, if they spent any time there, could see one another.

And there were a couple of extra doors to offices that could be allocated to additional staff.

Grayson waved his bunch to the chairs so they could start their discussion. Once they were seated, he glanced beyond them to his view of the street. All seemed fine outside.

His mind returned to the damaged cabin where he had left Savannah. Hopefully she remained okay—and there.

"Okay, who's first?" Grayson asked, putting that behind him for now and looking at Norah.

"You, chief," she said.

"Nope. I'm last. So tell me your experiences with the quake and after."

Norah didn't argue but leaned forward in her chair. Before joining First Hand, she had worked for the City of Phoenix as an EMT but always crowed about how she'd run right to Mustang Valley when she heard of Grayson's start-up of a private first responder company a while back. She was well trained and a certified expert in emergency medical techniques, and was doing a great job with FH. She was thin yet very strong, and she kept her light brown hair in a style that framed her face.

Most important? With her ongoing and always increasing EMT skills, she was excellent at helping to save lives.

"I was right here when the quake hit." She motioned toward her office door.

Since not too much around there was damaged, she had hurriedly driven to Mustang Valley General Hospital. The staff there had immediately assigned her to ride in one of the ambulances, to assist the drivers and hospital EMTs.

"Six different locations, and we helped over a dozen people, although their injuries were of different severities. Some weren't too bad off, but there were maybe four that probably wouldn't have survived if we weren't there." Her grin totally lighted up her slender face, and Grayson smiled back.

"Great job," he said, then turned toward Pedro. "Any fires?"

Pedro Perez had been a firefighter in Las Vegas—but he'd informed Grayson when he'd hired him that he was excited about the opportunity to come to Mustang Valley and be the premier firefighter for FHFR. Pedro was dark-haired, large and muscular.

"About five, across town. Only one was really bad, though. I heard about it in the news before heading there and helped the local fire department get it under control. They know me, of course, so they asked me to help with the rest. And after we got those out, I hung out with the gang at the station for a couple more hours just in case. I gathered that all the fires were electrical fires because the wiring in those buildings was badly damaged by the quake and aftershocks. And I remain on call now, too, with the department in case they learn of any other blazes."

"Excellent," Grayson said. They all then turned toward Chad and Winchell, his German shepherd. "So—what's your story, both of you?"

Chad had been a K-9 cop with Tucson PD before coming to work for First Hand. He'd brought along his assistant Winchell, who was a certified search and rescue dog as well as a police K-9. He was moderate height and wore glasses, and always asked if Winch and he could do more.

"There were a few reports of break-ins across town in the area where the quake hit worst—you know, the shopping area where stores are plentiful but not especially elite. I got a call from one of the dispatchers at the police department, and Winch and I headed there. We actually nabbed a couple of guys who dared to try to loot some damaged stores—those SOBs. Fortunately, they were scared of Winch, so we were able to turn them over to the PD."

Grayson intended to visit just such a shopping center soon, where he wouldn't be recognized as a Colton by store owners and other shoppers. There he could hopefully find all the supplies and the cell phone he had promised Savannah.

For now, he stood and approached each of his employees, reaching out his hand to shake theirs. "You know, when I went into this, opening a private first responders' outfit, I wondered not only if I could succeed, but if I would be able to find assistants who were okay working in the private sector but do as well, or better than, first responders working for the official departments. Well, damn it, I did great in choosing every one of you."

"And we did great choosing you as our boss," Norah responded.

Both of the guys vocally agreed.

"But we're not done here," Norah continued. "What did you find, Grayson?"

Grayson trusted these people with his life. And with other lives, those they worked so hard to save.

But did he dare mention he'd found Savannah?

Maybe eventually, especially if he wound up needing their help. Plus, if he was found out and there were any legal ramifications against him, his staff could be affected, too.

For now, he decided to be cautious. He sat back down and described finding the van and its deceased driver.

"Was there anyone in the back?" Chad asked—not surprising from a former cop.

"Apparently there had been at least one person there," Grayson said, looking Chad in the other man's dark brown eyes, which kind of resembled his dog's. "But no one was in it when I got there, and though I looked around for a while to make sure no one was injured or otherwise needed my help, I didn't discover anything or anyone that had to be taken care of or reported." He'd phrased that in a way that remained sort of true, at least.

"Sad," Pedro said, "but I gather there weren't a whole lot of injuries or deaths due to the quake. A lot of property damage in some locations, though."

"Like the older parts of town," Grayson said, nodding. "I'm going to go take a walk around there soon and size up the damage—assuming no new information comes in requiring us to do any first responding right now. Meantime, I'd like each of you to contact the officials in your areas of expertise again just to confirm that all's well for now, and to offer your services if needed, of course."

FHFR received most of its funding from the public departments they assisted, being paid a general retainer and getting more each time they helped out.

And when needed, Grayson supplemented his company's finances with his own money received as a Colton.

He always made sure to pay his excellent employees well.

"Yes, sir," Chad said, rising and saluting as if Grayson was his superior officer—which he was, in a way. Grayson, grinning, saluted back, and his smile grew even wider as Winchell held out his paw for a shake.

Grayson wanted to make a couple of calls, too, to his major local contacts—in case he or his people were needed now, so he walked up the stairs to the second floor to where his own office was.

But he looked forward to heading soon to the other side of town.

First, though, he decided to check the news on his computer. He wanted to see what the local media said about the quake and the havoc it had caused.

And anything about the destroyed van and its driver... and the passenger who had disappeared.

Sure enough, although most of the news was about the quake itself, the crushed van and the death of Ari, its driver, was out there, too.

Grayson turned on the sound on his computer and listened to a couple of those reports.

They all ended with the fact that the female prisoner being transported from court back to the local prison had apparently escaped.

The authorities suspected that the passenger, Savannah Oliver, had killed the driver so she could flee. Her handcuffs had been found beside the destroyed van, after all.

Oh boy, Grayson thought. The idea hadn't crossed his mind, since he had seen Ari and the van and the tree that had caused the driver's death. But not everyone had. And the photos on his phone wouldn't necessarily do away with the suspicion.

What would Savannah think of these additional accusations against her?

He felt certain he would soon find out.

Chapter 5

Savannah had previously looked around the cabin for a TV or radio or anything else that would allow her to learn what was happening in the outside world, but she'd found nothing.

The tall, unsteady-looking set of wooden bookshelves along one of the walls held quite a few volumes about the area and fish and traveling, but nothing that would provide her with the kind of knowledge she now sought.

And until Grayson returned with the phone he'd promised, she was on her own here.

Was that a good reason simply to leave in order to learn what she could about how the earthquake and aftershocks had affected Mustang Valley?

No, she intended to stay here, at least for today, and see if Grayson really did return. But she would of course remain alert and conscious—in case he wasn't the one to arrive first, or at all.

The cops, if they weren't overwhelmed with quake stuff, were probably looking for her.

And if she could figure out an inconspicuous way to do it, she wanted to be out there soon, somewhere, somehow, looking for Zane, or talking to any people she thought of as his coconspirators, like Schuyler Wells. As if she'd had any interest in him, social or professional.

Although, at the moment, she was definitely interested in finding—and talking to—Schuyler, too, since unlike Zane, he was still out and about. However, he was also the kind of person likely to call the cops to pick her up right away if he had any knowledge of where she was.

She had pondered why Zane would fake his own death, and figured that, if nothing else, it would be to spite her. To hurt her for dumping him. And maybe his finances weren't as good as he let on to the world, so he'd wanted to find a way to hide. She wasn't sure. All she knew was that he was a horrible person who lied and cheated and she should never have married him.

And, it seemed, Schuyler had become his coconspirator. For money? If so, Zane must still have some.

"I'll figure it out," she muttered to herself, again sitting at the table that had become a sort of refuge in this remote cabin, drinking another bottle of water—and hoping that Grayson brought some more when he got there.

If he got there.

But she couldn't stay here for long—certainly not after she came up with a viable plan to track down the people who had done this to her, and somehow extract the truth.

Now all she needed to do was determine how.

* * *

Unsurprisingly, downtown Mustang Valley was a mess.

Oh, in the nicer area where Grayson's office building and other newer, well-constructed ones were located, the earthquake damage was visible but not extensive. The cracks didn't appear too deep in some of the walls, although there were fractures in the streets and debris had fallen on the streets from the structures. Maintenance crews were already out there working on repairs, though Grayson assumed there would be more in upcoming days.

The sidewalks were at least mostly passable, so he walked toward the other area of town that had been around longer without upgrades. He'd assumed the damage would be more obvious there, and it was: deeper gouges in the streets often turning them from two-lane to one—or less. There were also larger portions of the buildings that were ruined, reminding him a bit of the cabin where Savannah was.

Savannah. She remained on his mind a lot, largely because of his promise to buy her supplies…but not entirely. He kept wondering how she was doing, if she trusted him to keep his word and was waiting for him to return. Whether anyone official had been looking in that area for her—or had found her there.

He figured he would hear about that if it happened. Her disappearance might be a result of the earthquake, but it had newsworthiness of its own, particularly under the circumstances of the driver's death. Grayson understood that. He'd be a lot more dubious about her innocence, too, if he hadn't talked to her. Believe her? Maybe. He hadn't liked, hadn't trusted her ex Zane, so maybe she wasn't making anything up.

As he continued walking, he thought about his siblings. He had only ducked into his wing at the ranch late last night and out of it fast this morning so he hadn't seen any of them, but he had called most of them as he left that day. He might not be close with them, but he wanted reassurance that none was hurt. Fortunately, he heard only good news.

He'd even spoken with Ace. He still considered him his brother, even though Ace had taken a DNA test after the email that the Colton Oil board received. It confirmed that he was not a biological Colton. Grayson might not be good buddies with all his family members, but he didn't dislike Ace.

Now he noticed he was far from alone here. There were more pedestrians than automobile traffic, but the few cars there proceeded slowly, causing traffic jams. No one looked at him, and he paid no attention to anyone else.

He did, however, notice a kid playing in some rubble near a damaged building. The kid wore an Arizona State Sun Devils T-shirt, which reminded Grayson of the Arizona State Sun Devils pin that had been found in his father's office after his dad was shot. Payne remained in a coma—and no one knew yet who'd done it. The pin might be a clue to the shooter's identity.

Grayson suddenly found himself uncharacteristically overwhelmed by concern for his father. He wasn't particularly close to him, but still, Payne Colton was his dad, and he had been shot.

Maybe his emotions were brought on by the earthquake and knowing people had been injured, sometimes killed, and parts of the town had been wrecked...

Well, despite never really feeling close to his family, or particularly fond of Colton Oil, right now Grayson felt even more isolated from his siblings than usual.

And why didn't he feel close? Because of nearly everyone's obsession with Colton Oil. Sure, it made a lot of money for the family, but he hadn't like the pressure he had felt while growing up to get involved with the business. In fact, he had wound up ignoring it, starting out in the military, then becoming a wilderness guide and ultimately a first responder instead. Which hadn't sat well with his dad or some of his siblings. Well, too bad.

Drawing his gaze away from the kid and attempting to shrug off those thoughts, he continued walking. He frequently looked down streets leading off the main road. Some homes appeared okay, at least from this angle. Others seemed damaged—and a few were destroyed.

What a shame, he thought.

He passed one chain discount store that looked closed, damaged, possibly ruined. Then there was an open pharmacy but he wasn't sure he could find all he wanted there.

Interestingly, he saw several tables arranged along what remained of the sidewalk, staffed by people he didn't recognize. The signs indicated they were members of a small self-help group he had heard of: the Affirmation Alliance Group. They seemed to greet everyone who walked by, although Grayson didn't stop. Some even called out to passersby that they were there to help them. They claimed to have a place for people to stay who couldn't go back home now, right at their own very special guest ranch. How had they gotten things set up so fast after the quake? Of course, from what Grayson had heard about them, they were supposed to be all about teaching others how to help themselves, so maybe they had procedures developed for all kinds of situations or disasters, including earthquakes.

He'd heard a lot about the good work the group and its founder, Micheline Anderson, did, including holding self-help seminars at that ranch, but something about them made him a bit uneasy.

Good thing he didn't need someplace else to live. In any event, if that group truly helped people in need around here, more power to them.

There. He had reached another chain discount store where he should be able to find all the supplies he intended to buy. It appeared fine, and open. He went inside and grabbed a cart, glad he didn't see anyone he knew as he started picking up a lot of basic stuff that most people, especially the Coltons, were likely to already have around their houses.

If anyone asked, he would claim that the earthquake was his rationale, since, although he knew his family ranch was fine, who knew when all the basic supplies would be available around here again?

So...he tossed into his cart cleaning supplies, paper towels, batteries, a couple of additional flashlights—the size of his and not Savannah's—and a lot more.

However, he'd thought this place also carried basic food items like bread, but it didn't.

When he got into the checkout line, one of half a dozen in a row, all with signs indicating they were open, he thought he recognized the clerk, darn it. And even if the man hadn't recognized him, Grayson had stuck a credit card in the reader, so of course his name appeared.

"Oh, hello, Mr. Colton," the guy, a senior with white

hair and a beard, said. "Did you find everything you were looking for?" He looked curious yet friendly.

Grayson decided not to mention the food. There was a store he would pass later that would be better for those kinds of provisions anyway.

Instead, he offered a bland explanation of sorts. "We're probably just fine, but I wanted to make sure we've got the basics at the ranch—especially since I'd imagine your headquarters' ability to deliver more to this store could have been affected by the quake."

"Could be, but I think we're fine. Anyway, come back anytime if you need anything else. We'll do all we can to accommodate you, of course."

"Thanks," Grayson said, not surprised by the guy's attitude. Grayson was a Colton, even if he maintained a distance from his family. But strangers wouldn't know that. And it might not matter anyway. The Coltons had power.

And they, and even he, had money, thanks to Colton Oil.

The clerk stuffed everything into three large plastic bags.

Fortunately, the store that was his next goal was only another block away. He just hoped it was undamaged and open, too.

Which it was. It sold tech, including computers and telephones—and of course the latter was Grayson's target. He was able to purchase a disposable one—a burner phone—without anyone asking questions. Although the woman who waited on him commented he wasn't the only person seeking this kind of phone today, since so many people had apparently lost their phones and technical connections in the quake that they'd come here to buy temporary phones till they figured out what to do next.

He simply nodded and put on a sad face, telling her, "That sounds familiar." He had enough cash with him so he did not have to provide a credit card here. He was glad he so seldom came to this part of town that no one in this store, at least, recognized him. Plus, he bought a battery-operated charger and extra batteries. He wanted to make certain the phone had plenty of time and power connected to it so Savannah would be able to use it for a while anonymously.

And when she couldn't use it any longer? Well, it wasn't really his concern, but he *was* concerned. He would just have to see where things stood then—and whether he would feel committed to acquire another of these important devices for her.

He walked back to his office building as quickly as he could, again relieved that he didn't see anyone he knew. When he arrived, he immediately went around back to the parking lot to place his purchases in the trunk before going back inside to check in with his staff again.

"I'm just going to do some looking around to see if there are any others, government agencies or otherwise, who need our help today," he told Pedro, the first of his gang that he saw in the reception area.

Then he got into his car and drove first to the nearby grocery store, where he would stock up even more on basics, then head toward the fishing cabin where he had last seen Savannah. Would she still be there?

As she'd anticipated, Savannah had spent the morning pondering what she could, what she should, do to get her out of this fix and find the men she needed to resolve it.

She focused on her need to find Zane and turn him over to the police. The real question, then, remained how she would be able to do that. Surely his anger at her wanting to be rid of him because of his lies and infidelities wouldn't keep him away from his former, normal life forever. Though his faking his death with the idea of getting her thrown permanently in prison... well, she didn't know how he intended to return and deal with that.

Or could he get people to continue to run his business for him here and give him access to its proceeds?

She eventually stood up, figuring she wasn't getting anywhere just sitting at the table. Now she was walking around outside the house for the second time.

Looking into the surrounding woods, enjoying occasional views of birds and the tree branches waving in the wind, inhaling the scent of the outdoors, and paying attention to her footing, hoping there wouldn't be any further earth movement that day.

Most important, she was thinking and trying to come up with different methods, different angles to get out of the mess she was in.

Attempting to dive into Zane's mind, despite his not being here, despite his being out of her life—at least as her husband.

Zane had run an investment bank and liked using social media and tech in many aspects of his life. He'd surrounded them with various security devices in their home, which at that time had helped to make her feel protected.

Yeah, from everyone but Zane.

Despite not being a techie, she believed she had a reasonably sharp mind. Sure, she was considered a socialite and didn't have a genuine, well-paying career, but thanks to her family resources, and, more recently, Zane's, she had spent her time learning about various charitable enterprises and participating in events where money was collected to help people in need.

Unlike her.

Before she'd been accused of murdering her husband, at least.

What would come next for her? Freedom, she hoped. And plenty of time to determine what else she wanted to do with her future now that Zane would be out of her life—hopefully in prison instead of her, for his chilling attempt to scam the authorities and frame her.

More charitable functions? Maybe, but if so she would get more involved, maybe even find a way to help manage one or more of them. She was unsure what her financial situation would be, of course, but it should be okay thanks to the money she had inherited from her grandparents that had supported her before, as well as her divorce settlement from Zane. She would deal with it, no matter what.

And—well, oddly enough, she was very impressed with Grayson and what he did. Would she want to learn to become a first responder, too?

She would definitely like to be able to save lives. She had always enjoyed helping people when she was helping to run charitable enterprises before. And now, she wished she'd been able to help Ari, no matter how indifferent he had been to her. And even if she hadn't been shackled inside the van, she doubted if she could have done much more for him.

Still…

"Okay, time to go back inside," she finally muttered

to herself, watching a crow in the air above her spread its wings and soar off, uttering a caw as if agreeing with her.

She entered the cabin again and locked the door behind her.

Though she had hand-bathed several times, she really, really wanted a shower. She had already begun using a clean towel that she had found in the bathroom, and recognized she could make even better use of it. Plus, she had peeked into the shower stall and seen a substantial bar of soap on a small shelf inside it.

Now was a good time to start her new life, whatever it might wind up being. And she'd just as soon do it clean.

At least, thanks to the bag she'd brought here, she had a change of clothes. So far, she hadn't changed, but she looked forward to wearing something different from the outfit she still had on that now reminded her of her latest courthouse appearance—and all that had happened afterward.

Of course, the other outfit looked very much like this one. And the shirt and slacks were a good reminder of her current freedom, which she hoped would now last forever.

She went into the bathroom and rinsed off the bar of soap, although it already appeared clean enough to use.

Then she stepped into the shower.

Not for long, though. She only wanted a short shower. And she knew full well that, despite the water working, the power wasn't turned on here, so it wasn't a big surprise that the water never warmed up. The April Arizona air around here wasn't extremely cold, but it wasn't particularly comfortable. She soon turned off the water and dried herself.

That was when she thought she heard a noise from somewhere inside the cabin.

Oh, great. She hoped she was imagining it. And if she wasn't—well, her next hope was that Grayson had returned.

But what if it wasn't him? She had figured out how to get inside through the window, and other people besides Grayson could undoubtedly do it, too—especially if they were looking for her and had reason to believe she was here.

She needed to get out of there. Protect herself, no matter who it was.

But here she only had a towel to keep herself covered.

Had she been foolish again? Maybe she shouldn't have showered. Or maybe she had just imagined the noise…and maybe not.

What was she going to do?

Well, she could at least confirm that someone was there—and that it was the person she had anticipated. Hoped for.

Grayson.

Wrapping the towel around herself, tucking the edges so it would stay wrapped—and also holding it—she opened the door just a crack.

"Who's there?" she called out. She still hoped her imagination was on overdrive and no one was there, but—

"It's me, Savannah. Grayson. I'm back."

Relief swept through her. "Since I know I locked the door, I assume you crawled through the window," she said, feeling amused and embarrassed, too.

"Yep. I'm getting to know my way around this place."

Savannah had opened the bathroom door wider at

the confirmation of who was there—and her easy recognition of his deep voice. Sure enough, there he was, standing by that dratted table again, his back toward her clothes on the chair. He no longer wore the neon vest, and his long-sleeved T-shirt today was dark blue, the same shade as his jeans.

He looked in her direction. Scanned her, with her towel, head to toe.

She barely knew the guy, but somehow his warm, interested expression turned her on.

That, combined with her happiness at realizing her visitor was the man she'd wanted to see again, caused her to dash toward him, smiling, arms open wide. "Welcome to my refuge—again—Grayson."

She threw her arms around him, and at the same time he grasped her and pulled her close.

Good thing she had done a reasonable job of securing the towel around her beforehand.

"Thanks, Savannah," he responded. "Good to see you again, too."

And before she could stop herself, she reached up, brought his head down to hers, and gave him one hot, sexy kiss.

Chapter 6

What the heck was he doing?

Kissing Savannah, of course. Or responding to her kissing him. And it felt wonderful. All over.

Sure, Savannah looked damned beautiful in only a towel framing her slender body that nevertheless suggested lots of curves, which were confirmed by the feel of her in his arms.

And, okay, she hadn't been the only one wanting a hug. Or more. From the instant he had seen her that way, wrapped only in that towel, smiling welcomingly at him, her shorter blond hair wet and forming a halo around her gorgeous face, he certainly hadn't objected to her grabbing him. And he had definitely grabbed her back. And joined in that amazing kiss.

But right now, he ended it. Let his arms drop. Then he backed slightly away.

She smiled but seemed to blush a little as she, too, stepped back and stood there looking at him. Or around him.

Oh yeah. He'd seen some clothes stacked on one of the chairs he now stood in front of.

"Hey," he said, moving sideways, farther from the clothes. "Wait till you see all the supplies I brought for you. Maybe that kiss will be the first of many." He was teasing, of course.

But he pictured her pulling that towel away altogether. And then imagined what happened between them…

Okay, he felt a real attraction to her. One that made a certain part of his body stand at attention, although his jeans were loose enough that he didn't believe that was obvious.

Or at least he hoped not.

But that attraction was highly inappropriate. She was a woman in trouble. He was a man whose main purpose was to help people in trouble—not add to their problems.

No matter how strong his urge to touch her beneath that damned towel.

And besides…well, he had no intention of getting involved with her other than to help clear her name. He had no intention of getting involved with any woman, possibly ever again. Not after the miserable way his last romantic relationship had ended.

"Thanks so much," Savannah said, and he knew she referred to his comments about the supplies he'd brought, not his simmering thoughts about her. "Let me get dressed now, and we can go out to your car and bring it all in." She walked a step toward the pile of clothes, then stopped. "Did you drive all the way here this time?"

"Yeah," he said. "No closures or major impairments

along the way despite the destruction in other areas. Not to mention all the downed trees and poles. Of course the dirt road that ends right here had some lumps and moderate rises that were probably the result of the quake."

"But your car is here," she said. She looked a bit pensive—another attractive expression on her pretty face.

Was she thinking about where to ask him to drive her?

But where could she go and remain safe, not grabbed by the law?

And he definitely didn't want to be seen helping her.

He decided instead to tease her about it. "So, do you want to drive my car off somewhere? If I let you, I'd have to say it was stolen. And everyone would guess who stole it, probably, considering the fact that you're the most likely flight risk around here at the moment."

"You're right." Her tone was so sad that he wondered if she was about to cry.

"Hey, I was kidding. Sort of. No, right now I think you're safer just hanging out here until we come up with some kind of plan to get you out of this mess." He purposely stressed the "we" a bit, so she wouldn't think that by bringing up her difficult situation, he was abandoning her.

At least she couldn't think he'd turned her over to the cops, since here he was, on his own, with stuff in his car to give to her.

And as a first responder used to helping people in distress, that felt damned good with this woman who, right or wrong, he still believed to be innocent. Maybe it was because he hadn't known anything particularly good about her husband, and couldn't ignore her claim that Zane was still alive, framing her. Not until there was more evidence either way, at least.

"I agree." Her tone was strong now, her expression somehow fearless—and he wanted to take a few steps toward her on the cabin's dingy wood floor and give her another hug.

He didn't.

"I'll go get dressed," she said. She maneuvered her way around him—almost, but not quite, touching his back with her own—and tugged her clothes off the chair.

He hadn't noticed before, but he saw some underwear peeking from beneath her shirt and slacks. It didn't look particularly sexy. Whatever she had here now was probably the same thing she had worn in prison, utilitarian and bland.

But just the hint of seeing it made him wonder what she would look like in something tiny, or without it…

Enough of this, he told himself, turning his back toward the bathroom door after she disappeared behind it.

He opened the cabin door and stepped outside. He stood there looking around and listening for a moment, just to be safe. He'd no reason to believe he was followed here, nor had he seen anyone else driving or walking around who might wind up here. But he wanted to remain safe—to have Savannah remain safe—so he needed to stay alert and cautious.

He heard and saw nothing to warn him of any problems, so he continued to the rear of his SUV and opened it. He pulled out the nearest bags, paper ones filled with the food he had purchased at his third store before returning here.

He had managed to find what he hoped would be enough to keep Savannah fed and healthy. Bread, yes, which had been his first thought, plus several different kinds of fruits and vegetables, which wouldn't last forever unrefrigerated, but she surely would be eating some of it fairly fast since it was the only food she would have here. He had additionally brought some canned meat—Spam and tuna—as well as wrapped and sliced meat, so she could make sandwiches. Plus, he'd bought some more bottles of water for her…and a little wine, just to make their meal more enjoyable, perhaps, if he ate here with her at all. And the food was in addition to some other essentials, such as a first-aid kit, paper products and some cleaning supplies, although he hadn't brought much of those this time.

Still alert for sounds, he heard his own footsteps crunch a bit on the loose dirt and leaves on the path back to the front door. A couple of crows cawed, but he heard no other birds or wildlife making any sounds. No breeze, either; the trees were still and soundless.

He soon was inside the house—and staring slightly down at Savannah, who'd been about to come out the door. She was fully dressed now, even wearing the black slip-on shoes he had seen her in previously. She was equally attractive with her clothes on, and Grayson was glad, for his own peace of mind, that she'd gotten rid of the towel.

She looked down at the bags he held. "What do we have here?"

"Groceries," he said. "I left water and other supplies in the car."

"I'll go get some," she said.

"No, show me where you want these and we'll get the rest together." He didn't want her alone out there, even while he was around.

But his protective instinct was controlling him, and he needed to use it for her as long as they were together.

"Okay," she said, fortunately not disputing him, although she did give him a quizzical look. And after he'd put the bags on the kitchen counter where she indicated, she said, "Is everything okay outside?"

"As far as I know," he said, realizing that probably didn't give her a lot of reassurance.

Even so, she was with him on their next couple of trips outside to bring in the rest. "Wow," she said as they both put down the bags they'd been carrying. "Why didn't you get some more?"

Of course she was attempting a touch of humor. He responded in kind. "Oh, I figured this was enough to hold you through tomorrow morning. I can bring more then."

"That's good," she said. Then she grew more serious. "I'd really like to have some sense of how long I'll need to stay here—and what I can do to figure out what happened to Zane. As fast as possible, of course."

"Of course," he acknowledged. "I don't know what to tell you, other than we need to discuss more of your sense of what happened, and its timing. Then maybe we'll come up with some ideas."

"Not just maybe," she contradicted. "We have to figure it out. Or at least I do."

"We," he said again. "I intend to help."

He went back outside again, this time to retrieve the phone. Savannah was in the kitchen area, standing on tiptoes in her black sneakers, placing packages of paper towels, paper plates, napkins and more into a floor-to-ceiling wooden cabinet.

"As soon as you're done there, I have something else to show you."

"What's that?"

"You'll see."

She seemed to speed up the pace of stuffing the still-sealed packages onto the shelves, stretching to thrust some into the areas above her, then kneeling to also use the lower ledges. He enjoyed watching her lithe form as she maneuvered. Not a good idea, he told himself, but observed her anyway.

Finishing in about two minutes, she strode over to him. "I can put the food in another cabinet and in the fridge soon. Even knowing nothing will get chilled there, it'll make a good storage area. But first—what else do you have to show me? I'll warn you, though. I have an idea what it is."

"Of course you do." He pulled the phone from his pocket. "Let's go to our favorite place here and I'll turn it on, then we'll make sure you know how to use it."

In moments, she sat at her usual spot watching him—and, amusingly, batting her eyelashes. She seemed to have a natural beauty that was entirely her own.

"What's taking you so long?" she asked.

He pulled out his chair and sat down beside her. "Here we are."

The phone resembled major manufacturers' equipment—black and rectangular, with a screen in front. He also pulled the new battery-operated charger from his pocket.

"Okay, here's how you turn it on. Nothing crazy or unique." He pushed a button along the narrow side of the phone. "I assume that doesn't look unusual, though I don't know what kind of phone you had."

"Not much different from that one," Savannah confirmed.

She held out her hand, and he placed the phone in her palm as the screen came to life. The wallpaper on that screen showed a blue sky with white cumulus clouds. When he swiped at the screen, a bunch of apps suddenly appeared. One was the play store from which more apps could be downloaded. Another was a camera. Then there were the standard ones for making calls on the phone, getting to the internet, and sending and receiving text messages. And though Grayson didn't know what internet connection there was at the cabin, there must have been something because everything appeared to work.

"Looks nice and familiar," she said again. "Can I get its phone number from you?"

"Of course." He pulled his own phone from his pocket and checked his list of contacts. He had added Savannah's new number at the tech store where he'd bought it.

Of course he didn't use her name in his contacts list. Not that he anticipated anyone would be checking his phone for it, but no sense taking any chances.

No, she was listed there under the name of a girl he'd been buddies with in college, Charlene Farmer. Not a girlfriend, but a girl who was a friend. That number had an area code for Arizona, but there wasn't anything else that should reveal its owner's location any more than her name.

After he explained all that to Savannah, she said, "Please give me a call. That way, I can save your number. I assume it's okay to use your real name as my contact."

"Absolutely. But I assume I don't have to tell you to be careful and not make calls to anyone you know without thinking it through first. They may not recognize your number or your name on the phone, but—"

"I understand. No way will I call anyone I don't trust. You can be sure I'll be cautious."

"Good," Grayson said, then he did as she had requested and called her from his phone.

She answered it. "This is Charlene. And who am I talking to?"

"Some weird guy who wants to know exactly where you are so I can come and hassle you."

"Okay, weird guy. I've got your number." And Savannah pressed the button to end the call.

"I think I'm in trouble." Grayson made a mock-nervous face and aimed a grin toward Savannah.

But what was next? He could leave now, but the kind of help he had provided that day wasn't all she needed.

To provide an excuse to stay longer, he said, "I think we deserve a late lunch now, don't you?"

"I certainly do," she said, rising. "And since you brought all the food and other stuff we need, I'll make us a salad and sandwiches. That okay with you?"

"Definitely," he replied.

It was an excuse, of course. Savannah was perfectly happy using the things Grayson had brought to prepare as nice a lunch as possible for them.

But mostly she didn't want him just to drop things off, show her how to use that critical phone—and then leave her here, alone and unsure what to do next.

Besides…well, she enjoyed having him around.

Especially after that kiss.

Of course, even if he stayed for a while, that moment when he left would come. He couldn't, shouldn't, stay here much longer. Yet she hated the idea of hanging out here alone again. Although, now that she had a phone she could use, it wouldn't hurt to try to do some research on Zane and what was being said about him on the internet. Would she find any answers? Well, she definitely wouldn't if she didn't try.

Without another word to Grayson, she went to the kitchen. She used the cleaning materials he had brought to scrub the sink, then washed some of the utensils she had found in the kitchen drawers.

She cut the head of lettuce Grayson had brought, along with a tomato, placing them into a clean bowl. Then she made sandwiches from the cold cuts and kept everything on paper plates.

While she was doing all this, she glanced at him now and then. Which wasn't a chore. Grayson's gleaming blue eyes seemed to sparkle when he looked at her, and particularly when he teased her and helped to keep her mood from becoming completely depressed despite her questionable freedom.

Plus, he was a first responder. Could he use his skills and help her figure out what really happened to Zane?

Plus, Savannah couldn't help thinking about before, when he had first arrived that day.

When she'd had no clothes on, only a towel around her, and had impulsively hugged, and kissed, him.

She had an urge to do it again now. In thanks for what he had brought.

In thanks for appearing to believe in her. For helping her. For bringing her food, and hanging out to share a meal with her. Unlike Zane. Oh, they sometimes shared meals, but that had become a lot less frequent before they separated.

During part of the time she prepared their lunch, Grayson seemed to be texting someone, maybe more than one. His staff?

He eventually stood and crossed to the far side of the room, where he conducted some phone conversations, too. Though he was talking to whoever was on the other end, he kept his voice low so she couldn't hear more than a few words of what he said.

At least his staying here didn't seem to prevent him from communicating with people he needed to.

And her? Who would she dare to communicate with using her new phone?

She might need to ponder that for a while.

For now, though…

She saw Grayson pull his phone away from his ear and cross the small cabin. He wasn't smiling.

Was something wrong?

But as he reached her, he said, "Okay, I'm free for a while. Talked to everyone I needed to. So when do we eat?"

Savannah waved toward the food she had clustered, still on the counter near the sink. "Right now," she said. "Take a plate and sit down."

She was so glad he was staying. She really enjoyed his company.

Not to mention the idea that he was the kind of person who just might try to help her prove her innocence.

Chapter 7

Grayson sat down to a pretty tasty lunch on a thick paper plate. Of course, it consisted of the stuff he'd bought, nothing even hinting at gourmet. Even so, Savannah had put it together in a way that looked appealing.

And that was what he told her. "This all looks really good," he said as he placed a second half sandwich onto his plate.

"It looks like what you brought here," she said dismissively, although he caught the smile on her face as she scooped up some salad.

"Ah, but your serving skills added a lot."

She laughed as she aimed her green eyes at him in an expression that seemed both amused and appreciative. "Taste it first," she said.

He finished filling his plate and went to sit down at

the table. He savored the food, such as it was, partly to keep her amused—and because he wanted to hang out here a while longer. He intended to discuss her situation and what he could do to help her not only survive, but end what was happening to her—and how he could help her uncover the truth about Zane.

She was most likely being hunted now by the cops. In their phone call yesterday, Chad had indicated that was in fact the case. Chad had heard that the cops, including the few who had K-9 partners, were mostly occupied with checking out damage, though a warning had been issued for people to be careful not only of potential looters, but also of a murderer who might be loose among them.

He also assumed from what Chad said that there hadn't been time to look for her...yet.

Now he took a significant bite of sandwich, watching Savannah watch him as he did so. It actually tasted pretty good, probably because he was hungry.

"So what's your favorite food when you aren't in the middle of nowhere helping an innocent prison escapee?" Savannah asked him. Although the tone of her sweetly feminine voice was light, the expression on her pretty face remained wry.

"Oh, I like sandwiches, though I'm fondest of really good, thick burgers. Roast beef sandwiches, too. Steaks and—"

"I get it," Savannah said, interrupting him with a laugh. "Beef and you are buddies."

"You don't like my faves?" He tried to sound as though his feelings were hurt, and he squeezed his mouth into a pout. He liked the idea of keeping this conversation light. For now. But soon they'd have to start discussing what was really on their minds.

"In moderation," she responded. "Along with good, healthy food, like salads and other veggies. Fish and chicken, too."

"You sound like a health nut," he said, shaking his head.

"Guess what, I prefer healthy."

"Well, I actually like sides along with my meats, and that can include the salads and veggies you mentioned. Good fruit, too."

"Then maybe your family did bring you up right," Savannah said. "Even though from what I've heard you can afford to eat anything, anywhere, that you want." Her turn to put down the plastic salad fork and take a bite of sandwich.

"That's what I gather about you and your family, too," Grayson said, and as she stopped chewing and looked down, he knew he'd made a mistake even mentioning them. Even though she had brought up his.

He had understood, meeting her at elite parties before, that her family had money, too. She was essentially a socialite, he believed, although he knew she helped to raise money for organizations that helped people who were less fortunate.

But his bringing up her family now wouldn't call into mind charitable events, or even just her parents and siblings, difficult or not, but also a particularly nasty, wealthy ex who was now apparently framing her for murder.

Family. Grayson, at age thirty-six, was the youngest of three from Payne's first marriage to Tessa. He had an older brother, Ace—the one to whom it now appeared he might not be biologically related—and an older sister, Ainsley, plus adopted brother Rafe.

Ace was still a Colton, genetically or not.

Then there were three more siblings from his dad's third marriage, to his stepmother, Genevieve: twins Marlowe and Callum, and Asher. In between his late mother, Tessa, and Genevieve, Payne was married to the sinister Selina Barnes Colton. Although they had been divorced for years, Selina still remained in a prominent position at Colton Oil, leading the siblings to wonder what she held over their father.

Grayson's second phone call earlier had been with Callum.

Callum had confirmed to Grayson that Payne remained in a coma. They still didn't know who'd shot him. And couldn't Grayson get a little more involved with helping to figure that out, or working with the authorities more, since he knew them better and interacted with them as a first responder?

That wasn't the first time Callum had suggested it. Or had prodded Grayson to get more involved emotionally, too—though he didn't phrase it that way. Callum had recently uncovered the nurse who might have swapped her own newborn son with a sickly Colton baby forty years ago. That woman, Luella Smith, might be Ace's biological mother. Callum had also fallen in love with a charming single mom, Hazel Hart, and adored her daughter, Evie.

But although Grayson was okay with the fact he was a Colton, he wasn't really close to the family and didn't intend to change that even now, partly for fear they would try to twist his arm to get involved with Colton Oil.

Although, close or not, he was really concerned about

his father and how he was doing—and whether he would survive.

With his mind off on that tangent, Grayson had been looking more at his nearly empty paper plate than at Savannah, even though he had last mentioned her and her family.

While his family and their father's situation might be important, they weren't why he was here.

Or involved with what he wanted to do here.

He tore his gaze from the boring plate he'd not really noticed as his thoughts flew around. He looked up at Savannah.

She, too, appeared to be studying her empty plate. Her face was pale, her expression pensive but leaning toward sorrowful. Maybe even distraught.

"Are you okay?" he asked.

She looked up at him. "Of course. It's just that you mentioned my family. They're a good group, my mother and brother. And yes, we have some money. But my father's gone now."

The thought clearly, and understandably, made her sad. It was time to put this lunch behind them and do something else. Something that hopefully would be productive—in improving Savannah's mood, if nothing else.

Better yet, they could discuss a bit of the past and hurl it into what they could do in the near future to change things drastically for the better for his lunch companion.

"Hey, Savannah," he said. "You ready to take a walk outside? We need to take a bit of a hike to work off some of the calories from this enormous, filling lunch."

Her family.

Ignoring the fact that it recently had included—been

usurped by—that jerk Zane, Savannah briefly let her mind wander further as she stood up and cleared the table, tossing their plates into the plastic bag she was now using for trash. She also picked up the bottle of water she had been drinking from and placed it beside, though not in, the refrigerator. Why bother?

She wondered what her mother and younger brother, Randy, were thinking now. Her dad was gone, and of course she was sad about that—but he'd been a major reason she had wound up marrying Zane.

Oh, she'd had an elite upbringing, despite there being no private schools good enough around Mustang Valley for the Murphy children. Her parents, Randolph Senior and Eleanor, had imported live-in tutors to work with them while they also attended those public institutions, like the local high school, part-time, to ensure they learned everything privileged children of their ages should learn. And their mansion at the fringes of town had plenty of room for live-in help. That had been largely due to her father's income as chief executive officer of a highly profitable manufacturing company, as well as his inheritance.

Her dad was gone now, but Savannah had not worried about her mother and brother after the earthquake. Neither would have been affected. Randy had moved to Phoenix to join a highly successful stock brokerage firm. Her mom was on an extended trip to Europe with some friends.

Savannah had lived in the family mansion until she married Zane, partying and enjoying her life, including getting involved with all the charitable events she could. She'd continued to help throw fund-raising events, which wasn't much of a career, she realized, but she'd enjoyed it.

And she didn't give a damn about what, if anything, was now left of the other mansion she'd lived in, her ex's. While, apparently, he was enjoying multiple affairs.

Well, she wasn't going to talk about any of those things as she took her walk with Grayson.

Still, she appreciated his company. And his apparent intention of helping her get through this and finding the truth so she would be exonerated. She didn't know what she'd do with her life then, but she would definitely be out of prison.

Or so she hoped.

Since they had eaten everything she had prepared as their small lunch, she just checked to ensure that she had encased the remaining meat and salad fixings as well as possible in the plastic wrap Grayson had brought. She put them back with the rest of the food, knowing they wouldn't last long with no power in the refrigerator, then turned back to him—only to find him right behind her.

Or maybe she wasn't so surprised after all. He certainly hadn't startled her.

"Are we ready to go?" she asked.

"Absolutely." He held out his right elbow, as if inviting her to latch onto it with her own arm, which she did—for the few seconds it took them to reach the front door.

She opened it, but Grayson stepped in front of her. "Me first," he said. Which she appreciated, especially when he began looking around, his head raised as if he was listening, too.

He was undoubtedly checking for intruders to the area.

"Okay," he said after a few seconds. "No obvious problems, but we'll stay alert."

"Of course," she agreed. Without even thinking about it, she, too, stopped for a moment to listen for anything that didn't belong there. But other than the breeze flowing through the leaves and branches of the fir trees around them, she heard nothing except for an occasional bird call, mostly crows.

Nothing that sounded like people stalking her. No cops on her trail…but she knew she had better expect the worst eventually.

Still, she also might as well enjoy her freedom for the moment and attempt to figure out a way to guarantee it in the future.

Grayson didn't offer to take her arm again as he walked slowly around the cabin on the narrow, uneven path. "Have you walked around this way before?" he asked.

She nodded, staying at his side as they strolled along. "Yes, partly just to get out of the cabin, partly for a touch of exercise—and mostly just to think as I walked."

"I can guess what you were thinking about. Did you reach any conclusions?"

She sucked in her lips as she considered the circumstances—as if she wasn't thinking about them all the time anyway. "I want to get out of here. But as much as I'd like to find a way to flee the area, what would I do then? I'd need a new identity, and I'd always be looking over my shoulder for someone to recognize me and drag me back here to stand trial."

"Not if you could prove that the only crime committed was your ex framing you for his murder."

Savannah stopped abruptly and looked at Grayson. He'd described what she really wanted. And of course he knew that, since she hadn't exactly kept it to herself.

But his mentioning it here and now felt—well, as if he had somehow handed her a key to the future she really craved.

Not that he'd offered any guidance about finding that proof.

Still, she had an urge to hug him for his understanding.

Heck, she had an urge to hug this kind man again for more than that.

This amazingly handsome, sexy man who could have just obeyed the law and turned her over to the authorities.

And as she looked straight into his intense blue eyes, even more striking beneath his thick, sculpted brows, she had an urge to do even more with him—like drag him back into the cabin and seduce him.

Possibly the last passionate encounter she would ever experience if she was, in fact, recaptured and thrown back into prison.

Instead, she turned and restarted their walk. She inhaled the fresh, April-cool air of the woodlands. "Yes, that's the current goal of my life. I really want to dig up the truth. Find my ex and show the world what a horrible man he is. And find out for sure why he decided to frame me, although I think it's just because I refused to stay married to him while he did what he wanted, like seeing other women."

"Okay, let's start trying to figure out how to do that."

"How?" Savannah blurted. Since escaping and hiding in this place, she had been racking her brain for ideas—and hadn't come up with any good ones.

"Good question." This time Grayson stopped, and Savannah immediately halted again, too. He looked down at her with an expression that suggested he was attempting to see into her mind.

To judge whether she was actually innocent?

She wasn't about to ask.

"I want to hear it all," he said. "From the moment your ex disappeared and the world started to believe he was dead—but you didn't. What happened? Maybe, if we brainstorm after we discuss it, we can come up with an idea or two."

Or hundreds, Savannah thought, since it might take that many to clear her. But she appreciated this man's concept.

She appreciated him.

And if—when—she did get out of this, she would do what she could to repay him.

At the moment, though, as they exited the path to walk farther into the woods, onto hard ground covered with clumps of leaves—and fortunately no visibly big cracks after the earthquake—she again tamped down any idea she still retained about having sex with him.

That could lead to...well, caring.

And she didn't intend to care for any man again for a long time, if ever. Not even one as kind as this guy.

"Okay," she said. "Although if I get choked up—well, it's a pretty emotional tale for me. And it's one I've had to repeat multiple times after I was arrested. I told it to the cops, to my attorney and to nearly anyone who asked, but if anyone believed me it still didn't help me get released."

"I get it." And damned if, as they continued forward, Grayson didn't reach over and take her hand—possibly for stability in their walking and possibly for emotional support.

Tightening her grip slightly, Savannah forced herself not to let her eyes tear up—at least not much.

"It was like this," she said. She explained that the night Zane had disappeared, she had been out in the evening at a friend's place near the Rattlesnake Ridge Ranch to talk about a fund-raiser for the Mustang Valley General Hospital's children's wing. "Nothing was decided that night, but the group I get together with for that kind of thing has put together that scale of an event before, so we were just touching base and getting the idea started for a new bash."

"Yeah, I think a couple of my sisters get involved now and then."

Savannah saw a thick tree limb lying on the ground in front of them, as did Grayson, who still held her hand. "Let's go this way, rather than climbing over," he said, and they turned to their right. "Okay," Grayson said in a minute. "Please continue."

And Savannah did, hating to relive that night and the next day as she yet again described what had happened.

"We had just finalized our divorce," she told Grayson. "I didn't want to move back in with my family, nor did I want to stay anywhere near Zane, but I hadn't yet figured out where to move. So I was living in a separate guesthouse on the grounds at the back of his house—our house—though he got it back as part of our divorce settlement. I avoided Zane for the most part, and he kept encouraging me to move out as soon as possible, which was fine with me. In fact, I already had someone helping me to look for a new place. Only in retrospect that turned out to be a mistake."

Savannah almost stumbled as she thought about that

particular mistake, and what it had added to the horror of her situation.

"Why was that a mistake?" Grayson prompted beside her.

"The real estate guy's name is Schuyler Wells," she said. She tried to concentrate on the crunchy sounds of leaves beneath their shoes to distance herself from the anger and frustration of what came next.

"I've heard of him," said Grayson. "He's a big-deal developer around here, right?"

"Right. He had ideas and connections and—well, as things went south I was accused of having a long-term affair with him. He even hinted to the cops that we had planned to run away together once my divorce was final, that we'd decided to even before…before Zane disappeared."

"And you weren't?" Grayson asked.

Again Savannah stopped, this time just long enough to stomp her foot on the ground. "No way." She remained quiet until they continued forward again. She hated the way this aspect of the horror etched its way through her mind.

"Go on, please," Grayson finally said.

Savannah explained how, living in that small back house, she hadn't kept track of Zane's comings and goings, so of course she wasn't aware of whether he'd been home at all the night he supposedly disappeared.

Not that his absence would be a surprise. Even when they were married, he often wouldn't come home at night, and Savannah assumed he was having an affair or several, although he'd always explained his absence the next day as somehow related to his business. Savannah had never bought that. Why would the owner of a highly successful investment bank need to conduct an all-night meeting? No, she'd heard rumors of his affairs and even caught him once, just before she filed for divorce, with another woman.

Still, as their relationship had deteriorated, Savannah didn't mind his absences. She'd been irritated, though, when he'd claimed she had been going out, as well—which she recognized afterward was probably his way of boosting the allegations of her affair with Schuyler. And of course Schuyler later claimed they spent a lot of time together looking for someplace for Savannah to move, but he implied there were other, sexier, reasons, too.

"But then—well, that night was one Zane didn't come home. The next day, late in the morning, I got a call from his office. He hadn't shown up there, either—and that was unusual. Nor did he show up later that night or the next day. Not that I cared about him that way anymore, but I became concerned, and apparently his staff did, too. Someone called the cops, who showed up and began questioning me about what I knew about Zane and his disappearance, and why was I still living there, and what had our relationship been like recently. And then—and then—"

She had to continue. She recognized that. And if Grayson was aware at all about Zane's alleged murder, he'd probably heard it.

"And then what?" he said.

"And then—the cops found a knife in my closet, hidden under a box. It was bloody. Of course they grabbed it and took it in and had it tested."

"I assume the blood had Zane's DNA in it," Grayson said, stopping and turning to face Savannah, who also stopped but refused to look him in the face.

"You assume right," she answered with a sob.

Chapter 8

Grayson wanted yet again to take Savannah into his arms, to hold her tightly against him as she cried.

Too bad the cops didn't see this. Surely she wouldn't be crying that way if she'd killed the SOB.

On the other hand, she'd probably told this story before, and might have cried then, too. They hadn't released her.

And they could interpret this as her being sorry about getting caught, not about her ex's apparent murder.

Instead of hugging Savannah, Grayson took her hand, pulling her closer on the dirt beneath them. "Let's go back inside," he said, attempting to keep his tone light. "Did you notice? I brought you some wine, and I think this would be a good time for a sip or two."

Savannah, now facing him, swallowed and appeared to attempt a smile. "I saw that. A nice, not-too-expensive brand that no one would particularly notice when you bought it."

"Exactly." He held onto her hand as she started leading them back to the cabin.

Once they got inside, Grayson made sure the door was locked as Savannah picked up the wine from the back of the counter beside the refrigerator. And yes, it wasn't especially expensive or high quality. It came in a screw-top bottle, since he'd doubted there was an opener here in the cabin and didn't want to search for one to buy when he was on that outing. There were a few glasses without stems that the owner of the cabin had left in a cupboard, so they didn't need to drink out of the bottle.

Grayson offered a toast. "Here's to getting all of this resolved quickly and well."

"I'll drink to that," Savannah said solemnly, clinking his glass with her own.

Grayson gestured toward the table. "Let's sit down and—"

"And talk about you for a change," Savannah asserted. "I'm sure I'll be the topic again soon, but I'd like to hear about you, Grayson. How did you happen to become a first responder in the first place, then start your own company?"

The explanation had its good and bad points. In any case, Grayson didn't want to talk about it now.

But sitting across the table from Savannah as she sipped her wine and regarded him with an expectant expression on her face that was beautiful despite the redness around her eyes from crying, he didn't want to tell her to mind her own business. She deserved answers, too. And he could keep things as light as possible.

"Well," he began, "I started out after high school in

the military—the army. Did my duty but decided I didn't want to make it my long-term career." But it had been a good way to get out of town briefly and begin his own life, away from his clinging Colton family.

"Wow," Savannah said, taking another sip. Her short blond hair fell forward as she tipped her head to drink, and he resisted the urge to reach across the table and push it back. "I'm impressed. A Colton soldier."

"Exactly. Did my stint as a private in basic training and a bit more. I left, though, as soon as my enlistment ended and came back here. Then I became a wilderness guide, but only for a short while." Though he had stayed in close touch with some fellow soldiers with whom he'd become good friends.

One such pal had been Philip Prokol, formerly of Tucson, who'd been sent overseas to Iraq, where he was wounded in the military and had come back with PTSD. That hadn't killed him directly, but his attempt to flee everything he had known before, including his hometown and family, had caused him to be out in the wilderness in northern Arizona in a major rainstorm. He'd died from being washed away in a flood.

Could he have been saved? Apparently there hadn't been enough first responders to deal with that disaster and the many people swept into the water.

Hearing about it, first on the news and then from Phil's family, had almost destroyed Grayson inside. He should have done more to help his friend. He'd already ended his own brief career as a wilderness guider and started college. He should have been with Phil when he'd run off to try to find himself again.

Saved him.

And remembering Phil's fate in the wilderness during a disaster was one reason Grayson had headed out of town after the quake…to save people who might be in similar situations.

"Are you okay, Grayson?" Savannah interrupted his thoughts, a good thing. It was probably better that he not dwell on why and how he had decided to become a first responder.

"Sure," he responded brightly. "Just thinking of what I did when I returned to the States. I'd decided first to become a wilderness guide, then ended that to go to college and major in business."

And when he'd dropped out, his family, especially his father, hadn't been happy, and Payne had made that very clear. But Grayson had done what he wanted.

"Sounds good. So did you get a corporate job when you got your degree?"

He laughed. "What degree? I dumped it all when I decided to become a first responder. I left the university for a smaller school where I could learn what I needed to get my emergency medical technician credentials, and I learned more than enough to get my official certification, and there I was."

Savannah's wine glass was nearly empty, and so was Grayson's. He picked up the bottle from the table and poured them each a little more.

"Thanks," Savannah said. She'd furrowed her brow, which didn't detract in the least from how pretty she was. "But why did you want to become an EMT? A first responder?"

"I just did." He had no desire to talk any more about it. "And you? Did you get a college degree?" From what he knew about Savannah, she didn't have an official job, although her charitable efforts were admirable.

"Yes, I had the fun of moving to Los Angeles for a few years to major in English at UCLA. I loved to read then, and still do, so that worked out well."

He wanted to ask her how she used her degree now, if she did, without a job. But before he decided how to phrase it, she said, "And in case you're wondering, I never really got a job where I could use my degree, but I do go to the elementary schools in and around Mustang Valley a lot to work with kids who are reading challenged. It's really a kick to see them improve and know I at least had a little to do with it."

So the wealthy socialite who was Savannah might not earn money to cover her own expenses now, but she certainly earned kudos by helping others.

"That sounds great." And it did, to Grayson. This woman had made good use of her time and family's money—and her ex's—to help other people.

Not a first responder, but definitely someone who gave a damn and attempted to do something about it.

To prevent her from asking more about him and why he was who he was, he decided to press her some more and get her to describe some of the kids she'd helped with their reading. Then he urged her to talk more about her favorite charities that she helped now, like the hospital children's ward.

She apparently liked kids. Maybe she'd intended to have some with Zane. Well, that clearly wasn't going to happen now, nor would it even if Zane wasn't ostensibly dead, since they'd already divorced. That could have been a motive for her to kill him, Grayson supposed, or the district attorney might approach it that way: anger that he hadn't given her kids.

Nah, too ridiculous.

Grayson didn't know what the terms of the divorce settlement were. Had it been fair, or had Zane's lawyers cut her out of everything?

He had a thought then. "Any idea what your lawyer might be thinking now that you've disappeared?"

Like was he—or she—now upset because Savannah wasn't currently racking up any fees? Or was he looking bad because his client had flown? Grayson assumed that, married or not, the socialite in front of him had money of her own to pay her counsel before and after her arrest.

"Who? Ian? I don't know. He'd warned me that the evidence against me looked grim, but he'd seemed to be completely on my side, eager to at least try to get me off."

"But he didn't think you were innocent?" Grayson shook his head, eyeing the bottle of wine again but deciding he'd had enough for now.

"I thought he did, although he kept enumerating all the evidence that could keep me from even having any bail set for me, let alone getting off at trial. He reassured me a lot, though, that he would do everything in his power to get me cleared."

Yeah, like spend a lot of time—and her money—to try to prove her innocent. Well, Grayson didn't know any attorneys named Ian, but he did know others, and even the good ones appeared to be money-grubbing. "What's his name?" he asked. "Ian what?"

"Ian Wright," Savannah said, "but please don't contact him." She sounded alarmed. "He's an officer of the court, like all lawyers, he told me, which means he might have to turn me in if he found out where I was. He asked me if I'd killed Zane, said it was okay for me to admit it to him. Because of attorney-client privilege, he wouldn't reveal it to anyone else. But of course I didn't admit anything, since I'm innocent. I trust him. I like him as a lawyer. But I don't want anyone, even him, to know where I am. Not now, at least. Or that you've seen me."

Grayson didn't like the sound of that. Not that he'd tell that Ian Wright anything. But even though Savannah trusted him, Grayson trusted no one on her behalf. Not now. Not until he'd learned a lot more about her situation.

"Got it," he said. "With your phone now, you can contact him if you decide to and not give your location away"

Savannah nodded and smiled at him, her expression more relaxed—and trusting. Damn. She shouldn't trust anyone right now, even him.

Still… Evening was approaching now. He needed to leave, get back to the office for a while before going home.

"Sorry," he told Savannah, drinking his last few drops of wine. "I'd better get on my way."

He was about to tell her he'd be back again soon, though he didn't think it would be tomorrow. He'd brought her enough sustenance for a few days, anyway. And wine.

"I understand," she said, nodding slightly. If he read her expression correctly, she probably understood but felt bad about his leaving. "That's fine. I appreciate our discussions today and think I might have an idea of what to do next, but I want to think about it more, so being here on my own will be fine. Only—"

"Only what?" he asked when she hesitated.

"I don't suppose you have a pen and paper in your car that you could give me so I can make some notes, do you?"

He laughed. He'd expected something a lot more significant than that, given the change in her expression to uncertainty, maybe fear—or worse.

She needed to jot something down, apparently. And he always kept a notebook or two in his SUV in case he got a call and needed to jot down quickly where to go and why.

"Sure," he said. "I'll bring them in right now—before I leave."

Grayson had left an hour or more ago, but Savannah had tried not to think about him as she sat at the same old table once more, making notes.

And realizing she needed to get out of there soon. In some ways, the cabin was as much a prison as her cell.

Not just because she felt lonely with her only current contact, Grayson, gone. She recognized that she missed him not only because he was attempting to help her but because…well, she liked the guy. Felt attracted to him, despite herself.

But she also recognized that was a mistake. He was a good man, dedicating his life to helping people, and at the moment that included her.

It didn't mean he liked her as anything more than someone who needed him.

Despite the hugs and the kiss they'd shared, which to Savannah had suggested more. A lot more.

But that wouldn't happen.

Savannah rose again to turn on the lanterns to avoid being left in the dark. She checked to make sure the door was locked and the windows fully closed. She had no intention of going outside again that night.

And tomorrow? Maybe. Hanging out inside here

alone could drive her nuts—even nuttier than she already felt. But what else could she do?

She would ponder that tonight where she could go, what she could do, to locate Zane and show the world what a horrible person he was. A living person. But how?

And what would she do if she didn't ever see Grayson again? After handing her the notebook and pen, he had said he might not be back tomorrow but promised she would see him again soon.

But *soon* could mean anything from another day to a week or more. And his saying he'd return didn't mean it would come about. Even when the food he so kindly supplied her with was gone.

So…now what?

She was a murder suspect who'd fled and was most likely being chased, or would be once the authorities finished with disaster relief.

If she left here, she would have to walk through these woods and beyond, in an area she didn't know at all—unless she found her way back to town, a horrible idea if she couldn't remain hidden somehow. She'd be recognized and arrested again, probably immediately.

But what was the alternative?

She had an idea, but it depended on Grayson's returning. More than once.

Which meant, yes, she relied on him. A lot.

She trusted him, sure. Because she had to. She needed him to help her hang on to the last shred of sanity she still had.

And if he didn't come back here even once?

Well, she could stay here until her remaining food ran out and then see what happened.

And in the meantime?

She decided to try to keep her sanity a bit by working out details for that idea she had.

She placed the notebook Grayson had given her on the table in front of her. Then she hurried into the bathroom and examined herself again in the mirror. At least she liked her new hairstyle—sort of.

Returning to the main room, she set a water bottle on the table and poured herself a small amount of wine before opening the notebook.

She began sketching on the first page.

Chapter 9

Grayson's mind remained on Savannah and what to do next to help her, as he headed his SUV back toward his office. He knew where he'd start once he sat down at his computer.

He was worried about her, unsure what she'd do without him hanging around and encouraging her to stay put while they worked out a plan. But even if no one paid attention to where he was going and he therefore didn't endanger Savannah further, he couldn't keep visiting there as much as he had without his company suffering.

But he didn't want her to suffer, either.

Would she run before he showed up again? It wasn't really his business, yet he felt like it was. He'd promised to help her get through this. And as long as he believed she was innocent, he intended to assist her.

But did he fully trust her? Maybe not, but until he found some reason not to, he'd act as if he did.

And help her. After all, that was his calling in life: helping people.

Plus, something about Savannah Oliver made him want to pull out all stops to clear her name. Her resigned yet hopeful attitude and this miserable situation were what did it, he told himself.

He could handle the unwanted attraction he felt for her. He had to.

Still, better that he do things quickly to try to clear her—like what he intended to do that evening and tomorrow.

He answered a few phone calls as he drove, mostly business-related but also concerning his family—darn it. Of course he was worried about his father, but at least Ainsley let him know that Payne was holding his own at the moment. And then there was the Ace situation. No matter what, the guy was their brother, even though not by blood.

He drove even more slowly once he reached downtown Mustang Valley. The earthquake damage wasn't what kept his speed low, or not entirely. The cracked streets he traversed had already been at least temporarily fixed, or detours designated. The sidewalks around them had been improved a bit, too. The buildings not so much, at least not yet.

But what particularly kept Grayson from driving at a normal speed was amazement at how many tables along those sidewalks he now saw that had Affirmation Alliance Group signs on them—even more than before. He still liked the idea that they were out there trying to help people who'd suffered damages from the quake.

But though he couldn't quite put a finger on why, he still didn't trust them.

His curiosity about them inflated even more after he reached his office building—and saw one of those tables on the sidewalk on the next block. The sign there was even larger than the rest—and it invited people to come and meet the group's founder, Micheline Anderson.

Grayson had heard of Micheline—all pretty good stuff. Maybe his opinion of the group going overboard would change if he actually met her.

And so, after parking his SUV behind his office building, he walked around to the front and crossed the street.

The table here was larger than the others he'd seen. There were lots of flyers on it, and several people sat or stood behind it.

One had an identification card folded in front of her: Micheline Anderson.

The woman behind it appeared to be a really attractive senior. She had long blond hair, dangling earrings with pearls at the ends and a face that resembled a movie star's. She wore a blue shirtwaist dress and stood behind the table.

Beside her ID card was a larger sign. It said Be Your Best You! Grayson had heard that before. It was her organization's slogan.

He approached her. Several other people dressed nicely, yet less formally than Micheline, stood around her, and a couple were talking to others lined up across the table, apparently handing out flyers and discussing the group with them.

"Hello," Grayson said to Micheline. She'd watched

him as he approached, a large smile on her face. Did she recognize him? If so, how and why?

"Hello," she said, drawing out the word as if she was happy to see him. "Welcome to the Affirmation Alliance Group. I'm Micheline Anderson." As if he couldn't tell, despite the others hanging around the long table with her. "And you are…?"

"I'm Grayson Colton." He watched both her eyes and smile widen even more as he said his last name. Evidently, whether or not she thought she knew him, she was aware of the prominence of the Colton family—as who wasn't around here? But not many people actually knew him…and his not-so-thrilled attitude toward most of his relations.

Although, on his way here, one of the calls he'd received was from his half brother, Callum. And after a bunch of arm-twisting, not easy over the phone, Grayson had agreed to join his relatives for dinner at the ranch house that night. The others intended to discuss some family matters and really wanted him there.

Which had also added to his concern about when he'd next be able to visit Savannah and help keep her motivated to stay where she was.

"How do you do, Grayson Colton?" Micheline held her hand out for a shake. "Thanks for coming to say hi. I assume you don't need a place to stay after the quake, since, from what I've heard, the Rattlesnake Ridge Ranch survived just fine. That's one of the reasons we're out here, you know—to let everyone know we have a place people can stay, if they need it. But can I convince you to come visit us anyway and participate in one of our seminars? We give them often, on a variety of subjects to help people achieve our goal to 'be your best you.' There's a charge, of course, since we use the money to help others."

She smiled as if expecting him to compliment her for that, but he just smiled slightly in return.

"And you—" she continued, "I know you're a first responder and like to help people too, right?"

Grayson realized it had been a mistake to come to this table, despite how curious he was. The woman might have good intentions—or not. But what she definitely had was an open hand in which she wanted money deposited, no matter what she intended to use it for.

His passing thought earlier, that meeting her might help him accept her and her group more, had been only that—a passing thought that definitely wasn't coming true.

He needed to leave here right now, but without causing any kind of scene. He assumed Micheline would stop at nothing to achieve one of her goals, so he figured he'd need to do this as politely as he could.

"That's great that you know who I am," he lied, looking into her blue eyes, which he'd have found attractive on a younger and more trustworthy woman. "And I appreciate your invitation. I'll definitely consider it." Like hell he would. "But for right now I'm still working hard on helping people affected by the quake, as you are, so I can't commit to doing anything else."

"I understand." Micheline's smile seemed to drop a bit and her eyes showed irritation. "But here." She picked up a bunch of flyers from the table and handed them to him. "Call anytime you're able to set something up. And I hope it's soon."

"Thanks." He accepted the paperwork, figuring he'd dump it into a recycle bin in his office as soon as possible. "And good luck to you in helping as many folks in need as you can."

He strode away, across the street and into his building. Only then did he feel as if he could breathe naturally again.

He stood in the large, empty lobby, not yet approaching any of his staff. Okay, Affirmation Alliance Group could be everything Micheline claimed. Maybe more. But it sounded too good to be true. Plus, he didn't trust people easily, partly because of ways his own family had tried to guilt him into giving up his own company and join Colton Oil.

Anyway, he didn't need to stay in touch with their leader or any of them. And he hadn't lied to her. He and his gang were still working hard on helping people affected by the quake. For him, that included the fugitive Savannah, and after he caught up on what he needed to do that day, he'd take another approach to helping her— and proving her innocence.

He hadn't thought in advance about which of his staff he'd drop in on first now that he was on the floor where their offices were, but as often happened, Winchell decided that for him. Winch was well enough trained that Chad didn't generally keep him leashed in the office, although his door was often closed. As it had been— till now. It opened, and Winch ran out toward Grayson.

As Grayson bent to pat Winch, Chad joined them. "Hey," he said. "Good timing. Winch and I just ended our assignment for the day from the MVPD. And guess what?"

Grayson had a pretty good idea, considering the big grin on the retired cop's face that moved his glasses up a notch on his cheeks. But he let Chad inform him. "What?"

"This excellent K-9 of mine found a survivor who'd been buried in rubble from an apartment building just outside town."

"Good boy!" Now Grayson knelt on the floor and gave the dog a big hug. "Tell me more." He stood again and faced Chad, as Pedro came out of his office, too. "I assume you've already heard the story," Grayson said to Pedro.

"Not all of it," the former firefighter said. "I want to hear more. Fortunately, though I helped to get rid of several fires, there weren't any casualties—survivors or otherwise."

"Let's sit down here, then." Grayson gestured toward the seats in the reception area. "Is Norah here, too?"

"No, I gather she's back at the hospital, since the EMTs needed more help today," Chad said.

His hand still on Winch's head, Grayson listened to the story of the old and not particularly well-maintained apartment building in the part of town worst hit by the quake. And yes, it had been a couple of days, but the authorities were aware, thanks to info from others in that building, that at least one resident had remained missing. A couple of others, too, though they likely were out of town.

"The victim was elderly," Chad said, "but word was that she exercised a lot and was in fairly good shape for her age. And nearly as soon as the neighbors pointed us in the general direction of what was left of her unit, Winch began reacting—though a small distance away, which was probably why the woman hadn't been located before. Some firefighters and city staff were there digging, and in a short while they located her. She'd fortunately had an air pocket and had been able to breathe."

"So Winchell's a search and rescue hero," Grayson said with a grin, still petting the dog.

"You've got it," said his owner and handler. "Media folks were there, too, so I made sure to let them know Winchell and I were part of First Hand First Responders."

"Then you're our hero, too." Grayson stood again and held out his hand for Chad to shake it.

After making a fuss over Winch some more, Grayson excused himself, letting his staff know he'd be in his office for a while. He had a lot of work to do there.

First, he sat down at his desk and faced his computer. He researched the location of the buried senior and saw exactly what Chad had described, including some videos of Winchell at work—and Chad's mention of First Hand. Grayson virtually applauded.

The woman they'd saved, Susan Black, had suffered some significant injuries and was still in the hospital, but she was expected to make a full recovery.

Good. Grayson was glad the woman would be okay. He was also glad to see positive publicity for First Hand.

He next plowed through his emails, answering a lot of questions in them about what his company of first responders had done during and after the quake.

He was also glad to see that a few were from contacts from police and fire departments they'd worked with outside but not far away from Mustang Valley. But some were strangers, inquiring into what his first responders could and couldn't do in emergencies. Fortunately, Grayson kept his billing amounts within reason.

Finally, he got to what he had intended to do all along: research the people involved in the case against Savannah.

First, he searched Zane Oliver online. No surprises there. From all Grayson found, the guy had disappeared and was presumed dead, murdered by his ex-wife. A knife had been found in her home with his DNA on it.

Grayson tried a little further digging. It appeared that Zane's investment bank was still alive and profitable even without his presence. If so, Zane probably hadn't been trying to run from a career gone bad.

It was a shame, though, that Grayson couldn't instantly find information about Zane's personal finances.

Maybe Savannah's ex had invested his money back into accounts in the company to keep incurring further profits, still growing on behalf of his heirs, whoever they were, now that he was divorced.

That was something Grayson would have to look into, too. But not right now.

Next he researched that real estate developer Schuyler Wells, with whom Savannah had been accused of having an affair during her marriage. The guy was featured on a lot of websites mentioning construction and property sales, primarily around Mustang Valley. His picture was included in several of them, as were videos in which he described what wonderful homes and apartments and office buildings he'd been involved with planning and constructing—and now selling, undoubtedly for a nice profit, Grayson assumed. From what Grayson could see in the photos the middle-aged guy looked earnest and dedicated, with eyes staring straight into the camera, a tenor voice, and a hint of a knowing smile on his long face. His hair appeared short and impeccably groomed.

He appeared to be of moderate height and mostly wore suits. A real real estate agent.

But Grayson began getting bored with all the hype, finding nothing particularly exciting about Wells. Grayson figured it was nearly time to go on to his next subject—

Only, oddly, he found something on one of the sites he next checked. Or not so oddly. Real estate moguls, with lots of construction and sales to their names, undoubtedly needed good attorneys to handle issues with buyers who found flaws or were otherwise unhappy with their purchases.

Therefore it wasn't a huge surprise to learn of a lawsuit that had been filed against Schuyler Wells Real Estate—or that his defense attorney in the tort action had been none other than Savannah's criminal lawyer, Ian Wright.

So the two of them knew each other. That didn't necessarily mean they discussed Savannah.

But of course they could have. And the impression Grayson had gathered was that Schuyler Wells had lied about an affair with Savannah to make her appear to have a stronger motive to kill her ex—although that didn't make complete sense, since they were already divorced. Even if Zane had heard about a supposed affair and used that as a reason to divorce Savannah, once they were no longer a married couple, there'd be no reason for Savannah to murder Zane. He would have had more of a motive to murder her.

Although of course Grayson didn't know what the settlement of their assets involved. Even so, it was unlikely Savannah would become better off with Zane dead. She wouldn't inherit anything since they were divorced, and it might be even harder for her to obtain whatever their divorce settlement was, if she hadn't received all of it yet.

Anyway, Grayson compiled the information that he had found on researching all three men. He'd show it to Savannah tomorrow.

And then? Well, Grayson thought he might pay a visit to at least the lawyer, Ian Wright. Maybe just indicate that, since he'd found the van that had been transporting Savannah, he'd become interested in the murder case against her—and where would Ian go with it now if and when Savannah was found. What were his thoughts about that bloody knife that had become so vital in the case against Savannah? What else would he do to prove her innocent?

Of course the guy would undoubtedly rant about attorney-client privilege. But even so…well, maybe he'd say something that would give Grayson a better idea of whether it would make sense for Savannah to turn herself in—or to run far, far away.

Only then would Grayson let her know what he'd found out from Ian.

And he wouldn't be at all surprised if that lovely, determined woman who definitely thought for herself would listen to what he hoped would be his sound advice.

It was late afternoon. Savannah sat in her usual spot, reading an article on the Mustang Valley city government website about the history of the town. She already knew most of it, but at least it occupied a fragment of her mind. She'd used the battery-operated charger to make sure her new phone continued to have power.

So far, no new ideas about chasing down Zane. And

she hadn't admitted it to herself, but she'd hoped that Grayson would come visit her sometime that day.

That was just because she now had something else to ask him. Or so she told herself—even without believing it.

Added to that was that she was lonesome, of course, with no one else around to talk to, no one she could trust enough to call even just to say hi.

And—well, she refused to admit to herself that she really enjoyed Grayson and his company. His obvious determination to help her.

His appealing looks that she could speculate about for the future...

Not.

Okay. Enough of this. She exited the website and pushed the button to make the phone's screen go black, saving at least a little power.

She glanced down at the notebook on the table beside her. Oh yes, she'd been making notes.

Notes about things she would ask Grayson to do to help prove her innocence, though those remained sparse, and she couldn't be sure he would do them anyway. More of her notes contained items she would ask Grayson to purchase for her—and of course she would reimburse him. Eventually. As a Colton, he undoubtedly had enough money to buy it in the first place.

But he shouldn't buy it anywhere in Mustang Valley or in a town near here, because she had listed a lot of things she needed to disguise herself so she could at least escape this cabin. Maybe go into town and eavesdrop or snoop around to find evidence against Zane. Even ask questions without being recognized. Or so she hoped.

She grabbed the notebook and returned to the bathroom, where she again looked in the mirror.

Good thing she'd been a thespian in a local high school, though she hadn't followed up afterward. She'd acted in a couple of different plays, even starred in one during her senior year.

The English teachers had been in charge and they'd taught the actors—including Savannah—how to put on makeup that helped them resemble their characters.

Savannah's favorite role had been as a grandmother to a bunch of kids in a comedy. That meant she'd learned how to apply makeup to look older, which she intended to take advantage of now.

She usually wore makeup to enhance her appearance, which she considered attractive enough.

Now she would only ask Grayson to buy certain shades of foundation, eye shadow and hair dye, of course, since she planned a new haircut that would help disguise her even more. And she would be less recognizable if she wasn't a blonde.

She could always return to her original coloring in the future, when this was all behind her.

As she had before, she studied her face and imagined what it would be like once she added lines to make her appear older, though her eyes would remain green, which could be a problem. But she didn't want to suddenly start wearing contact lenses and possibly damage her vision.

She looked at herself, then down at her list, and up into the mirror again.

Okay, the list seemed good enough. Particularly because it also included the kind of clothes she would generally only wear while cleaning or on a hike or something—ratty T-shirts and jeans that already had holes in them, or whatever else was available at a discount shop.

And as embarrassing as it was, she would also have to request more underwear. She hated to provide her size, but what else could she do? They should not be the luxury kind she usually wore, though no one but Grayson would know that.

And yes, a new pair of athletic shoes, again not expensive but different from what she had now, the ones she had worn leaving the prison.

Now all she had to do was wait until Grayson showed up again. Sometime.

Surely he would. He'd promised.

And she could request then that he leave town and go buy her all she needed.

She only hoped he didn't get caught. For her sake, sure. But also for his well-being, which was becoming more and more important to her.

Chapter 10

Grayson sat on the swanky beige coverlet on the antique bed in his room at Rattlesnake Ridge Ranch. Sort of. He had his own small wing on the second floor of this mansion, and so did each of his full siblings Ace and Ainsley.

He'd seen Callum on his arrival, but no one else so far, since he'd kind of edged his way in via a side door as he mostly did. That was a good thing.

But soon it would be time for dinner, the main reason he had come here at this time. After Callum's coercion.

Those who were here would discuss not only their dad's dire medical condition but more about the current status of the family mystery: the true background of their oldest brother, Ace—and what had happened to his parents' biological firstborn, for whom Ace had allegedly been swapped at birth.

It had been a common topic of conversation among the group, ever since someone had sent those allegations to the Colton Oil board, which had shocked them all. But were they true? Even Grayson, despite his intentional distance from the family most of the time, wanted to know.

He was curious.

For now, he sat on the bed and surveyed the masculine headboard of pale wood, matched by the nightstand and the dresser with a mirror. He had picked these out when he was a lot younger, before he had even joined the military. He still liked them. And even if members of his hot-stuff wealthy family weren't thrilled with them, they hadn't gotten rid of them.

After all, at least some of those family members still encouraged Grayson to actually live here full-time.

His cell phone rang, and he pulled it out of the pocket of his dressy gray slacks. He'd been dressed fine for work before but here, at the Colton digs, he always felt he needed to shine.

It was Callum again. "Everyone's starting to arrive. Come on down to the dining room."

"Right," Grayson said and hung up.

He took a deep breath. Would all of his siblings be here? He'd soon find out.

He considered checking how he looked again in the full-length mirror in the bathroom—and ruled that out. Heck, even the change of clothes was more than he should have done. He was here, and that was all his family should care about.

He strode out the door leading to the rest of the house. Before he reached the stairway that led down to the first floor—where the dining room was—he saw Ainsley approach from her wing, next to his. Ace's wing was on this floor, too. All three of them had the same mother, the late Tessa Ainsley Colton.

Maybe. That remained a question as to Ace.

"Hi, Grayson," Ainsley called, clearly hurrying to catch up. Ainsley was slightly older than Grayson, thirty-seven to his thirty-six. Their only other full sibling was Ace—or so everyone had thought before questions arose.

"Hi, Ainsley."

Grayson waited till she reached him. She was much more involved with their relatives than he was—particularly as an attorney for Colton Oil. In fact, Grayson found her maybe a bit too devoted to the family, but that was just him. Ainsley was a pretty lady, well groomed even when not dressed in attorney clothes, like her current long-sleeved floral T-shirt and slacks. She was shorter than Grayson, with light eyes and hair an attractive chestnut shade.

"So you did come." Ainsley continued to walk toward the stairway as she patted him on the shoulder. "Callum said you would. I hoped so, especially because all of these horrible questions about Ace and whether he shot our father. Or not."

"I gather someone has more information, and that's the reason we're meeting up, right?" Grayson asked. He figured that if anyone knew anything around here, the smart and involved Ainsley would be it.

"Yes, but—"

"Hi, you two," Callum called from the bottom of the steps. Younger than Ainsley and Grayson, he was a product of their dad's relationship with his current wife, Genevieve. Callum was a big guy and a former Navy SEAL, and currently a bodyguard.

And he was definitely a Colton.

"Good evening, Callum," Ainsley called, and Grayson just waved since they'd already seen each other since his arrival.

"Hurry up," Callum said. "Dinner is about to be served."

They walked through the amazingly decorated living room. Its wooden floor matched the trim on the walls. In the middle was an ornate table surrounded by upholstered chairs. It had a fireplace and an attractive vaulted ceiling, and a wide window overlooking one of the ranch's pastures.

The dining room connected with it via a rounded wall. It had an impressively carved table in its center, with upholstered chairs for diners, and splendid chandeliers above.

Grayson headed there, with Ainsley and Callum behind him. Their other siblings were already seated.

Grayson greeted Marlowe, Callum's twin, and their older brother Asher, who was also Genevieve's child. Genevieve wasn't there, though. Was she at the hospital with their dad?

Selina wasn't there, either, but that was no surprise. Even though she was a big wheel at Colton Oil, their father's second wife hadn't had any children and wasn't that close with Payne's actual offspring. She did have her own house on this property, though.

Grayson sat down beside Ace, slightly surprised he was there. But heck, no matter what his actual DNA might be, Ace had been brought up as a Colton, their oldest brother, and that was who he still was, at least in Grayson's mind.

Still, on hearing about the discrepancy, which was

proven by a DNA test, their dad had immediately fired Ace as chief executive officer of Colton Oil, due to company bylaws.

Even worse, because of their ensuing argument, Ace was also a suspect in their father's shooting—probably another false allegation, like the accusation leveled at Savannah of her ex's murder.

Ace hadn't been arrested, at least not yet, so Grayson supposed he could do whatever he wanted, at least for now. Although he had also heard that Ace had been told not to leave town by the MVPD, including Kerry.

Would any of that be brought up this evening? Most likely, or why was Callum so insistent he join his siblings tonight?

What did they all want to talk about?

"Hey, bro." Ace gave Grayson a high five. "Long time no see." Ace's light brown hair was more unruly than Grayson was used to seeing it. Of course, when he'd represented Colton Oil, he had to maintain a professional look. He studied Grayson with his closely set dark eyes, as if trying to figure out what was on Grayson's mind.

"Lots going on as a first responder after the quake," Grayson said, figuring that was a good enough excuse— though he'd been avoiding seeing people at the ranch even before that.

He considered asking Ace more about how he was doing, and what he was doing now that he no longer ran the company. But as interested as he was in his brother's answer, he decided to hold off for now.

Water glasses had already been left by each place setting—all antique crystal, as far as Grayson could tell. Now a member of the kitchen staff whom Grayson hadn't met previously placed salads arranged on fine china out in front of them.

This was definitely a formal dinner.

Grayson appreciated sitting between Ace and Ainsley, to whom he was closest, since they shared a mom.

They had become even closer after their mother died, especially when their father began remarrying. Grayson had never become close with either of his stepmothers, though he had made himself get along with them. But the additional marriages, and siblings, had also contributed to his distance from the family, along with the urging by many of them for him to get more involved with Colton Oil.

Now, the family members who were here all dug into their salads, conversing with the others around them. For a while. For a frustrating while to Grayson. And so he was the first to speak up.

"It's good to see all of you," he lied, looking around. Well, maybe it wasn't a total lie. He didn't enjoy much camaraderie with his family members, but it was okay to see them now and then. "And I know something is going on around here, which is why I'm here. But first thing—I'd really like to know how Dad is doing."

There. That should get them talking. Grayson glanced first toward Ace, who stared at him as if he'd been slugged.

"He's still alive, at least," Ainsley said from between them. She clutched her salad fork, then placed it on her plate. "But he remains in a coma."

At least their father still held his own, Grayson thought. That was a good thing. He wanted to ask about the investigation into the shooting but, for Ace's sake, hesitated.

Ace spoke up, though. "And in case any of you still wonders if I was the one to shoot him, the answer is no. But I don't know where the cops stand on their investigation, other than to make assumptions about me because I'd argued with him."

"An understatement," laughed Callum. "Oh, I'm not accusing you, bro, but you certainly weren't pleased when he fired you from Colton Oil."

"Can you blame me?" Ace countered loudly.

Their adopted brother Rafe, son of the ranch's old foreman, got into the conversation. "I don't imagine the cops believe you're the source of that Arizona State University pin," he said to Ace. "That's got to be something in your favor." The pin, found near their father when he was shot, was considered a possible clue.

"Certainly nothing I had anything to do with, either," Ace said.

"Besides," Callum broke in. "So what if Ace wasn't a Colton by blood? The bylaws should be changed. And one of the reasons I wanted to get you all together was to give an update on our investigation into who actually was the baby Ace was swapped with."

For nearly the rest of the meal, Grayson listened to the discussion going on.

Callum had narrowed in on Luella, a nurse at the hospital, who had also given birth to a baby on the night of Ace's birth forty years ago. She had left quickly, allegedly to find better medical care for her baby, since that infant had major medical issues.

No one had yet been able to find Luella to learn any more. One good thing, though, was that the nurse who'd first identified Luella had recently let Callum know she'd finally remembered Luella's last name: Smith. Of course that wasn't great news because the name was too common. But Callum hadn't given up.

The conclusion at the end of dinner that night? The search continued. Callum told them he'd tracked every Luella Smith in Arizona and bordering states. Three had seemed like possibilities because of their ages. But none had panned out.

"The last time Luella Smith seemed to have existed was on Christmas Day forty years ago," Callum said, "and then she vanished off the face of the earth. There's no birth record of her son, since those records were destroyed in the hospital fire. And since she apparently switched babies and took one that wasn't hers, she must have forged a birth certificate for him."

"She must have taken on a fake name, don't you think?" Grayson asked.

"Yes, that's what we think," Ainsley replied. "And we'll find her one day, somehow, someway. Turning over rocks always reveals something."

Grayson's siblings had also begun trying to track down the other babies born locally on Christmas morning forty years ago by checking through newspaper microfiches and doing online searches. Maybe one of them was the real, missing Ace Colton.

Well, Callum had said that one reason why this dinner had been called was to let them all know the status of the search. And it was an interesting update, kind of.

Fortunately, the meal included some great-tasting steaks. When Grayson finished eating, he tried to excuse himself.

He wanted to return to his office and do a bit more research.

His intention was to hurry to see Savannah in the

morning, let her know what he had already found and discuss with her what to do next—although he figured he knew.

But before they let him go, Callum said to him, "You can't leave yet. We all want to hear more about how our first responder brother did after the earthquake—and the man you found dead."

Grayson remained seated and refrained from rolling his eyes. A lot of this had already appeared in the media.

But this was his family, so he described how he had found the crushed transport van with the dead driver.

"But the back was empty inside, right?" Ainsley asked.

"That's right," Grayson agreed.

"But they said there'd been someone inside being transported," Ainsley pressed. "Savannah Oliver, right? She'd been arrested for murdering her husband and was on her way back to prison from the courthouse."

"That's what I understand." Grayson tried not to grit his teeth.

"That whole situation is sad," Marlowe said. "I've known Savannah for a long time—Savannah Murphy. Some of you have, too, right?" She looked at Ainsley, who nodded. "She's a nice person. I find it really hard to believe she's a murderer."

An accused murderer, Grayson wanted to say but kept quiet. He didn't want them to figure out he even knew Savannah, let alone that he was attempting to help her.

"People snap and do terrible things sometimes," Ainsley said. "But I have to agree with you, Marlowe. I find it hard to believe that Savannah's a killer."

That, at least, was good, Grayson thought. And fortunately the topic of conversation moved to how Colton

Oil was doing now that their dad Payne wasn't in charge of even his executive staff. Marlowe was now CEO. And Rafe was CFO.

Which was of some interest to Grayson, but not much. Especially since all seemed to be going relatively well.

"No dessert for me," he said a little while later as the staff began clearing plates and bringing out sweets. "I've got to get on the move." He ignored the irritation on his siblings' faces as he left. "See you again soon," he said—lying somewhat again.

He was interested in what they might eventually discover about their missing oldest sibling, so he might meet up with one or more of them again soon about that.

And he wanted to stay informed about how their father was doing.

But otherwise—well, he wasn't hanging out in the dining room here. He was going back to his wing to spend the night.

So he could get up early the next morning—and head for a certain fisherman's cabin.

Savannah's eyes popped open. What time was it? Daylight poured into the cabin through its multiple windows, illuminating its shabby but utilitarian contents that she had come to know too well.

She thrust the sheet off and sat up in bed. She had actually slept last night, at least for a while. Amazing!

She wore a long T-shirt, the one that had been in the bag she had rescued. It felt good to get out of the other clothes she'd been wearing pretty much all the time since her flight from the van—and before.

And with luck, she would be able to convince Grayson to buy her the things she had listed to help turn her into someone who appeared quite different from the fugitive Savannah Oliver. That would include utilitarian nightwear of her own.

Before leaving the bed, she sat there listening for any sound that could have awakened her. There were a few birds tweeting outside, but nothing suggested she was about to have any human visitors.

Unfortunately, not even Grayson. But he'd already told her not to expect him that day.

And if he did turn up tomorrow or the next day? Should she really just continue to stay in this cabin waiting for him—and imagining that no one else could find her here?

On that miserable thought, she finally stood and headed toward the bathroom, where she stepped into the shower. She had left her clothes on the bed, and when she was done washing she dried herself and opened the bathroom door again.

Yesterday, Grayson had been there, and she'd kissed him. She listened once more, just in case, but heard nothing. Saw nothing. And so she got dressed.

She wasn't especially hungry, but she'd seen some cereal bars with fruit filling that Grayson had brought, and so she took one out of its small box in one of the kitchen cabinets and brought it to the table, along with—what else? A bottle of water. She wished she had caffeine, but with no power here, let alone any kind of coffee maker, she was out of luck.

One of these days, though…especially if she accomplished what she wanted to and started looking like someone who wasn't her at all. Could she then work directly with Grayson and somehow investigate what had happened to Zane? If not, she would still ask for his advice on how to prove her innocence.

As she was eating, she considered what she would do that day—assuming she didn't just go crazy and flee this place. But if she did, where would she go?

No, it made more sense to hang out here one more day and see if Grayson did show up tomorrow. Then she could make her request for disguise material, and if he agreed and got what she asked for, that would be the time to leave.

If he showed up.

After all, the men in her life such as Zane, and even Schuyler, had betrayed her. Could she believe that Grayson wouldn't do so, too?

For now—well, she noticed that her burner phone was fully charged, fortunately. She quickly added more batteries to the list she'd been making, though. She had no idea how long these would last.

Then she decided to take a walk around the cabin for a modicum of exercise before starting whatever research she could come up with on the phone.

She put the phone in her pocket, just in case she needed it, then headed to the door. She opened it, and gasped. Grayson.

Chapter 11

Savannah reached out, grabbed Grayson's hand and pulled him into the house.

She closed the door behind him and did what she'd vowed never to do again. She hugged him. Tightly. And looked up into his wonderful blue eyes. Which also looked down at her, but only for an instant, until he bent his head…and they kissed.

Oh, what a kiss. Savannah felt Grayson's hard body against her, his heat surrounding her, his slight beard scratching her face just a little, his—well, she definitely knew that he was as aroused as she.

Bad idea. Bad idea. The words started circulating through her brain even as she pulled him even more tightly against her, her mouth absorbing every heated moment of that kiss.

But this couldn't go on forever. And that it had happened at all felt foolish.

And amazing...

She gave him one more kiss against that hot mouth of his, the slightest, most wonderful of pressures, then pulled away.

"Wow," he said, looking at her once more.

"Well, that's what you get when you show up when you're not supposed to," she said, then realized how absurd that sounded. "I mean—"

"I get it," he said. "And I'll remember it. Maybe what I should do is tell you each time I come here that you won't see me again for a while, and then come anyway the next day."

She made herself scowl at him, though it wasn't real and he undoubtedly knew it. "I don't like being lied to—even when the results are...are...well, good ones." She stepped back even further. "Anyway, why are you here today? I had the impression you had a lot of things to take care of at your office, or whatever."

"Well, I got quite a bit done after I left here yesterday. And part of it made me want more answers that maybe you can give."

"Oh," Savannah said. "What are the questions?"

"We'll discuss them in a minute," he said. "For now—well, I'm not sure if you like coffee, but I brewed some in my apartment and brought it in two insulated travel mugs so it's still hot. And none of my family was around when I left, so no one saw me carrying two, so don't worry about that. But if you don't want any, I'll—"

"I'd love some coffee," Savannah said, feeling herself smile as if he'd offered her a bag of diamonds.

Diamonds. They made her think of commitments—

although she of course no longer wore the one Zane had given her when they'd gotten engaged. She'd kept the ring with the big, expensive jewel, though. It served him right for being such a jerk while they were married.

And that was also part of their negotiated divorce settlement.

Not that it would do her any good now, especially since she had it locked in a safe deposit box at her local bank. She couldn't just show up there and claim it, even if she got access again to the code to let her in.

Divorce. Relationships. She never wanted another one again, after Zane and his nastiness and infidelities. Not even with a man who looked and kissed like Grayson, who seemed so nice, who was helping her...

Enough.

She looked at Grayson. "Hey, can I come out to your car and help you carry the coffee in?"

"No thanks, but in case you didn't eat breakfast, or even if you did, I also brought a half dozen doughnuts."

When things normalized a bit, Savannah figured she'd be able to eat more sensibly, more healthfully. But considering everything, including her mood and lack of much appetite, she doubted she would gain much weight right now.

"Sounds good," she said, then watched him head back out the door.

She returned to the bathroom again to see what she looked like. She'd used her fingers to comb her hair, as was her norm right now. But even with no makeup, she figured she didn't look too bad.

Maybe she would look a lot better soon. Or at least a lot different.

Grayson was gone only a few minutes before coming

in with two metallic coffee mugs with caps, as well as a plastic bag containing the doughnuts he had mentioned.

They both sat down at their now-regular places at the table. Savannah immediately took a nice, long sip from the mug Grayson placed in front of her. It tasted good, not too strong or too light, and it had maintained a sufficient amount of heat. She closed her eyes for a moment to savor it.

"I gather you don't mind drinking coffee," Grayson said.

"Not at all." But after taking a glazed doughnut from the bag, along with a napkin, Savannah said, "So what brought you here today? What questions do you have?"

"Well, out of curiosity, how did you happen to hire Ian Wright as your lawyer? Did you already have a professional relationship with him?"

"No. I…well, I did have a local lawyer, John Morton, representing me in my divorce. When I recognized that I needed a criminal attorney when…when it appeared that Zane had been killed, I asked him for a referral. He suggested a couple but said that Ian, whose office was also in his building, had experience in different legal areas but had recently successfully defended a client in a murder case in a nearby town. I looked that up on the internet, thought he sounded good, so I called him and he came to see me at my home before the cops came for me, and I hired him."

"Got it," Grayson said.

"Why did you ask that?" Savannah felt a bit puzzled.

"Well, I spent some time on the computer yesterday checking into Mr. Wright's background, as well as Schuyler Wells's. And funny thing."

Both curiosity and anticipated dismay rocketed through Savannah. "What?"

"It turned out that your supposed buddy, Schuyler the real estate mogul, had a lawsuit filed against his company a few years ago. Nothing criminal, but a civil suit. And guess who his attorney was?"

"Ian." Savannah knew better than to turn that into a question—not with the way Grayson was staring at her with both inquisitiveness and compassion. "But... but Ian never mentioned that, despite all the lies about my supposedly having an affair with Schuyler leading me to murder Zane."

"My initial reaction is to assume they were in collusion over this," Grayson said. He reached across the table and grasped Savannah's hand with empathy. "Maybe with Zane, too, if he really is alive, though I didn't find anything specific to make that more than a possibility."

"So Ian had a reason to not represent me fairly? He was somehow in cahoots at least with Schuyler, and possibly Zane, too? But why? Though that would explain why he wasn't able to get me out on bail..."

Savannah felt like putting her head down on the table and crying. What was she going to do now? How could she ever prove her attorney was a phony? Especially when she didn't dare contact the authorities for any reason, at least not at the moment.

"I... I don't know what to do about that," she finally said to Grayson.

"I have some thoughts," he said. "No one is aware that I know where you are, but since I found the van you were in I can certainly express professional curiosity as a first responder. In fact, I have an idea how to introduce myself to your lawyer to see his reaction. I can lie a little and tell Mr. Wright I've been hired by local authorities to try to help find you since I did discover the van you were in, plus, thanks to my background, I know the area pretty well. We'll see what his reaction is to that. But I won't do it without your okay."

"You've certainly got my okay," Savannah said, feeling shocked by this new twist on her situation. "I'll be eager to hear his reaction."

"I'll let you know how it goes as soon as I can," Grayson said.

"I... Things keep getting crazier and crazier." Savannah shook her head, partly to keep the tears welling in her eyes from falling. "I just don't know how I'm going to get out of this."

"We'll figure it out." Grayson captured her gaze with his own.

"I wish I could be there when you question my wonderful lawyer. Maybe he really is as good as he tells me, and the fact he once knew Schuyler is irrelevant."

"Well, I'll tell you what he says when I can."

"Right," Savannah said. "And ask him who he thinks the most likely suspects are in Zane's murder, excluding me, of course." Savannah had already expressed some of her ideas to Ian, including members of Zane's bank staff, since she'd gotten the sense from some things her ex had said, that he might have played games with the company's income and blamed it on them, or maybe some of the women he'd had affairs with, but she had nothing that even barely resembled evidence.

And even if she got all the things she was going to request Grayson to get for her, it wouldn't make sense for her, whoever she became, to accompany him.

But she would broach the subject of his obtaining a good disguise for her before he left.

That greeting. Grayson had been only partially kidding when he'd told Savannah that from now on he'd say he wasn't coming, then show up. Both times he'd visited her now, they'd wound up kissing.

He took a long swig of coffee as he remained at the table with her, half wishing it was alcohol, even at this hour of the morning.

He wanted to hang out here a lot longer, but he needed to leave now to get started on his upgraded research for Savannah. Also, he had to spend a few hours in his office getting in touch with some of his police and fire contacts to make sure they were happy with First Hand's response after the quake, and to seek more assignments.

Besides, he wanted to make some suggestions regarding official preparations for any future quakes. After all, he wanted, needed, to keep a good relationship with all of them.

So, as much as he regretted leaving Savannah, he said, "I'd better get on my way now. I can see you're doing okay, and I'm glad you consented to my talking to your lawyer the way we discussed—although he's likely to claim attorney-client privilege and all that if I ask him some of the pertinent questions I have in mind."

"About his knowing Schuyler, the liar who convinced the cops I killed my ex? Good old Schuyler—and good old Ian. I'll definitely be eager to hear what Ian says. But—well, I have something to ask you before you go."

Her expression after she said that appeared both eager and apprehensive. What was she going to ask?

"I appreciate all you've been doing for me, Grayson,"

she began, picking up the pad of paper he had given her previously and fiddling with it somewhat nervously. He could tell that she had written notes on it. "And that you're continuing to help me. But I'm sure you can imagine that I'm going nuts hanging out alone here, knowing that if I go anywhere else I'm likely to be spotted and taken back into custody."

"Yes, I'm sure that's difficult," he said, wondering where she was heading with this. And he did sympathize with her. Even with her ability now to look things up on the phone he'd brought her, watch videos on it, read free magazines on it and whatever, she remained alone out here in the middle of nowhere.

"And I hate to ask you to spend more money on me now."

He began to react, since that wasn't a concern to him and she knew it.

"But," she continued, "as I said before I'll repay you when I'm able to. The thing is, I don't want to be me any longer. Or at least I don't want to be recognizable in any way."

"What do you mean?"

She immediately jumped in to explain, showing him the list of items she wanted him to purchase for her—and suggesting he not shop anywhere near Mustang Valley, where he could be seen, and where people would know he didn't have a significant other to buy all of this for.

And those people could become suspicious.

She jumped up from her seat then and motioned for him to follow her into the bathroom, where she looked in the mirror and gave a better explanation of what she intended to do with the makeup and all, pointing out what changes she would make.

He had to hand it to Savannah. Of course, as a former debutante and someone who had apparently been featured in a few high school acting roles, she'd come up with a lot of good ideas for disguising herself.

"So, if I'm able to find all this stuff, I gather that your nose will look longer." He reached over and touched her nose softly with his index finger. "Your hair will be deep brown instead of blond—and in this style that no one but me has seen you in anyway." He gently touched the side of her hair. "Your eyes will appear larger, with dark lashes and brows over them that match your hair." He touched those brows, too.

As he was doing this, he realized how ridiculous it was—and yet how sexually stimulated he was becoming. And Savannah's eyes widened as she met his gaze in that mirror.

It was as if he was getting emotionally attached to her. In some ways, maybe he was. But he knew only too well that he didn't want to get involved with any woman.

This one had particularly gotten under his skin with her sad situation. Well, he didn't need any kind of relationship with her except as her helper. Anything else would be way out of bounds.

He still believed she was innocent, believed it enough to continue to help her.

Bu what if he was wrong? What if she actually was guilty of killing her husband?

Nah…although he hoped that confronting her attorney and learning more about her that way would convince him even more of her innocence.

It had better. He didn't want to get caught abetting a genuine murderer.

And touching her here and now? He had to stop. And

so he did. He took a step back though he continued to look at her in the mirror.

"Sounds like a good idea," he said. "But once you look that different, what do you intend to do about it? Run away? Unless you have someplace specific in mind and means to get there, it's a bad idea."

"Even so, I really can't just stay here forever." Her usually sweet voice had turned into a bit of a wail, and he couldn't help putting an arm around her.

But she wasn't having any of that, at least not now. She pulled away and returned to the table, where she sat back down and put her hand on that notepad.

"So what do you suggest?" she demanded, her tone harsher.

"Well, here's what I think we should do." He purposely emphasized the "we." He had already dived into this situation on her side, and she certainly should recognize that—and listen to him.

But would she?

"What's that?" she prompted.

"I'm going to go see your buddy Ian first, assuming he'll grant me an audience. I'll go get the things you've asked for, but only after that discussion and some business I need to conduct, when I have some time to get away from the office without anyone questioning where I am. That means I'll have to get a few things done first. Until then, you need to stay here. Okay?" That, of course, was important.

"Sure, as long as you call me when you can to let me know what Ian says, or tell me if you didn't get to see him."

"Sounds fair." But now he was going to impose a condition she probably wouldn't like at all—even though it was for her own sake. "The other thing I want you to promise is that, even after I buy the things you want, and you change your looks, I'll want to give you the once-over before you leave here, to confirm that you really do look like someone else."

"Fine, as long as you get here quickly after I notify you. I'll just send you a text message that says 'Done.'"

"Okay," Grayson said. "That was the first condition. The second is that you don't leave until I agree it's the right time, and then only after you've told me where you're going and how long you'll be there—and I will also have to agree with that. Might even come with you." He stared at her hard across the table. He recognized that was being pretty restrictive, but as a professional first responder he had a better sense of where she should or shouldn't go.

"You're awfully controlling, aren't you?" Those amazingly attractive green eyes were hard and she was clearly irritated.

"Yes," he said in as jovial a tone as he could muster. "When it makes sense." He hunkered down then, leaning across the table toward her. "And you can be sure that in this case it does. Do we have a deal?"

Savannah sucked in her lips and closed her eyes for an instant, obviously reining in her emotions and most likely her inclination to say no. She finally opened her eyes and took a deep breath before continuing. "Do I have a choice?"

"No," Grayson said.

"Well, under the circumstances, then I guess we have a deal." She put her hand up, and he noticed the shortness of her plain fingernails, probably required while she was in prison. Did she usually wear polish?

"Good," he said, standing and reaching for her hand to give it a businesslike shake. "I'll get on my way now and let you know as soon as I can what happens with Ian—and also go on your shopping expedition as fast as I'm able."

Her hand grasped his a bit more tightly than he'd anticipated, and didn't let go immediately. "Thank you, Grayson," she said in a soft voice. "I might not always agree with you, but you do seem to have my best interests in mind."

"Yeah," he said, pulled her closer around the table and gave her a quick hug before he left.

And as he walked out the door, now locked behind him and headed to his car, he wished he could do something to reassure Savannah that everything would be okay for her, and soon.

But first, he needed to do whatever was necessary to start believing that himself.

Chapter 12

Okay, now what? Savannah trusted Grayson. She had to.

But she had also trusted Ian Wright—and she'd had to do that, too.

She was outside the cabin now, walking around it in the open air as she had done with Grayson because she had to do something. Physically, at least. She didn't want to just wait inside, playing with her phone like a kid.

Not at this moment.

Soon, Grayson and Ian would meet. Savannah had no doubt that Grayson would convince the attorney to see him—especially because of his plan to tell Ian he needed his guidance in tracking Savannah down.

If Ian was the horrible person she now feared he was, a cohort of Zane's and Schuyler's, he'd undoubtedly open his office door wide and invite Grayson in so they could discuss where in the world Savannah was likely to be now. He would be keen to find her, professionally or worse.

And Ian might use his lawyerly arguments to state why Savannah should turn herself in so she could go through the legal system as she should.

With Ian still representing her, of course.

Not.

In fact, what would she do now if she were caught again? Would the courts let her fire her current attorney? Probably. But then, who could she hire in his place who might actually help her?

She realized her pace had increased. She was now stomping her way around, possibly noisily, to help calm her inner thoughts—but she was instead igniting them further. If there was any wildlife around, any birds, she had to be scaring them off, even though a sighting of them might help to calm her. They represented ongoing life.

She looked around at the trees surrounding her, through their branches where she could, toward the blue April sky.

She was free now, despite the kinks in her ability to go places. She had to remain free.

Would Grayson actually bring her the disguise items she'd requested?

If so, would they work at all?

Okay, enough of this. She had to go back inside and—

And what?

Survive. Think.

Maybe plan what she could, and would, do once she donned a disguise and left this place.

And determine what Grayson might approve. No, she didn't need his approval, but she trusted him.

Could that turn into more?

Definitely not, especially when all of this was behind her and she could finally connect again with other people—in a friendly way.

But even then—well, at least for the moment, she hoped Grayson would remain in her life.

She sighed as she turned the corner again from one side to the front of the cabin. Time to go inside again. Get her mind off all of this—or at least try to.

Would she ever be able to?

Not likely until this was all worked out and her innocence was no longer in question.

And she could only hope that would occur very soon.

Grayson drove a longer route back to his office. Not that he thought anyone was following him, but since he kept coming into the area where the cabins were, he didn't want to take any more chances of being noticed than necessary.

He checked often into his rearview mirror and saw nothing unusual.

Of course, taking a longer route also meant more streets within Mustang Valley, many of which were easily drivable now despite the quake just a couple of days ago. That also meant some additional views of tables and signs from that Affirmation Alliance Group. Oh, well. He didn't stop to talk to anyone and didn't see Micheline Anderson. Maybe she was out assisting more people today. He had done a little additional research on her group and noted that they had a reputation for doing all sorts of useful things, including helping out in other natural disasters besides earthquakes, even heat waves, handing out water and supplies and generally trying to make things at least a little better in whatever situation they found themselves.

Sounded quite good—and yet, especially now that he had met Micheline, he felt glad he didn't need to deal with them—or her—again.

He parked his car as usual behind his office and walked around to the front door.

As he looked through the windows, he saw Norah sitting at the reception desk against the far wall. Not a surprise. Even though all his employees knew to act as greeters if anyone came in off the street, Norah seemed to like it best. She spent at least part of each day staffing that desk, unless she was off on an assignment as an EMT and not around to help.

They were getting busy enough now, and not just because of the earthquake, that Grayson was considering hiring a receptionist.

"Hi," Grayson called after pushing open the front door and walking into the large room. "Anyone out on a job?" When he was around, he always had all assignments run by him. But in urgent situations, he never required that anyone wait for his approval when a job came in.

"Yep." Norah leaned forward. Her light brown hair was pulled up in a bun on top of her head, and she wore a First Hand First Responders T-shirt in red today. "We got a call from the MV Fire Department about an accident on a nearby freeway, possibly caused by quake damage. A big rig and a couple of cars caught fire. There's a bigger blaze downtown they're working on, so they asked for Pedro's help at the accident." Like the Mustang

Valley police, the local fire department knew how well Pedro could help them in a difficult situation.

"I hope no lives are lost," Grayson said automatically, but meaning it. "Are Chad and Winch here?" He sat down in one of the blue chairs nearest the reception desk.

"No, they were called out, too—this time a sad follow-up from the earthquake. An eighteen-year-old kid is apparently still missing from one of those less affluent areas that had the worst damage. His parents think he probably fled into the desert since he was out on a hike by himself around when the quake hit. They've been looking for him and so have some of the official PD first responders, including one of their K-9 cops, but everyone's getting worried and desperate and asked Chad and Winch to get involved."

"I hope they find the kid," Grayson said.

"Alive and okay," added Norah, and Grayson nodded.

They talked a little longer about how things were going around here—and what Grayson had been up to. Only he didn't tell even his probably most discreet and reliable employee the whole truth. "I've been in touch with the police to see how things stand in their investigation of the death of the truck driver I found." That part, at least, was true. Maybe because the local media kept prodding the cops for answers about the missing passenger. "Not much new so far."

"Do you think they'll ask us to bring Chad and Winch in on that, too?"

"Could be." Grayson didn't want to talk about it anymore with Norah. She was too smart, too insightful. No way would he encourage her to find out what was really going on with Savannah. "Anyway, I've got a few things I need to take care of, so I'll see you later."

He raised one hand in a wave as he headed for the stairway.

Once inside his office, he closed the door. He got on the computer for a few minutes to look up where his staff members were assigned.

He then searched for news about the crushed transport vehicle. There didn't appear to be any new information, at least not as reported by the local newspaper or other media—which of course didn't mean things weren't happening that were being kept confidential.

He also looked up the website of the office of Ian Wright. He studied the photo of the man before he prepared to call him.

Wright was an older fellow whose hairline had receded, but who still had enough graying hair to provide a nice frame to his face. He stood there in a suit, arms crossed, clean-shaven, staring with intense eyes beneath stern brows into the camera. Grayson continued to look at that picture as he pressed the law office number onto his phone.

As he anticipated, a receptionist answered. Grayson identified himself as the CEO of First Hand First Responders—and also the person who had located the destroyed vehicle that had apparently been transferring Mr. Wright's client from the court back to prison. He wanted to speak with Mr. Wright about that and ask him some questions.

The woman got off the phone for a minute, then returned. "Mr. Wright is about to start a meeting here that will last for most of the afternoon. Can he call you back later?"

"Sure," Grayson said, then left his number and said

goodbye. And smiled. It appeared that Wright was in his office, after all.

Well, Grayson wouldn't know for sure until he got there. Wright might call him back soon, if he thought the first responder who found Savannah missing could be of any help getting her back, assuming the lawyer was attempting to help Zane and Schuyler. In any case, Grayson prepared to go to Wright's office as soon as he finished some other calls. First, he sent a few follow-up messages to professional contacts in nearby towns, reminding them that First Hand could help them if they needed any assistance now, particularly after the earthquake.

That was the kind of email message he sent often, though he'd never needed to mention something like a quake prior to the last couple of days. But he always remained in contact as closely as possible with the various local groups who might—and did—use their highly qualified and well-certified services.

In a little while, he closed down his computer and headed downstairs to the reception area.

"I'm about to leave for a meeting," he told Norah, quickly averting any questions she might have about that meeting. "And—well, I'd love to check in with Chad and Winch later. Do you know where they are?"

"Kind of." Norah described the desert area northwest of town where the young man was thought to have disappeared. She also showed Grayson a report she had found on her phone about the missing guy.

"Please text that link to me," Grayson told her. "If I get a chance, I may even head there after my meeting."

The area was on its way toward Mountain Valley, a

nearby town whose police and fire departments sometimes requested their help.

It was also someplace Grayson wouldn't be recognized, so he could at least start acquiring the disguise materials Savannah had requested.

But Wright's office? It was right in downtown Mustang Valley, not far from Grayson's own building. And as Grayson had already figured, Ian Wright was apparently in his office right now, unless he'd instructed his receptionist to lie.

Which was entirely possible.

Grayson decided to drive there anyway, despite its proximity.

He pulled his SUV out of the parking lot behind his building and drove the few blocks to the ornate yet professional-looking structure that housed the law firm of Wright & Jessup. It had a parking lot behind it, too, and Grayson easily found a spot there.

He went around to enter the front of the building, where he checked out the list of businesses it contained that was hung by the elevator. No receptionists here, just a few glass doors with signage beside them describing the offices they opened into.

He saw that the building housed a couple of other law firms, as well as a local office for a tech company based in Phoenix, and a few other groups Grayson didn't recognize.

Ian Wright's firm was listed as being on the top couple of floors.

Grayson pushed the button and the elevator door opened. He touched the number for the lowest floor of Wright's offices. The elevator was slow but not especially noisy.

When it arrived and the door opened, Grayson got out and looked around. Sure enough, the door to the law firm's offices was straight ahead, and that was where Grayson headed. He opened it and walked in.

A large black laminate desk took up most of the front room. Behind it sat a fiftyish lady with clearly bleached golden hair. She looked up, regarding Grayson from behind her blue-rimmed glasses. A sign on the top of the desk read Connie Glasser. She was probably the person he had talked to when he had called Ian Wright earlier.

"Hello," she said, greeting Grayson. "May I help you?"

"I'm Grayson Colton. I assume you're the person I spoke with before."

"That's right," she said. "And—"

"Well, after we talked, I called Mr. Wright directly, and he told me to come right in. I assume his meeting is over, right?"

Even if it wasn't, Grayson intended to slip through the door behind the reception desk. And he didn't have Wright's direct line, but Connie didn't need to know that.

"Well, yes, but he didn't mention—"

"Oh, that's okay. Thanks." He figured he might as well be polite as he walked around the desk and behind Connie Glasser, even though there wasn't anything to thank her for.

Fortunately, the large, paneled wooden door with Ian Wright's name on it wasn't locked, and Grayson slipped right in.

There sat Wright behind a large and angled mahogany desk. He had a phone pressed to his ear and held a file that matched the many piled on the desk.

Of course Grayson recognized the man from his website—sort of. Sure, he looked like the same handsome, professional older man depicted online. But this version looked even older, his face lined and pale, the divots in his cheeks deeper, his blue eyes narrowed and dipping down at the corners.

"Hi," Grayson called to get his attention.

That happened immediately. Wright looked up, straight toward Grayson, and appeared to blanch even more as he hung up his phone. "Who are you? How did you get in here?"

"Just walked in," Grayson said, answering the second question first. "I'm Grayson Colton. Did your secretary let you know I called earlier? I need to talk to you about your client, Savannah Oliver."

"If you know anything about the legal system, you know I can't talk to you. Attorney-client privilege applies, and—"

"I haven't said what I want to discuss with you. It won't involve anything covered by attorney-client privilege." With no invitation, Grayson walked farther into the room and planted himself on one of the upholstered leather chairs facing Wright's desk.

"But—"

"Here's the thing. You might know that I'm the person who discovered the ruined transport that was supposed to be moving Ms. Oliver from the courthouse back to prison. It was way out on a road that was affected by the earthquake. I also found the driver dead, and no one in the back, where presumably Ms. Oliver had been secured. She's apparently escaped, and— Well, you may not know but I'm the owner of First Hand First Responders, a private first response company, and the local authorities know it. They've hired me to try to find Ms. Oliver, since I also know that wilderness area pretty well."

"I see. But I can't help you." Ian Wright stood and clearly glanced toward the door behind Grayson.

Interesting. Grayson figured that Wright would want Savannah found, or at least would give that impression in public. But, then, he already figured the lawyer was hiding things for Zane.

"Oh, I'm sure you can. You see, what I need you to tell me is the location of the rendezvous places where Savannah Oliver met up with her lover, Schuyler Wells—all the places you know about. She might have returned there because those spots were familiar. I at least need to check them out."

Would Wright's knowledge of any such place be privileged? Grayson didn't know but he'd take the position they weren't. And he hated suggesting Wells was Savannah's lover, but taking any other angle now might affect this conversation.

Wright looked even more uneasy now, a nervous wreck, maybe. He was sweating. "I wouldn't know the answer to that. Ms. Oliver and I talked a lot, of course, but not about where she might have seen Mr. Wells. And that assumes she did see him."

"Ah, then you question that, too? I understand from what I saw in the media that Ms. Oliver denied the affair, denied anything unseemly with Mr. Wells."

"Sorry, but we're getting too close to attorney-client privilege with that."

Which could give the impression that Savannah had admitted the supposed affair to her attorney. Clever guy for suggesting it. Grayson continued, "Oh, but I assumed you also spoke to Schuyler Wells for information that could help in her defense, right?"

Wright grew even paler, Grayson thought, if that was possible. "Well, I did talk to him a little, but he wasn't much help. He admitted to knowing Savannah and—well, that they'd had an affair and had even considered marrying after Savannah's divorce became final. He also said he was acting as her real estate agent to help her find a new home. But he never mentioned when and where they might have met up, even at sites he was showing her, and neither did Savannah."

Wright seemed to be bouncing back and forth regarding what could be privileged information. What was he trying to do—convince Grayson that Savannah was guilty without getting into anything she might have discussed directly with him?

"Then please tell me all you know about Schuyler Wells. Since you've spoken with him, maybe he told you, or hinted about, some of the places he and Savannah allegedly got together."

"I don't know anything!" Wright was standing now, and seemed to be shaking. He appeared more than nervous.

Was he hiding what he knew, not only about the nonexistence of Savannah's affair with Wells—but also about whether Zane remained alive?

Was he representing his client adequately? Even if he was on Zane's side, could Zane or Wells be blackmailing him into making things worse? Could Wright even be withholding evidence he knew that would get his client off? Failing to file motions that could help her? Anything else?

Hell, Grayson knew his imagination was running

wild—maybe because he was searching for ways to get Savannah vindicated fast and completely.

But he doubted he would learn any more right now.

"Okay," Grayson said. "I'll leave now. Here's my card." He reached into his pocket and drew one out, handing it to Wright, who acted as if it was covered with fatal bacteria. "Please contact me anytime you think of somewhere I should look to locate Ms. Oliver. Surely that's to your benefit, too, and hers. If you do your job well, you might even get her found innocent, but it'll be harder if she's spent a lot of time on the run. Even if she is innocent, she could look guiltier that way."

"Exactly." Wright let his breath out in a sigh. "And I understand you're just doing your job, too. For her benefit, I'll let you know if I think of anyplace she might have gone, though as I said, I don't know of any possible rendezvous points."

"Then maybe I should talk to Mr. Wells directly to see if he will give me that information. I'll let him know that I have spoken with you and that you suggested I contact him."

"Oh no. Don't do that." Wright's tone seemed almost frantic, but then he seemed to force himself to calm down. "I think it would be better if you just let him know why you're trying to find Ms. Oliver, since they were apparently at least close friends. And now, I hate to chase you out, but I am expecting an important phone call on another case and need to prepare for it."

Sure, he hates to chase me out, Grayson thought. But he said his goodbyes, said he would be in touch again—and watched Wright's face grow stony—then left.

Chapter 13

Grayson fought the urge to call Savannah as he got into his car. After meeting that awful attorney, he felt even more worried about her.

Sure, he could rush right out to the cabin and visit her, but what good would that do now? No, he had to act normally—or as normally as possible.

Since the quake, and the dinner with his siblings, he had been meaning to go to the hospital to visit his father. He'd received plenty of text messages from his siblings reminding him but no updates on Payne's condition.

Why not go now? He wouldn't stay long. And so Grayson drove to the Mustang Valley General Hospital, which wasn't far from the law office. He parked in the lot at the back and walked around the large, well-respected hospital to the front entrance.

And was surprised, and unhappy, to see Selina

Barnes Colton there, walking toward the outside door in the wide hospital lobby.

Selina had been his father's second wife, disliked by all of Payne's kids and his current wife, Genevieve. She was on the board of directors of Colton Oil, none-theless, and also its VP and PR director. From what Grayson understood, that was because his former step-mother was holding something over his father, but he didn't know what.

Grayson had an urge to leave. Or at least enter the hospital another way.

Selina saw him, approached the door where he stood, and came outside. He drew in his breath as he stood there.

Selina was a pretty woman, with long brown hair and blue eyes that always seemed to be amused. She had perfect cheekbones and a lovely chin, all touched up by attractive makeup, and her left ear and its earring were often exposed by her hairstyle.

Too bad her personality didn't match her looks.

"Well, Grayson, what a surprise. When was the last time you've been to the hospital to see your dad? He was shot in January, and now it's April."

He thought about making excuses, but why do that with her? "Not everything is done with the purpose of being recorded for posterity or on cameras, security or otherwise. I may not be viewed as a perfect son who vis-its often, but I think of my dad often and privately send him all my best thoughts." Or at least some. He might not adore his dad, but he certainly didn't want him to die.

Selina laughed. "How adorable. That sounds like hokum from that Affirmation Alliance Group. Those do-gooders are all over town spouting their positivity—

and that makes me want to barf." She gestured across the street from the hospital. Sure enough, Grayson saw one of those Affirmation Alliance tables there, where two members sat. In front of them was a banner that said Displaced From The Earthquake and Need Assistance? Let Affirmation Alliance Group Help! There was even a line of three people waiting to talk to the men behind the table.

But Selina had started talking to him again. "Enough of that. And your being here? You know, Grayson, your dad figured before that you think he's a corrupt jerk, so why be fake and sit at his bedside and pretend to feel something you don't?"

He'd come here to see his dad, damn it, no matter what this woman said. He wanted to push past Selina and do what he'd set out to.

But he also recognized that Selina was right. He was being fake by coming here, and he'd be fake if he visited Payne and spouted platitudes his father probably couldn't hear.

It wasn't that he really hated his father. But he did hate how Payne had tried to make Grayson obey him even as an adult, rather than live his own life. Maybe things would be different if his mother had lived…but why even contemplate that now?

Without saying another word to her, he stalked away to return to his car—hating that Selina had won.

Once inside his car, he pondered what to do. Something to improve his state of mind, certainly.

As a result, he headed his SUV out of town toward the desert outside Mustang Valley, where Norah had said Chad brought Winch to look for the missing young man.

Had they found him yet? Could Grayson help? Even just trying would make him feel better.

And help him forget this fiasco of an attempt to see his father.

As he drove along the main road that wound through the area, Grayson figured that without more information, he was unlikely to locate any of the searchers, let alone his employees. Of course, this was also the direction toward the town of Mountain Valley, and if he couldn't find the search group, he could at least spend a little time there looking for the items on Savannah's list.

Which would give him a better excuse to go visit her later than just to tell her what a jerk her lawyer seemed to be.

It didn't take long to get outside Mustang Valley and onto the road through the desert. Grayson became more determined to meet up with his first responder employee who was out there and see how things were going. He called Chad on his car phone system.

"Hey, Grayson." Chad answered immediately. "Can't talk. Looking for a young guy missing since the quake, and Winch just alerted on a scent."

"The kid's?"

"Yeah. His family thought he went in this direction, and some locals saw some footprints in this area earlier today, though they didn't lead to the kid."

"How do I find you?" Grayson quickly told Chad where he was and got directions—about ten miles ahead of him. "Thanks," he said but realized Chad had already hung up.

Grayson saw no additional cars out here—not until he reached the general area Chad had described. Several cop cars and an ambulance were parked there. Grayson parked, too, and got out.

He introduced himself to an officer standing beside his vehicle, staring into the distance. The area was mostly covered with sand and light patches of dirt, with quite a few cactus plants rising toward the blue sky that way, in the direction Grayson assumed Chad and Winch had gone.

Which turned out correct, according to that cop. And so, after putting on his sunglasses, Grayson rushed ahead.

In a few minutes he saw a small crowd ahead, some in uniform. He sped up to join them, then hurried to the front of that line.

Which was where Winch, at the end of the leash attached to the back of his K-9 vest, pulled Chad along behind him. Chad was holding a T-shirt, presumably one worn by the missing kid and provided by his family. One of K-9 Winch's skills was following a scent.

Chad saw Grayson then and motioned for him to catch up. "Looks good," he shouted.

In seconds, Winch found the missing kid he'd alerted on. Grayson couldn't believe his good luck—he'd happened to be there just at the right moment. The teen was sitting on the ground in the shadow of a cactus.

Seeing the dog, the young guy screamed and rose and stumbled toward Winch, throwing his arms around the dog's neck as he began crying. "Thank you, thank you," he managed between sobs. Thin and pale, he wore jeans and athletic shoes and a gray T-shirt, all of which appeared filthy and in bad condition—and no wonder. He'd apparently been wearing them for around three days out here with no food or water or shelter.

"You're Marty?" Chad asked.

"Yes. Yes, I am. I want to go home."

"Absolutely," Chad said, and Grayson noticed that a lot of the people who'd been back around the vehicles had now joined them, including an EMT who began examining the young man. Then there were a few people filming what was going on. Were they live on social media or just recording everything?

In any case, it didn't hurt to give First Hand a little publicity. They'd earned it, thanks to Chad and Winch. And since Chad was being kept away from Marty by those tending to his health, Grayson approached and held out his hand to his employee. "Great job, Chad. And Winchell." Grayson bent to pat the sitting, panting dog on the head between his pointed ears. He was glad Chad was wearing a First Hand shirt—a blue one—and he gestured toward it. "Our company, First Hand First Responders, is really proud of you." And Grayson was bold enough to smile at the cameras.

Chad laughed. "That's a bit over the top, boss—but you know we're both proud to be private first responders for your company. Aren't we, Winch?"

At his name, the dog looked up at him and gave a quick bark, causing nearly everyone around there to laugh as Chad stroked Winch's back.

Grayson had an urge to pat his human employee on the back and to let Chad know he'd get a bonus for this. He didn't do either...yet. But he would.

Grayson told Chad, "Go ahead and hang out here for a while in case more help or information is needed. I've got to run—but I can't tell you how glad I am that I saw Winch and you in action and doing so successfully."

"I can guess, boss." Chad aimed a salute his way, and Grayson, saluting back, turned to head toward his car.

Well, something, at least, had gone well that day. And now it was time for Grayson to start picking up those supplies for Savannah.

Savannah. If only he could help her reach as successful a conclusion as this.

But how? Getting her inept attorney into the media the way this had been picked up?

He just wished he had more answers—and could get them quickly.

Okay, Savannah thought. Patience. She needed patience.

She also needed to hear from Grayson.

It was late afternoon. Had he seen Ian Wright yet? If so, what did he think now about her lawyer?

When would she hear about it?

When would she see Grayson?

She was inside the cabin, going crazy as she usually did these days. Was Grayson at least getting her the disguise items she needed?

If not, she still had to get out of here, soon. Sitting at that darned table nibbling on apple chips that Grayson had brought wasn't doing her any good.

Neither was thinking about Zane, and why he was so angry with her that he'd decided to fake his own death so he could frame her for murder. They could have found a way to get along as time went on after their divorce, couldn't they?

Zane clearly didn't think so. And though Savannah thought he could have disappeared to someplace as far away as Bali, she wondered if he was instead hanging out around here to laugh at her.

Okay. There was one thing Grayson had brought that could at least get her mind occupied so she wouldn't feel so nuts.

Maybe.

She pulled the burner phone off its charger. Again. She was doing that a lot. She certainly hoped that Grayson continued to keep her well supplied with batteries for the charger.

What she needed to do now was figure out where to go from here and how to get there—notwithstanding whether Grayson actually came through with her disguise.

Too bad she couldn't just place an online order for what she needed. She preferred actually shopping in person, enjoying the outing, but she had used the internet for acquiring plenty of things before.

But even if she wanted to shop online, where could she have anything sent?

She needed to decide at last where to go.

Maybe to Phoenix—still in Arizona and not extremely far away.

Or Los Angeles—so big and crowded she could surely get lost there.

Or Mexico. It was just across the border from Arizona, after all. But just being in another country wouldn't solve her problems, especially since she didn't really know its language. And she didn't have the ID she would need to leave the United States.

Or—where else? New York City? Washington, DC? But how would she get there...or anywhere? And how could she live there on her own, with no money since she didn't dare to try to access any of her ample accounts? They had probably been frozen anyway, considering that she was accused of committing a murder and had even been denied bail.

No job. No identity she could use.

She sighed. Maybe looking at the news or some feature stories would help. Would she be able to learn how other fugitives got away—successfully?

She started her search this time at the local level. On her phone, she found a link to stream the news on the local affiliate of a national station. She turned up the sound on the phone and started looking.

And she immediately gasped aloud.

The story that came up wasn't at all what she was expecting. It couldn't be true. And yet, how could it not be?

With a photo in the background that seemed much too real, too familiar, and a banner at the bottom that said "Breaking News," the female newscaster with the solemn face was saying, "The police are not giving details yet, but the body of attorney Ian Wright was just discovered by his secretary inside his office building. More details to come. Ian Wright was representing murder suspect Savannah Oliver, now a fugitive. Although police have not publicly commented on potential suspects, we understand Oliver might be a suspect in this murder, as well."

Savannah sobbed as she closed the browser. She pushed the buttons on her phone to call Grayson, whether that was smart or not.

He answered right away. "Hell. You heard?"

"Yes," she managed to say. "Had you met…had you seen Ian?"

"Yeah, I did. I'll tell you about it later. Right now—well, stay where you are. I'll see you soon."

And then he was gone—when she perhaps needed to talk to him most.

He'd seen Ian. Talked with him.

Murdered him? Surely not. Why would he?

But the only thing Savannah could be sure of was that she hadn't been the one to kill Ian.

Damn.

He had just stopped making calls and turned on the car radio, driving along one of the nicer, four-lane downtown streets in Mountain Valley, from a discount store to a more posh one a couple of blocks away. Grayson had earlier bought some of the disguise makeup that Savannah had asked for, as well as a few other supplies like batteries. When he heard about Ian Wright on the radio, he nearly drove into a car parked along the curb.

Which was when Savannah had called. He pulled over and answered immediately, wishing he was with her to comfort her.

What the hell had happened? When he had left Ian, the attorney looked nervous yet had definitely been in lawyer mode. He'd done whatever he had to do to get Grayson out of his presence.

But he had definitely been breathing. And Grayson might have been the last person to see Ian alive. Except for his murderer.

Apparently the SOB had been shot—but who had done it?

Savannah had sounded scared on the phone, and no wonder. The media probably didn't know all the details yet but the reports indicated that Wright's cause of death was gunshot wounds. Whether or not the cops had suspects in mind, the media had taken no time to latch onto Savannah as their prime suspect. Even though she presumably had an alibi—being at the cabin—for this period of time, which they wouldn't know.

That was logical. Grayson admitted it to himself. Savannah theoretically could be mad at her lawyer for not getting her out on bail or clearing her name.

Grayson had wanted to keep talking with Savannah now but knew that wasn't a good idea. Instead, after ending their call, he continued to listen to the news as he drove toward the fishing cabin.

Even though no one was likely to be aware he had any connection to Savannah or Ian other than having found the van and visited Ian, Grayson recognized he could be under some kind of official surveillance regardless, as a result of those events. Or unofficial surveillance by Zane or his cronies attempting to frame Savannah.

And so, again he took a circuitous route to the cabin, keeping an eye out for anyone behind him. He even looked up to see if someone might be overhead in a helicopter or following him with a drone, since the authorities might be even more inclined now to be conducting a search for Savannah.

It might make them look bad if they didn't.

But Grayson had to continue to act normal, or at least appear that way.

Through the city streets he drove, going the speed limit while wanting to race. Into the suburbs, then along a road circling the town and back toward Mustang Valley. But instead of heading into town he aimed his car to the back roads that had been affected by the quake—

out toward the fishing area and the cabins abutting parts of it.

All the time watching out for anyone following.

He shut off the news and called Chad, again congratulating Winch and him. Then he called Pedro to hear about the vehicle fire he had helped to put out, the drivers and passengers he had helped to save, along with the town firefighters and EMTs.

Finally he called Norah at the office and calmly discussed with her the successes of the others that day—and thanked her for being the backup in charge.

"I guess no one's in big trouble today," she said, "or I'd have been called out as an EMT, too, to help save a life or two."

He heard the humor in her voice and said, "Or three or four. Well, wait for it. You're always on call, you know, like the rest of us. And you always do your job well."

"Like you, boss," she countered.

He hoped so. But if the world knew what he was up to right now, who he was trying to help—well, his company would be in big trouble

He soon hung up from that call, too, and continued driving slowly, carefully, along the narrow and uneven road into the wilderness that had come to mean a lot more to him these days than it had when it simply contained old fishing cabins, trees and wildlife.

Now, it contained a woman on whom he had bet his life, his ongoing existence, in a way. And despite how absurd, how dangerous, it might be, he was glad.

He had come to really believe in Savannah. To care for her. To cherish those kisses they'd shared and hope for more. A lot more.

Well, hell. All he had to do was figure out the best

way to exonerate her from all accusations against her. Clear her of two murders—one of which might not even have occurred, according to her.

And the other?

The sky was growing darker along this remote road; he occasionally saw another car going the other direction. He was nearing the cabin. He would soon see Savannah—and prove to himself that she was indeed there and could not have buzzed, carless, into town, murdered her attorney and returned to eventually cry on his shoulder.

Right?

What was he doing? Why was he risking so much to help this woman? Why did he believe in her and her innocence, despite there apparently being plenty of evidence against her?

Well, heck. He hated to admit, even to himself, that he was attracted to her…despite himself. For now. But he would slough that off soon, when he no longer needed to do things for her.

There. He had reached the turnoff to the cabin. He slowed to make sure he saw no one nearby, then drove in that direction.

He soon parked beside the cabin. He didn't see Savannah outside, at least. Was she inside? Was she hiding?

Was she okay?

He realized he needed to stay calm and act certain that all would be well, or he would just make things worse for her. She must be freaked out, justifiably so.

Well, as far as he was concerned, another glitch had occurred that they would need to deal with, but life would just go on and they would find a way to fix things for Savannah.

He had to. His mind leapt to why he had become a first responder in the first place, how he hadn't been able to help his friend Philip Prokol, who'd come home from military service with PTSD, which had killed him.

Well, nothing like that would happen to Savannah. Grayson would help her. Somehow.

He got out of his car and pulled out from the trunk a couple of bags of things he had bought for her.

Then he went to the cabin's front door. It was locked—a good thing. He knocked.

"Yes?" called a familiar voice from inside. Or was it familiar? He had heard Savannah in distress before, but the quiver in her tone and higher pitch suggested she truly felt tormented now.

"It's your deliveryman Grayson, Savannah," he called out, keeping his tone light.

The door opened immediately. Savannah appeared as anxious as he had imagined, her face ashen, her lips straight and tight. "Come in," she managed to say, and as soon as he was inside she closed the door behind him and locked it.

He looked down at her in the light from the lanterns, holding out a few bags.

She didn't reach for them. Instead, she headed for that same old table and sat down.

And put her face in her hands. "What am I going to do, Grayson?" Her voice was a wail—although a sweet, despairing one.

He wished he had an answer for her. A good answer.

For now, he placed the bags on the table in front of her and reached down, encouraging her to stand again.

Which she did. And again looked up at him. Her eyes

sought his. Her mouth opened slightly—as she reached out at the same time he reached for her.

Their kiss was soft at first, as he attempted to use the contact to reassure her physically.

But then it began heating up, their contact growing fiercer. He felt her arms pull him closer as his did the same. He allowed his hands to range along her back, touching her buttocks, then released her slightly so he could reach between them and feel her wonderfully firm breasts.

He grew harder, even as Savannah pushed her body against his even more. She clasped him tightly to her, then moved enough so she could first grasp his butt, too, then move her hand forward to touch his erection as their kiss became hot and all-encompassing. He couldn't think of anything else but her.

Except—

"Please, Grayson," Savannah said, stepping back only enough to start unbuttoning his shirt.

So what could he do but do the same with hers, while leading her toward the cabin's bed?

Chapter 14

This was such a bad idea. A stupid idea. And yet Savannah wanted it, wanted Grayson, more than anything else at this moment.

No, it wouldn't last long, but for now all she needed to think about was how being near him this way set her body ablaze with desire. Concentrating on what was here and now and not happening anyplace else, whether or not it concerned her.

She had tamped down her interest in him from the moment he had arrived at this cabin. It had seemed so inappropriate. It didn't matter that he was the only person she could communicate with in her current, small world. That wasn't the sole reason she found him attractive.

She had forced herself before to ignore any interest in him, or at least keep it deep inside.

No longer.

"Are you sure, Savannah?" Grayson's voice was raspy, totally sexy in tone and it stoked her desire even more, even as she considered her answer to him.

"Yes," she said with no hesitation.

Would this wind up being the last good memory she had of freedom before she was caught again?

Would it be the beginning of something new and wonderful?

Or would it be a huge mistake? After all she had gone through, she still had no intention of getting involved in the long term with Grayson or any other man, no matter what the circumstances were now...or later.

But she needed this.

She needed him and what he could do for her at this moment.

And she would do all she could to reciprocate.

They were sitting on the bed now, on top of the sheets. As soon as she pulled his shirt off, he did the same with hers. At the same time she gazed at his muscular chest, she rejoiced in his hot stare on her breasts and wished she wasn't wearing a bra.

That wish immediately came true as he reached around her, hugging her close but only for an instant as he unhooked her bra and drew it off.

She trembled in anticipation as he drew in his breath, looking at her as she felt her nipples grow taut—until he reached for her, bringing her close to him once more as he dipped his head to kiss and suckle those sensitive tips.

They weren't the only part of her that reacted to him now, but she wanted to see him, feel him, before she bared the rest of herself. She reached toward his pants, intending to maneuver him as he sat facing her and pull his clothes down, but instead connected with his erection again. She rubbed at the fabric outside it with the heel of her palm, then grasped at it—as Grayson pulled back.

"Oh," Savannah said.

But the delay was only for an instant as Grayson used it to pull down his dark slacks and the shorts beneath them.

His thick, enticing shaft was revealed, causing Savannah to reach for her own pants. She had help as she pulled them down and pushed them away.

"Grayson," she gasped aloud as he began stroking her, moving from her breasts slowly downward as he again kissed her mouth.

His fingers were hot, probing, magnetic, exciting her even more—especially when he reached her hottest, most female area and explored it with his touch, his grasp. Those fingers were long and thick and utterly engaging, and when Savannah felt one, then two, inside her, she began to writhe, to beg internally for more.

For everything from him.

For that amazing erection of his inside her, pumping and—

Suddenly he pulled away again, farther this time, and she felt like crying—and demanding more at the same time.

Was that it? Would he be the one to regain sanity and call this off?

"What—" she began, and heard him give a short chuckle that was somehow also sexy.

"Hey," he said softly, rolling over and reaching for his pants, which were now on the floor at the side of the bed. "I'm a first responder. I come prepared."

In moments Savannah understood. He had pulled his

wallet from a pocket and removed a condom from inside it.

Her turn to laugh. "I should have expected that from you." This man anticipated everything.

Maybe.

Before he could unwrap the package, she pushed him back on the bed until he lay there, fully exposed. She bent over until she could take him, still unsheathed, into her mouth—and enjoy his heated groan. She continued playing him, but not for long.

This time, he was the one to roll her over, positioning her on the bed till she lay beneath him—and he had the freedom now to wrap himself in that condom, then press the head of his erection exactly where it belonged.

Savannah drew in her breath as he entered her. It stung just a little until her body stretched to take him in, since he was so large and she hadn't engaged in this kind of experience for a long time. But the discomfort faded quickly. She wanted him. Now. She moved her hips to encourage him, and in moments he was pumping inside her and she was matching his eager motions with her own.

Please let this last, she begged silently, even as she knew it couldn't. For now, she would enjoy and appreciate every moment of it.

This was what she wanted.

This was here and now.

And it was all she could and would think about.

But much too soon she reached the critical, wonderful climax, even as Grayson, too, moaned and stopped moving. She managed to open her eyes enough to see that his remained closed, but that gorgeous body of his had risen somewhat and she could see the tension in it as he, too, came.

"Wow," he said as he gently lay down partly on her and partly beside her.

"Wow," she agreed, reaching to hold him tightly against her.

Wishing this moment could stay just like this—forever.

This had not been the reason Grayson rushed to the cabin this evening. In fact, it hadn't even been on his mind when he had headed here. Or at least as nothing more than a whimsy at the back of his mind that he'd never thought would come true.

But it had happened. He had helped to initiate it, had kept it going, and now they were lying in bed together.

Did he regret it? No way. Savannah was quite a woman. She had impressed him before with her attitude in a situation that appeared no-win for her—at least not without his help.

And so far, he hadn't really helped her.

But he still believed in her. Although he couldn't allow a miraculous bout of sex to swing his beliefs beyond what was logical as reality.

Still...

Bad idea, maybe, but he certainly had enjoyed it.

Wanted more, though not right now.

He would need to be careful, though. Sex could lead to long-term relationships if one wasn't careful.

Long-term relationships could lead to nothing but trouble. He'd seen that in so many other people that he had minimized getting too involved with anyone. His own recent failed relationship had been short-term. He was a first responder, but that didn't mean responding too deeply, too long, to a woman who attracted him.

Now Savannah was breathing deeply beside him, her head pressed against his chest.

Neither had donned any clothes, although they now were under the sheet. It was growing a little cooler—but he hardly recognized that, thanks to their combined body heat.

It was late now, dark outside.

He moved slightly, though his intention was to stay the night. Not for more sex, but to try to be there for Savannah during this difficult time.

Okay, he had come to care for her. Maybe too much.

On the other hand, it would probably be better for both of them if he left and pursued further leads.

And maybe got the rest of the disguises he had promised Savannah.

What else could he do to help her?

What—

"Grayson? Are you awake?" Savannah was moving now beside him, though she still remained close against him.

Which caused a certain part of him to react, despite how busy it had already been that evening.

"Yes," he said in response to her question.

"I—as much as I've enjoyed our time together, I'm worried again. Still. I—I can't just stay here and wait and maybe be found this time. Did you get any of the things we discussed?"

"Some, but—well, I heard about what happened to Wright while I was shopping and just headed here. I figured you might need the company." And he needed to see her, too, out of his caring for her, his concern for her.

"Thank you." Her voice sounded low. Humble, even. He turned to pull her tightly into his arms as they remained lying there. Her body heat, and the feel of her flesh against him once more, turned him on again.

But what they had done before, as wonderful as it was, had been somewhat inappropriate. He realized that adding to it now would only be more so—and they needed to focus on her case, not their chemistry.

"Hey," he said. "Let's get up and have some of that wonderful food I brought tonight and I'll show you what disguise stuff I've already bought. And then—well, we can talk about what comes next."

Grayson had some ideas about what should come next—but wished he could just whisk Savannah out of this place and...

Hey. He did know of someplace he could potentially move her if necessary.

More to think about, more to discuss, he thought.

"Sounds good," was Savannah's reply. Sadly, but not unexpectedly, she moved away from him and got out of bed on the other side.

And started pulling her clothes on. So of course he did the same.

After leaving the bed, they ate dinner. It consisted mostly of a couple of sandwiches already put together and purchased in town by Grayson—roast beef, pretty good. She enjoyed hers.

She enjoyed the company even more.

Her mind kept hopping back into bed with him, though they had put that behind them, at least for now.

And every time her thoughts started back on what had happened that day in town, what the possible consequences to her might be, she forced them back on the good things that had happened today instead.

Or at least she tried to.

Once they'd finished their meal, Grayson went back out to his car for some additional bags, which he handed her. "Sorry, not everything is there since I didn't have time to get it," he said, "but you can start working on your disguise with this stuff. I'll try to find the rest tomorrow."

Which meant he would leave tonight, of course. She would be alone again—with her thoughts.

She could handle it. She had to.

Forcing herself not to think about that, she looked inside the bags, took some contents out and laid them on the table. They included a lot of the eye makeup she had asked for but not all of it. Nor were the cream and foundation there.

"I think I'll wait right now to see if you are able to get the rest before I start experimenting," she told Grayson, although if this was all she acquired, she would make the best of it.

"I want to get some of the clothes you mentioned, too—the droopy, casual kind of things that you've likely never worn before—but no one you know is likely to recognize you in."

"Right," she said. "After all, I'm a society girl and always looked that way." She shrugged. That was the truth, after all. She figured her casual clothing generally cost more than a lot of women's dressiest stuff did. She'd sometimes wondered if she should start dressing "normally" but was glad now she hadn't.

Not when she didn't want anyone to know who she was. Except Grayson.

Grayson. Was she trusting him too much? She certainly was relying on him a lot. But what else could she do—at least for now?

After she went through the things he had brought, they jokingly discussed it, trading ideas on how she could change her appearance the way actors were changed—into zombies or superheroes or gorillas or anything other than who they were.

Their discussion morphed into the kinds of TV shows and movies they were fondest of. "So what do you think I like best on television?" she asked him.

"Sitcoms," he said decisively, and he was right—but that wasn't all.

"Add news specials to that," she said. "And some talk shows, depending on the host."

"Got it."

She told him more. In theaters, her favorites were romantic comedies, even though she knew they were all fiction, especially the ones where the main characters fell in love and anticipated, at the end, a happily-ever-after.

A happy few minutes, maybe, or a few days. Or even a year. But she'd married a guy she believed she loved, and who claimed to love her. And what had she gotten? A torment-ever-after, as long as they were together. Once they were divorced, she had assumed that would be the end of thinking about Zane and his infidelity and everything else about him.

And it was, for a brief time. Until he'd framed her for his murder, probably just to get even with her for divorcing him.

But she didn't want to think about that now.

As Grayson probed for her likes and dislikes, she

turned the tables on him. She wasn't surprised that he liked cop shows and superheroes, and he didn't even mention shows with romance in them.

Which was as she'd anticipated. Sex was one thing. Staying together? That wasn't on his agenda either, she felt certain. All the more reason to just enjoy his company—and maybe his body, too, again sometime. Meanwhile, she would hope he continued to help her as long as she was unable to help herself.

And expect he would soon be gone from her life one way or another. With luck, by then she would be free and exonerated.

But until she could find out how to clear herself, the burden of potentially being convicted of Zane's murder—and now Ian's—was hanging over her head.

Their conversation wound down. Savannah tried to figure out something else to talk about, but she was actually getting tired.

Not that she would mention that to Grayson.

She didn't want to encourage him to leave. She liked his company too much.

She needed his company, someone to talk to and to help her feel a good ending to all of this could—would— occur.

Not that they were discussing any of that. Not now.

But she wasn't surprised when Grayson stood up. "It's getting late," he said.

All she could do at first was nod and look in his direction without meeting his gaze. "Yes, it is," she finally agreed.

"I think we need some sleep, don't you?"

"Yes," she said again, feeling a bit puzzled. Why hadn't he said he was about to head home?

He must have seen something in her expression that concerned him, for he sat back down again. "I mean, let's head to bed here, okay? Together—and I'm not talking about having fun to keep us awake again. Not now. But I can sleep here, stay till tomorrow morning. I'll go back to town then, to my office, and get some work done. And find out how other things are going in town, too."

"Like the investigation into the latest murder," Savannah said, not making it a question. He—they—could find out more tonight, she realized, on their phones.

Not that they were likely to learn that way the motive for someone to have killed Ian. She assumed it had been Zane or Schuyler, but why?

And maybe they should, or at least she should, learn all she could to make sure that potential number one suspect—her—hadn't been discovered here in this cabin.

Although if she had been, there'd be some activity outside, and probably inside, too.

"That's right," Grayson agreed. "I'll determine what else we need to do, then head to another town to finish picking up your disguise materials. And come back here with it. Okay?"

"Sounds good," she responded as casually as she could, but her insides almost melted in relief. Although she recognized she couldn't, shouldn't, count on anything, not even his return as promised, until it happened.

But oh, how she hoped he was serious. Because her latest problem was that she was becoming much too serious about him.

"So, let's go to bed now, shall we?"

"Yes," she said, "Let's."

Grayson joined her in bed soon after, and drew close enough to her to put his arm around her.

She turned, snuggling against him.

They shared a wonderful good-night kiss, and although Savannah felt her body churn a bit in lust again, she didn't pursue it. Sleep sounded like a good idea.

Tomorrow could be a big day—even if she remained stuck here for all or part of the day.

"Good night, Grayson," she whispered against him.

"Good night." She felt him kiss the top of her head.

And hoped that wouldn't be the last time, either tonight or on future nights together.

Though she knew better than to count on that to count on anything,

Even regarding the wonderful Grayson.

Chapter 15

Grayson didn't fall asleep for a long time, and judging by her breathing, neither did Savannah. But it felt good, really good, to hold her like this with no current worries menacing them.

Wouldn't it be great if this was the beginning of some real time together? A future they shared.

Yeah, right. He recognized that he was beginning to care for her too much. Once the danger to her was over, so would any chance of a relationship between them. Which was for the best.

And that danger? When he had gone into the bathroom earlier to prepare for bed, he had brought his cell phone and checked for updates on Ian Wright's murder.

The media seemed to be having great fun with the idea that it was a follow-up to Zane Oliver's murder. They suggested that since the poor, hard-working, by-the-book attorney had failed to get his client out on bail for that killing, Savannah would have wanted revenge on him, too. Or so the various stories mostly asserted.

Grayson had seen that kind of hype and accusation before, of course. He would look into it more tomorrow when he was no longer here—and would also do further checking into the status of the murder investigation with his professional contacts.

And now...

Now, finally, he felt his body relaxing enough to let him drift into sleep. He concentrated on the feel of Savannah against him once more before he allowed himself to drop off.

"Sorry I don't have anything more exciting for breakfast than an English muffin and jam," Savannah said to Grayson the next morning. He was going to leave soon. She knew it.

And he would also be back. He had told her so. He had been reliable—and more—so far, so she believed him. Or at least wanted to. But how long could he help her without someone noticing his trips to the cabin?

She knew better than to assume that them being together in such a special manner last night would happen again.

But, oh, how she had enjoyed it.

And couldn't recall ever feeling that close to Zane.

"Sorry I didn't bring anything more exciting for breakfast than English muffins and jam," Grayson countered, and they both laughed.

What would she do today after he left, Savannah wondered.

For now—

For now, she ate slowly, not being especially hungry but knowing she needed to get something down. She mostly watched Grayson, who wolfed down his muffin enthusiastically—also watching her as he did so, as if attempting to set an example so she would eat more, too.

She didn't, though she appreciated his apparent concern. She simply wasn't hungry. Especially knowing he would be leaving soon. And would he be back to stay with her that night? She certainly couldn't count on it.

"Hey," he finally said. "The sooner I leave here, the sooner I can get back with the rest of the things you asked for."

"Right," she said, attempting to sound pleased. The sooner he left, the sooner she would once more be alone here with her thoughts, and for how long?

They would undoubtedly be worse now. She'd assumed the cops were looking for her when she'd fled the destroyed van, but then they also had things to do regarding the earthquake. But now, if they actually believed she had killed Ian, they might focus more on finding her.

"Hey," Grayson said. "I have an idea. I already brought more batteries, although I probably should get even more to make sure your phone charger remains usable."

"Right," Savannah said, not sure where this was going.

"I'll leave you some additional paper, too, that I have in the car. I'll find you a small but powerful tablet computer, too, if it looks like you'll be here much longer. Although—" He hesitated, and Savannah figured he was weighing the pros and cons of her remaining in the cabin while the authorities might ramp up their search for her. He clearly was aware of that possibility, too. "Anyway, taking notes on paper should work okay for now. Here's what I'd like you to do."

It turned out that he wanted to start a website chronicling first responders' achievements, both his employees' and others'. Their actions would be described in detail so other members of the public could learn more. He wanted to explain what they did, why they were important and what went into the certification process.

"I don't want accolades for myself or my company, but I want to inform the public so they'll know who to call and when, and what to expect. And maybe contribute money to the public emergency departments to help them increase their first responder involvement. But I haven't had time to even start researching what would need to go into this kind of project," he finished. "You have some time, at least for now. I would really appreciate it if you'd start it for me."

Savannah liked the idea. A lot.

Spending her time compiling achievements by first responders, how they jumped in and saved endangered lives, put out fires, and more?

Oh yes.

Including him, but he'd said he didn't want to applaud First Hand.

She hadn't thought much about first responders until the earthquake—and meeting Grayson. Now, she was highly impressed by them, by him, and would love to learn more. And help him.

And have something to do besides sit here and stew over what her life had become—and what would happen to it in the future.

"Yes!" she exclaimed. "I'd love to start your research." She didn't bother reminding him that it might be a pipe dream she would never be able to accomplish, thanks to what was going on with her.

She had to remain optimistic. She *would* remain optimistic. And a lot of that was because of Grayson, and all he was doing for her. At least she could pay him back just a little this way. Plus, maybe she could come up with additional ideas for helping first responders achieve even more.

"Excellent." He pulled his phone out of his pocket and looked at it. "Time for me to go. But I'll see you later."

He rose and approached Savannah rather than heading straight to the door. She stood, too, and quickly found herself in his arms.

Their kiss was quick but hot and seemed to promise more. Or at least she hoped so.

But she knew better than to count on anything right now.

Even Grayson.

She would wait here for him, though. At least for today.

First things first. Grayson took a long detour, all the way to Tucson, fifty miles away from Mustang Valley. But it was early and traffic wasn't bad—and no one there knew him.

He checked his surroundings a lot, though, in case he was being followed, unlikely as that was. Still, his paranoia wasn't a bad thing since he was aiding an escaped prisoner. And he had a lot of experience and knowledge about how to spot anyone who oughtn't be there.

He used his car phone system to check in at the office. He told Norah, who answered his call, that he was engaged in some promotional work in nearby towns.

She sounded happy because she had an assignment that day working with some high school kids who wanted to learn more about being first responders. The school system had hired First Hand to present a program to a club for teens who were interested in future medical careers at Mustang Valley General Hospital. Chad and Winch would come along for a short while, too, and Pedro would most likely stay in the office attending to calls and whatever else needed to be done—unless a call came in. Or more aftershocks occurred.

"Thanks," Grayson said to Norah before hanging up, meaning it. He loved owning the company, being in charge—and having such skilled and dedicated employees at his back. And what Norah was doing would be a great addition to the website he planned to work on with Savannah.

Finally reaching Tucson, he visited several shops, high-end makeup, low-end clothing and more, just to be sure he was getting the right stuff and not forgetting anything. This time, he would bring everything else Savannah had asked for, plus several versions of some things like items of clothing and slightly different colors and quality of makeup.

He also found a tablet computer for Savannah, assuming she remained interested and hung out at the cabin enough to work on his project. He needed help, she needed something to do. It all seemed perfect for the moment, assuming Savannah remained free.

When he was finished, he secured it all in the back of his SUV in a crate installed there for carrying any equipment needed on the job. No one would be able to see its contents.

He'd been pondering how to look into the investigation into Ian Wright's murder and decided to visit the Mustang Valley police station when he returned to town. He'd been seen in Wright's office, after all, so it shouldn't be too over the top for him to express interest in what happened.

He hoped that his usual primary contact, Senior Detective PJ Doherty, was there. Grayson felt more comfortable asking PJ questions than any of the other cops, even his distant cousin Spencer, although Grayson knew most of the pros respected him there. He decided to call PJ to check on his availability and was glad when his friend answered.

"Yeah, I'm here, and unless something comes up I should be around when you get here," PJ said. "No first responder stuff going on at the moment that I know of, but I suspect I know what you want to talk about."

"I suspect you do, too," Grayson said. Of course PJ knew he'd found the destroyed vehicle and dead driver, and therefore might have a continuing interest in the escaped prisoner who was being transported. That same escapee who was in the news once more.

It took Grayson longer to get back to Mustang Valley than it had been to drive to Tucson, thanks to midday traffic, but he soon parked in a lot near the police station. No problem walking to the one-story brick building on Mustang Boulevard. Cops in dark blue uniforms filled the lobby area, a few talking to visiting citizens. Grayson stepped up to the front desk and asked the officer there to let PJ know he was there. "He's expecting me."

The cop got on the desk phone and in moments PJ came out, dressed in uniform. "Let's go out for some coffee," he told Grayson. A chain coffee shop was within easy walking distance, and they headed that way along the sidewalk.

PJ was tall, a few years younger than Grayson. He had blond hair and blue eyes and kept glancing toward Grayson almost impishly, as if he was trying to read his mind. They'd talked a few times since the earthquake but this was the first time they'd gotten together.

"Okay, what do you want?" PJ finally asked after they entered the shop. They sat down at a small round table near the door after getting their drinks.

"All that stuff in the news about the murder of Ian Wright. Has anyone mentioned I went to see the guy yesterday?"

"Yeah, we heard about that. What did you talk about?" PJ's eyes narrowed a bit as if he was working even harder at mind reading.

Grayson knew he would need to be careful. "Well, I understood the guy represented Savannah Oliver, that prisoner who escaped from the van I found after the earthquake. I don't have any professional reason to be interested."

Despite what he had told Wright, PJ would definitely know that Grayson hadn't been hired by the police department to help find the woman.

Grayson continued. "But I feel a connection anyway. I talked to him about his representing her, what he could tell me that wasn't attorney-client privileged, which wasn't much. I still got the impression he thought his client could be guilty. And now I've heard on the news that Savannah Oliver is a suspect in his murder, too. Logical, I guess—but is that true?"

"You know we don't talk publicly about ongoing investigations for a while, till we believe we have sufficient evidence for a conviction and all, and we don't talk about that evidence much, either. And we certainly don't have need for a first responder in this situation. But hell, I can understand your interest, even though it's remote. You could have found that woman in the van. Even been attacked by her if she'd been there. And now you do have a sort-of connection with her next victim."

Grayson forced himself not to object to PJ's assumption, but the detective must have seen some kind of reaction on his face and held up his hand.

"Okay, she's only an alleged killer in both cases. But...look, my friend, can I trust you to keep a secret about the evidence we found?"

"Of course." Grayson forced himself to stay calm and not push PJ to talk more and faster. What secret?

"We haven't revealed much to the media, but in case you're interested, Mr. Wright was found with two gunshot wounds to the head, definitely not self-inflicted. Not sure why others in his building didn't hear it, but the walls at his upstairs office were soundproofed. The weapon wasn't left there, either. But something else was."

Grayson wanted to shake it out of PJ, whose tone and teasing expression suggested that was what he wanted Grayson to do.

"You going to tell me, or do I have to wait till I see it on TV eventually?" Grayson kept his tone cool and calm as he grinned as wryly as he could toward his friend. "So why do you think she put those gunshot wounds into her lawyer's head?"

"Because," PJ chortled triumphantly, "he didn't get her off the charges against her right away, didn't succeed in even getting her bail. I've seen photos of her."

Not anymore, Grayson thought, but didn't say so. "And we know she kept her long hair pulled back into those decorative clips some women wear. Because—" he said again.

"Because?" Grayson prompted.

"Because it must have fallen out of her hair at the latest crime scene. Maybe Wright and she fought for a while before she shot him, or maybe she was just careless. But one of those clips was found under Wright's desk, a pretty thing made of what I was told is called tortoiseshell plastic—and it had initials on it."

"Let me guess," Grayson said, his hopes falling. It was a setup, sure. But it seemed to be working. "Were those initials SO?"

"SMO," PJ contradicted. "Including her maiden name."

Grayson's head was spinning. Savannah was being framed—again. Her ex? Probably. But since he couldn't show up in town there had to be someone else. Wells? That was more likely.

What could Grayson do to protect her? To put the cops on the right trail?

He didn't know.

"Very interesting," he said to PJ, trying to sound somewhat excited. "So you really do have a viable suspect." Should he suggest that the clip could have been planted?

No. That might give away whose side he was on.

"Yep, we do," PJ said. "Still don't know where she is, though. But we're putting together a bigger task force to search for her. Maybe she's still hiding out in the woods near where the van went down. Meanwhile, we're out there. Expanding our search. And we'll find her."

That was what Grayson was afraid of.

"And good thing we're together now," PJ said. "We'd intended to contact you to interview you about your meeting with Wright. Can you come to the station when we're done here? From what we have found so far, you were one of the last people to see him alive."

"Sure," Grayson said, his heart sinking. Well, he wouldn't have anything helpful to say. "And after we're done, I'd appreciate it if you would keep me informed about your investigation as much as you can. I'm interested, especially since Wright was killed so soon after I saw him. And if you need a first responder or two or three in your investigation, be sure to let me know."

Chapter 16

"What do you mean, we're leaving?" Savannah demanded.

It was late afternoon. Grayson had just returned to the cabin and said he'd brought everything else she'd requested, and more.

But he was acting strange. His expression was worried. Very worried.

And that worried Savannah.

Of course she was more than emotionally ready to leave this place. But practically?

Where could she go?

She hadn't changed her appearance yet, so she would most likely be too identifiable to go nearly anywhere.

Even so, since he was pushing this, Grayson had to have someplace in mind.

"Look, everything's probably fine," he said, "but I do know they're looking for you in earnest right now."

Savannah felt herself both stiffen and shudder, looking at Grayson's face. Its features were the same, utterly handsome and appealing—except for the unnatural frown.

"Who is looking?" But of course she knew.

"The police. I'll explain shortly. But right now, go ahead and change into one of the new outfits, including the shoes I brought."

He'd shown her some athletic shoes that looked pretty inexpensive, unlike anything she would have chosen for herself before.

He had also brought her some cheap-looking T-shirts and other tops and jeans, nothing anyone who knew her would expect her to wear, which was perfect.

He had just brought her some hair dye, too, but she hadn't had time to use it.

But how did he know the police were after her right now? Not that it should be a big surprise.

And if they were, did she dare leave here? Or were they more likely to find her here than someplace else?

Grayson seemed to have taken charge—again. Was he truly on her side? He still appeared to be, but how could she be certain?

Well, she didn't have much choice if he believed the cops might come looking for her here.

And at least she might get an opportunity to run.

She closed herself in the bathroom and did as he directed. She changed clothes and modified her makeup, adding eye shadow, eyeliner and mascara, although she didn't try aging herself. She also practiced slumping, especially her shoulders, since most women she'd associated with from successful families walked and talked like models, with gentle waves of their hands.

Not that she felt certain how people of a lesser public status held themselves, but she would give it a try. In addition, she forced herself to practice walking in a way that stuck her stomach out more than usual. She felt highly uncomfortable, not so much physically as mentally. This wasn't her—yet it was, for now.

In a short while, she exited the bathroom with her new clothes and less prideful demeanor. She tilted her head slightly and looked up sadly and uncomfortably toward Grayson.

"Hello, Mr. Colton," she said, making her voice rasp. "Do you know who I am?"

He smiled at her. "If I didn't know, I definitely wouldn't recognize you now. Great job, Savannah! Now let's go."

Though Grayson doubted anyone would recognize Savannah the way she looked now, he couldn't be sure. As a result, after they quickly cleaned the cabin to make it look as close as possible to how it had when Savannah moved in, leaving no extra food but replenishing the water bottles, he had her lie down on the back seat of his car.

He hadn't bought her a hat, though maybe he should have for when—if—they were out somewhere with other people around. Later. But he did have a baseball cap in the back of his car—fortunately not one branded with the First Hand logo, but a gray one that just said Mustang Valley. He handed it to her to put on eventually and at least partially shield her face.

He explained their destination to Savannah as he drove as far as he could beyond the lake area where the cabin was, twisting his way through the forest in the direction of his family ranch. He'd decided that, first and foremost, he needed to get her out of there. If the cops did a better job of fanning out from the location where the van had been destroyed, they could easily wind up near the lake—and its nearby cabins.

He drove toward the bunker he had found ages ago as a kid and used as his refuge, to hide from the family when he could. Even when he was younger, he'd needed time and a place away from his sometimes overbearing and controlling family.

And now, he had visited the bunker briefly after the earthquake to ensure that it remained undamaged and no one had been caught there.

"Here's what's going on," he said to Savannah. He told her first about his conversation with his buddy Detective Doherty. "The cops have what they believe is good evidence—a concrete reason to put you at the top of their suspect list, Savannah."

"What?" she demanded, her voice muffled from the back seat.

Grayson wished he could watch her as he spoke, hold her in his arms to comfort her as much as possible. He could imagine the frightened expression on her beautiful face anyway. But he'd been a bit spooked and his mind had gone in many ugly directions while he drove back to the cabin.

The bunker should be a safer hideout. Even though a lot of people knew about the many abandoned mineshafts in the area, no one else to his knowledge was ever aware he'd used that one.

"I'll tell you soon," he said. He wanted to soothe her as he told her the situation as he knew it—and his further fears about it. He wanted to hold her tight, and not just to protect her, although that was most important at the moment. But later? He could imagine their making use of the bunker to engage in more of the wonderful sex they had already experienced. He didn't know how things would be in the future, but he definitely craved keeping Savannah in his life.

A few cars passed on the remote street until he turned off and headed down a dirt road beyond the Rattlesnake Ridge Ranch, between it and other ranches. He drove as far as he could into a grove of trees near the side of a fair-sized hill and parked behind bushes that obscured his vehicle.

He got out of the car and looked around, listening.

"Okay," he finally said, opening a back door. "Time for you to visit the next exciting mansion where you'll hang out for a while."

"I'm not sure I like your sarcasm, Grayson," she said, stepping out of the car and pivoting to look around them into the woods.

He noted that she retained her disguise, slouching and frowning and sticking her gut out to appear heavier than the lovely, slender woman she was.

She'd have made a great actress, he figured. But he didn't tell her that. Not now, at least. Not until they'd put all this behind them and she could return to her life as an heiress with contacts and charitable instincts—and then decide if there was anything else she wanted to do. He could only hope it would still involve him.

"So where are we going?" she asked in a moment.

"This way," he said and took her hand.

It still felt the same to him—warm and sweet and sexy as she held onto his while they began walking.

You're doing this because you're a first responder

who does all he can to help people, he reminded himself. And this woman needed help.

Eventually, no matter what he wished for, they might both go their own ways, and he could only hope, at this point, that hers didn't involve prison.

His either, since if anyone caught him he could be charged with abetting a fugitive.

He reminded himself that he shouldn't care for her beyond someone who desperately needed his help, but recognized that was no longer entirely true.

Ignoring the calls of birds and the sound of twigs cracking beneath their feet, the only noises out here, he led Savannah around the rise at the base of the hill—and beyond some bushes he pushed aside to reveal the opening into the bunker. At first it was like walking inside a cave, and Grayson still held Savannah's hand as they entered, using the flashlight function on his phone in the other. But at the back was another opening, and it led farther inside to the area Grayson had made his own.

It had no windows, of course, or other openings to the outside, but over time he had brought in folding chairs and a cot and shelves where he stacked foods and chips and things that didn't go stale fast, and of course bottles of water.

Not to mention a whole variety of battery-operated lanterns, better than the ones he had brought to the cabin.

Over time, he'd also brought in ornate draperies to hide the stone walls, and vinyl tiles resembling wood to cover most of the floor. He had walled off the end that led to the actual mineshaft. And he'd spent enough time here that he had brought in a tall bookcase that was now loaded with books he had read—even though now he used an e-reader more.

He had even worked out an area that could be used as an off-the-grid compost bathroom retreat, with another drape as a doorway.

It was his haven as a kid and occasionally now, too.

And it was about to become Savannah's.

"What is this place?" she asked.

He explained his childhood retreat. Yes, he was a Colton and lived at the Triple R with the rest of his siblings and his father and stepmother, but he'd needed to get away, too.

"I was never particularly close to any of them," he said. "I'm still not, though I can't explain it entirely. I knew I didn't like taking orders from them and would eventually have my own life, and so I did—but this former mineshaft became my refuge when I needed it as a kid. I call it my bunker."

"It's amazing," Savannah said, looking around. She turned back to him. "And I appreciate your sharing such an important place in your life with me."

"Any time," he said, meaning it. He figured she might have wanted a refuge like this when her relationship with Zane began to deteriorate, but he didn't ask.

"So now I want to hear what you learned in town that made you decide I couldn't stay in the cabin anymore."

"It may be fine," he responded. "But…well, maybe we'll go back there depending on how things work out over the next day or so. But here's the thing."

They sat in folding chairs across from each other, and Grayson told Savannah about his conversation with PJ—and the hair clip that had been found beside Ian Wright's murdered body.

"Oh no!" Savannah looked frightened and reached for what was left of her hair. "That does sound like one of mine I had monogrammed. Obviously, it was planted there. I'm being framed again."

"So I figured." Grayson reached toward her and took her hands in his once more. "I was pondering that on my drive to the cabin. If you're being framed, it has to be whoever framed you for the first murder—most likely your ex, if you're correct about his still being alive. He'd have been recognized going into Wright's law office, but then so might Schuyler"

"I agree," Savannah said, nodding. "Do you think it could be both Zane and Schuyler working together?"

"Exactly," Grayson agreed, "since it appears they were co-conspirators before and that relationship most likely continues. Now all we have to do is figure out a way to point the cops in that direction rather than at you. My suspicion is that it was Schuyler who murdered Ian since he's more likely to be out in public than Zane, though it's not clear how anyone sneaked into the law office and got past the receptionist without being seen. I guess that will come to light when the case is finally solved. I just wish we knew of a way to show the cops the way to go with some genuine evidence."

Savannah sat back, letting go of his hands, her expression thoughtful. "You know, I may not have mentioned before, but dear old Zane liked to think of himself as a techie genius. He hid security devices on his computer and phones, mostly to protect the security of his investment banking interests, though he only used one main camera in the house since he didn't want to be photographed. He recorded conversations on the phone and in various rooms and all, but I didn't know what happened to it all after we divorced. I didn't particularly like it when we were married, and as things went downhill

I figured he was recording me. I confronted him to try to protect my privacy, but he mostly ignored me. I assumed the equipment was still there but once I wasn't living in the house I didn't care. But right now—well, it may be a stretch, but if my disguise is good enough I'd like to sneak into his place and find out if there's anything there of his conversations with Ian and Schuyler about his disappearing or me or anything."

"Didn't the police check for stuff like that?"

"I don't know. I heard in court that they did conduct some investigation at Zane's house, but any particularly valuable stuff might have been well hidden. I got the impression from Ian that it wouldn't be a good idea to mention it since Zane could have said things about me that would implicate me even more, so I kept quiet about it. And now that I know Ian wasn't really on my side… Well, since I've been sitting around thinking so much, I've come up with some ideas where those kinds of things could be. They may lead to nothing, of course, but I'd feel so much better if I could at least try." She looked at him with a hopeful grin on her face, which looked so different with the makeup. "Could you imagine that? Finding proof to exonerate me?"

"Sounds like a great idea."

"So…later today or tomorrow, I want to go to town, disguised even more thoroughly than I am now. I need to figure out a fake name in case someone asks, but I want to go to a store or fast-food place or something near where I used to hang out and see if anyone recognizes me. I know it could be a mistake, but I don't think so. Once I feel secure in my disguise, I can go places and do a whole lot more to try to locate Zane and find evidence that he and his friends framed me."

Grayson stood as adrenaline spiked and mental alarms went off inside him. "I don't know—"

"I do," she said. "Just for a short while, and I don't want you anywhere near me after you drop me off someplace secluded, so no one will know I was in your car. But now that I look at least a little different, I'm finally feeling some hope, despite all the awful things going on and what you told me about the cops... I need this, Grayson. To give it a try. Please."

Her appeal was echoed in her pleading expression. "Well—" He felt himself giving in.

"Please, please," she repeated. "Pretty please with lots of sugar on it, or first responder good stuff or whatever. I promise that, no matter what, I won't mention you or how you've helped me if I do get caught. I need to take the chance. I just need to do something at last."

He could understand what she was saying.

He also knew he wouldn't just drop and desert her. He would act as the first responder he was: he would help her.

Because she would need help, he told himself. Not because there was anything other than friendship—and lust—between them.

"Well, okay," he finally said. "But I'll be there, too, in the background at least. We have to agree on when and how you should contact me so I can get you out of there if it becomes necessary. And—"

"Of course," she interrupted. "Thank you, Grayson, for this and everything else."

He was surprised when Savannah stood and moved to put her arms around him. "Hey," she said. "You have a cot over there." She gestured toward that part of the room. "Wouldn't you like to enjoy this new person? I'd like to see what it's like to make love in this new persona of mine."

Grayson laughed. "I liked your previous self, too, but I'm always interested in variety." Not exactly true—he liked her in every incarnation—but that fit the moment. He stood, too, and took her into his arms.

Their kiss was long and hot—like the others they had shared when she was just Savannah. Not *just* Savannah. She was a lovely person, no matter what her face looked like, no matter how she held her body.

Savannah eventually pulled back and looked up at him. Despite the bit of makeup she had used so far, her eyes remained the sharp, sweet, sexy green he had come to know. "So what do you think about this new me?"

"I still have a lot to learn about you," he said and, taking her hand, led her to that cot she had pointed to.

A while later, Savannah wriggled her naked body against Grayson's, feeling his waning hardness, feeling his heat. They were quite close together, since the cot wasn't very large, but they hadn't needed a lot of room.

He wriggled back and pulled her closer, his arms still around her body.

Who knew? Before the events of the last few days, she wouldn't have imagined herself making love so soon after her divorce, if ever again. And with a man she hardly knew? Grayson was not one of the men she would have anticipated getting physical with. Though he and his family had money, she believed he had only appeared occasionally at her social functions. He, unlike Zane, hadn't seemed to be excited about appearing in public at events held for the town's elite. But who cared?

He was a first responder, and he definitely had responded to her in many ways.

"So," he said to her. "That was a first for my bunker, and it certainly was memorable."

"Good. I'm glad to have helped you make history here." But her mind was zooming. "Even so, there's still some daylight outside, or at least I think so. None apparently penetrates this place."

"Nope. But are you suggesting you're already prepared to get out there and test your disguise, like you mentioned before?"

"I am, but—"

He read her mind. Or maybe it was obvious. "But do I think it's time, and do I think you look different enough to give that a try? Yes, I do, if we're careful. And we will be. Both of us."

"That's good." There wasn't much she could say to that except, "I agree. And believe you, Grayson. Thank you so much for everything."

He again pulled her close, and she loved how her body reacted to his naked presence, from her nipples to the warmth of her most sensual parts below.

Well, heck. It was late in the day. She figured waiting till tomorrow to start checking on Zane would be the better plan.

Plus, this way she could practice putting on her disguise again in the morning.

Tonight she could attempt to seduce Grayson again.

And so she did.

Chapter 17

This had to work and provide her with the information and optimism she needed, Savannah hoped the next morning as she again slid into the back seat of Grayson's car, being careful not to rub her glasses along the surface as she lay down. If all went well, if she had done a good job with her makeup and clothing and all and looked as different as she hoped, she might be able to go out in public and learn all she needed to fix her life now and prove she was innocent of all accusations against her.

If not…well, she didn't want to think about that.

She did want to think about last night, though. It had been wonderful spending it in the small bed with Grayson, even between their fantastic bouts of sex. Grayson had been fine with hanging out with her that way. In fact, he had seemed happy about waiting until they had a whole new day before beginning their latest plan. They had eaten a brief breakfast of things he'd brought to the bunker, and Savannah had gotten into her disguise once more before they left.

Grayson hadn't initially mentioned it, but he had also bought her two pairs of glasses—one, sunglasses, and the other, regular glasses with a dark, wide frame but with no prescription

She had checked out her appearance again before coming out to the car. Grayson's bunker also had a large mirror in its bathroom, and thanks to the lantern in there, she was able to see herself well enough to confirm that she looked quite different from the usual Savannah Oliver.

Which wasn't her name right now, nor was Savannah Murphy. She'd chosen a new name out of thin air in case she wound up talking to someone and needed to identify herself: Chloe Michaels.

Savannah had done a quick search on her phone for the name and saw quite a few faces come up, which was a good thing. The more, the merrier. That way, she was unlikely to be confused with any other person, or so she hoped.

It was time to get started. That hopefully would include sneaking into Zane's house and looking for…well, whatever she could find that might tell her who her ex recently communicated with, and how and what they'd said. She at least had some ideas about what types of high-tech gadgets he had used.

Fortunately, she knew more than he'd realized

Those he talked to could, and probably would, involve at least Schuyler and, most likely, Ian.

If so—well, she could hope there was enough there to turn over to the police as evidence of her own innocence.

Would anything show that Zane wasn't in as excellent financial condition as he'd let on to the world? Would there be any evidence of plane tickets he had booked or hotel reservations he had made?

Savannah had already informed Grayson about what she intended to seek, and he sounded happy to help. Grayson had started driving. "Are you okay back there?"

"I sure am," she responded.

They had already discussed where they would go first. Savannah had an urge to visit one of the stores she had once frequented, where she hoped the sales staff and patrons wouldn't recognize her.

Grayson had talked her out of that. "Let's start small," he said, convincing her to go to a convenience store she sometimes visited for things she needed at the last minute, where maybe someone could recognize her usual appearance but they didn't know her well.

Savannah had agreed to do things Grayson's way. After all, he was the first responder. He knew a lot more about police investigations.

Besides, if all went well at the convenience store, they could follow it up by doing things Savannah's way—

Before she did as she intended, whether Grayson agreed to it or not. She would sneak into Zane's house, her former home, and do the search she had been thinking about, which could help her get out of this mess. Maybe. At least she had a plan that shouldn't call attention to someone entering the house.

As they had discussed, Grayson pulled into a parking structure at the edge of town, on one of the middle levels. He got out first without locking the door.

Savannah—Chloe—had her burner phone with her, sound turned off. About five minutes after Grayson left, he called her, and her phone vibrated. "I'm at the stairway and don't see anyone else around," he said. "You can get out now."

She stuck the cap Grayson had given her over her head above the glasses. She also pulled on a bulky, old-looking jacket he'd given her over her T-shirt. Keeping her phone in her pocket with her hand over it, in case she needed to yank it out and call Grayson again, she did her best to sneak out of the car from her prone position on the back seat. They had decided she could take the elevator downstairs—her first experiment with being seen and, possibly, recognized.

Which she wasn't. A woman rode with her in the elevator, and she didn't seem to know, or pay any attention, to Savannah.

Step number one—a success!

The convenience store that was Savannah's target was a couple of blocks away, and she headed there at a good, strong pace without, she hoped, appearing too fast or too slow. In a few minutes, she arrived and pulled open the glass door at the front.

The first person she saw was Grayson. They ignored each other. But Savannah liked the way he looked. Today he had on a long-sleeved blue T-shirt he must have kept at the bunker.

Savannah walked around and picked up supplies like water, wheat bread and cheese slices. Normal stuff. Nothing to call attention to her. Grayson had given her cash to pay for it, which she did.

"Did you find everything you were looking for, ma'am?" the young guy at the checkout stand asked. He looked familiar and looked at her as he spoke but didn't react in any way.

"Yes, thanks." She tried to keep her voice from shaking. The kid was just being polite by talking to her, as sales clerks were supposed to do. If she remained cool and just acted like a regular patron, everything should be fine.

"Good." He handed her the plastic bag containing her purchases, and some change. "Have a nice day."

"You, too."

There. That interaction was normal. He undoubtedly asked the same question of all the customers and wished them each a good day.

Everything still was going fine.

Until she walked outside.

She'd met Grayson's eye where he stood near the door. He was thumbing through a local newspaper, but she had seen him glancing at her now and then.

She had ignored him as if he was a total stranger. Which he was, to Chloe.

Now, as she moved onto the sidewalk, a police car drove slowly by. She tried to keep her gasp inside and keep walking.

Were the cops inside it looking at her? Did they know who she was? Had someone in the store called them?

Well, she knew she didn't look like the Savannah they might be looking for. She made sure she used the relaxed posture she'd been practicing. Her hair was different. Her face, too.

She wore those glasses.

Still, she had an urge to run. To call out to Grayson—assuming he was within hearing distance. But what could he do anyway?

Instead, she kept walking. She glanced curiously in the direction of the police car. Normal people would do that, after all. The officer on the passenger side was looking in her direction, but the car continued on.

It didn't stop. Surely, everything was fine.

She'd fooled them!

Maybe. She couldn't allow herself to get too excited, too confident. They could just have been headed to get more backup, then come after her.

Savannah remembered only too well what it felt like to be taken into police custody. To be swept off to jail. To be questioned and—

She forced herself to put as many of those thoughts aside as she could. She walked at a normal pace, glancing into a clothing store as she passed it, then a furniture store—like any normal pedestrian.

No cop car drove by again. No one showed up to confront her.

Maybe this had worked out. She felt jubilant—but quickly tamped that down again.

She soon made it to the parking lot, where she took the elevator back up to the floor where Grayson had parked. No one was around, so she called him.

He answered at once. "I'm already in the car and don't see anyone around. Come on over and get in."

Which she did, opening the unlocked door, putting her package on the floor, and again lying down on the back seat.

"How did it go?" Grayson asked as he started driving.

"Fine, though I was worried when the police car drove by. Did you see it?"

"I did, but I figured your disguise, including your posture, wouldn't let them recognize you. You're quite an actress."

"Me? Not exactly the career I'd choose if I decided to

really work for a living." Which actually sounded good now. She could make more choices for herself that way—assuming she was ever exonerated of these murders.

Which was definitely what she intended.

And so, she told Grayson, "Since I don't resemble myself and I'm such a great actress, here's where I want to go right now."

She gave him Zane's address, which he apparently already knew.

"It's a big house in a neighborhood of big houses but not many people. This car looks enough like a delivery vehicle that I doubt any neighbors will pay attention if you pull onto the street a little distance away and we get out there. I'll pretend to be a new cleaning lady if anyone pays attention to us, and you can bring a bag or something to deliver. The house is on a middle lot and we can get through the gate and inside in a way I know. Zane isn't that friendly with anyone on the street anyway."

"Okay, Chloe," Grayson said. "I understand this is important to you, and why. I just hope we find what you're looking for."

"Me, too," Savannah-Chloe responded.

And she was very glad he had said "we."

Grayson had agreed to do as Savannah wished, despite a whole lot of reservations. But he understood why she wanted it.

And it truly did make sense, if they could actually find something to prove the guilt of Schuyler Wells—or even Zane Oliver himself. Even though Savannah's access to the property as a resident of the guest house was now most likely limited since she was a fugitive.

He only wished he could somehow do this on his own,

keep her fully out of danger as he cleared her name. But that couldn't happen. She was the one who knew the house and where Zane might have hidden anything that might absolve her or indicate that Zane had faked his own death.

But if things went wrong…

Well, they couldn't. But in any case, he would keep his distance, mentally at least.

He would also help her as much as he could. But he'd additionally have to convince himself that she was just one more person he helped as a first responder, no matter how much time they had spent together in the past few days.

No matter how much he enjoyed her presence, and in so many ways.

After all, he wouldn't develop an ongoing relationship with this woman, even if things worked out as he hoped. She might not want to be with him anyway, since he might remind her in the future of all that was happening now.

This time, he had her ride in the front seat with him as he followed her directions to the house. It wasn't in an area he visited a lot. He wasn't likely to be recognized. Hopefully, neither would Savannah in her Chloe disguise.

He drove to one of the most upscale residential areas of Mustang Valley. It didn't include ranches, but it did include large estates that fronted on a well-maintained road, Vista Lane. Not even a sign of earthquake damage here. Along the road were large homes including mansions, most set back behind fences. Grayson knew where Zane Oliver had lived, but though he'd looked up the address again, he mostly counted on Savannah—no, Chloe. He had to start thinking of her that way.

They had already decided they would park some distance away, maybe a quarter of a mile, for unobtrusiveness. There was also an alley behind the homes that paralleled the main road. Savannah would walk that way back toward the house, while Grayson would carry a box he had stashed in the back of his SUV to make it appear he was delivering something, if he was approached.

As they drove by the huge gray stone house, Savannah pointed out where she would enter the yard, through a gate at the side where she would be less noticeable.

Grayson would go that way, too, since the neighbors would undoubtedly know that Zane had allegedly died and no one would be at home to open the front door for packages.

Looking at the place made Grayson remember who Savannah Oliver was, notwithstanding her being a murder suspect and fugitive. She came from wealth and had married into it, too.

Not that Grayson, a Colton, was unfamiliar with having a lot of assets.

But seeing where she had lived exemplified her background, and he could hardly imagine what it had felt for her to be in police custody, incarcerated with a lot of people who were undoubtedly guilty of the crimes they were charged with.

He had an urge to take her into his arms again at that thought. Good thing he was driving.

"How about there?" Savannah pointed toward a road veering to the right. It was a short distance from Zane's home, and there were other vehicles parked along it, too. The cars varied from relatively new ones like Grayson's

SUV to older ones, and he figured some household help, or maybe handymen, parked here.

Good. His car wouldn't be obvious, even though it was in better condition than most.

He made the turn, then parked in the first available space.

"Okay," he said. "Here we are. You go your way first, and then I'll come down the street beside the house and you can let me into the yard, too."

"Sounds good." She tossed him a smile behind the sunglasses and disguising makeup she now wore.

She might not look as beautiful as before, but he knew who was beneath that disguise. He pulled her toward him and gave her a quick kiss, then moved away.

"See you soon," he said.

Chapter 18

The walk along the back alley to Zane's house—and her guesthouse—seemed to take forever in the Arizona heat. Savannah kept her pace fairly fast along the even cement in her new clunky shoes, while holding the kind of posture she had assumed along with the rest of her disguise. The wind had suddenly grown strong so the jacket she wore, and even her jeans, seemed to blow and flutter around her, making her feel even more uncomfortable. At least the cap on her head, which was part of her camouflage, along with her glasses, stayed on. Hopefully she looked different enough that even if she was seen, no one would associate her with Savannah Oliver.

Fortunately, no one else was around. But if someone did appear, if anyone saw her or talked to her, she could let them know that she was a maid by profession and Mr. Oliver's family had asked her, Chloe Michaels, to do some housecleaning and to come in this way.

Zane had often had workers arrive through the side gate, after all, and when he knew they were coming he would leave it temporarily unlocked and without enabling the security alarm.

But who in his family now would ask for help that way? Good question. Big-time investment banker Zane had staff as well as executives at his company whom he must've trained well enough to keep the place going. When he'd discussed traveling with Savannah, long before their divorce, he had indicated he wanted that kind of professional support in place.

That had never happened. And now that he was "dead," perhaps living in one of the far-off areas he'd thought they might visit someday, his allies were undoubtedly keeping the company successful for what they believed to be their own benefit, as well as Zane's heirs.

Oh, he still had parents and a sister. They were most likely his official heirs now, as long as people believed him to be dead. Savannah certainly wasn't one, and might not have been even if they were still married as a result of Zane's ungenerous attitude. In fact, her allegedly wanting to get her hands on more of his assets, despite her own wealth, was one of the motives the authorities had ascribed to her for his murder, as well as revenge for his affairs. They'd never put an estate plan together, even though she'd suggested it, thanks to her father.

Arizona was a community property state, so she had been entitled to at least some of what Zane earned while they were together, but she'd gotten some money from him when they divorced that was supposed to satisfy the law. She assumed it still sat in the bank where she had deposited it.

Thoughts of her dad brought to mind why she had married Zane in the first place. It had largely been her father's idea. He had advised Savannah to marry soon and marry well, and when Zane Oliver had shown some interest, her dad had jumped right on it, urging her to go out with him. A lot. And marry him? Oh yeah!

Oh, she had thought she loved Zane, but she hadn't felt the kind of passion she'd anticipated having for the man she married and intended to spend the rest of her life with.

Grayson's face suddenly popped into her mind.

Ridiculous. She was grateful to him. She enjoyed sex with him. And rightly or not, she trusted him.

But she didn't love him. Couldn't, either now or later. He didn't seem to want a relationship, and she certainly didn't want one on the heels of what had happened with her terrible marriage and afterward. She needed time and space…and trust, which would be really difficult for her now.

She turned the corner into the narrow outdoor passageway between Zane's property and the one next door, both lined with fences. That was where she would open a gate and get inside. She knew where Zane put the key to that door, so even if he had changed locks, there should be no problem, assuming he hadn't changed hiding places or the code for the security alarm.

She hoped.

She glanced toward the neighbors' side and was glad to see the row of cacti still there. They apparently didn't use their gate here, and hopefully didn't stare at the plants along the fence.

And she wouldn't even glance toward the guesthouse.

Fortunately Grayson had brought them both gloves

to don to avoid leaving fingerprints. Savannah pulled hers on, then quickly searched for the key to the fence lock. There. It was where she'd anticipated, in a small box buried to the right of a fence post. This had been intended to be an emergency way to get on and off the property—and it worked right now.

The main house's front door? It was much more likely that neighbors would see her there, even if they didn't recognize her. Plus, she didn't have the front door key any longer. And the house's main security camera was aimed there.

As Savannah stepped inside the fence, in the shadow of the vast and lovely mansion she had called home for a couple of years, she saw Grayson approach from the direction of the main street. She waited for him. He, too, wore gloves.

"So far so good," he said as he reached her side.

"Yes. And—well, I never told Zane, of course, but I kept a key to the side door of the main house hidden on the grounds, too. I didn't think I'd have any need to use it, but it just—it made me feel a little better, a bit more in control. And I never disposed of it when we got divorced."

As they talked, they approached the side of the house. A key pad was attached to the wall near the door, and Savannah pulled it open and pressed in some numbers— and waited.

"Good," she said. "He mustn't have changed the alarm code, either, or we'd hear a buzz to indicate we needed to try again."

"Really? Then we wouldn't have been able to get in the house, even if you know where the key is." Grayson sounded unhappy.

"From what Zane told me when I moved in, that code hadn't been changed in decades, so I wasn't too worried." There was a garden area off to the side, with a hopbush hedge nearly against the house. Savannah walked five steps with one foot in front of the other, then bent and dug a small hole in the sandy dirt. Sure enough, she found the key in a small box and stood up. Waving it toward Grayson, she said, "Let's go inside."

She used the key in a side door, and soon walked into the kitchen—an appropriate entrance for the help, the way she wanted to appear at the moment, she thought.

This was a swanky kitchen, with ornate and imported tile on the floor, and ebony wooden cabinets surrounding the most expensive major appliances, all in gleaming metal.

"We're in," she said, knowing her grin was huge. Grayson smiled back, then grew serious again.

"Okay, now that we're in here, what are we looking for that might have evidence of Zane's collusion with Schuyler Wells and even Ian Wright?"

Savannah felt her face drop. "Well, I have a couple of ideas, but— Look, here are the possibilities I thought of." She proceeded to tell him about Zane's security camera, which was always aimed at the front door, as well as his proclivity for recording all phone calls—or so he'd told her. He'd never let her listen to any. But he did maintain a landline in his home office, so it was worth looking for it and grabbing anything that could have recorded calls. "He probably recorded some or all of his cell calls, too, but I've no idea where that phone is. I assume the police have it—or he still does."

Grayson looked at her. "So first thing, we need to

go check out what's recorded on the security camera at the front door."

"Maybe," she said. "But we need to be really careful. The way it's hanging high up on the wall, I don't know if we can get to it without having our photos taken, too."

"Not good. Well, if we do, we'll just have to bring the whole thing with us so no one else will see us."

She nodded, though she said, "I'm not sure that's possible. Getting to it, even with a ladder, isn't easy. Besides, I think that the recordings of landline calls will be the most likely to include any conversations he had here with Schuyler and Ian. They might not have come to the house at all."

"Got it. Now, where's the front door?"

Savannah led Grayson out of the kitchen and through the wide hallway decorated on both sides with modern artwork. They soon were near the front of the house, but she stopped before taking him into the large, open entry area. She pointed toward the wall to indicate where the camera was mounted, though they couldn't see the device from here.

He got it. "Do you have any ladders?"

"Yes, in the basement. Let's just go up the back stairway to Zane's office for now. Maybe we can find what we're looking for there."

She thought that was a better idea, especially since past conversations she'd had with Zane were now tiptoeing into her head—where he talked about phone calls he'd had with friends or business associates while he was working here in his office. He'd laughed and said he figured they'd all feel screwed if they knew, because he got them talking about things they would never admit if they thought anyone else had the possibility of hearing them.

In other words, he'd recorded them. But he hadn't mentioned how, or where he kept the audio files.

Still, when they got up the stairway and Savannah led Grayson to the closed, ornate wooden door into Zane's home office, she said, "I assume you're more techie than I am. I'm not sure what to look for, but we can check to see if there's any kind of recording device." She hesitated. "Although—well, Zane never seemed to trust anyone."

She was glad when Grayson preceded her into the office and began looking everywhere, starting around where the phone sat on Zane's huge but far from ornate wooden desk. Nothing there, nor inside the drawers. Or on any of the shelves behind the desk, or under the comfortable-looking desk chair or any of the other furniture in the room.

Grayson sat at Zane's desk, pulling some of the drawers out beside him. He extracted files and laid them on top of the desk, going through them and checking out the now empty drawers.

Then Grayson looked toward Savannah. "I gather you're not sure Zane had any kind of recorder here, though he implied it." As Savannah nodded, Grayson shrugged and shook his head. "Unfortunately, I don't see anything here that would do what you hoped for."

He somehow looked cute in his frustration Cute? Why was she even thinking in that way?

To pull herself out of this situation, out of here? Out of her own frustration at not finding what they needed— something to clear her, right away?

That was ridiculous.

"We should probably look other places, though, just in case," Grayson continued. "If he was trying to hide something, his office would probably be too obvious, after all. Where else did he spend time?"

"He liked to watch the big-screen TV in the den," Savannah said after realizing that Grayson was right and pondering an answer to his question. "We were kind of separated for a while inside the house, both emotionally and physically, even before we got divorced. He had his own bedroom then, before I moved into the guesthouse, so that's another possibility."

"A potentially good one," Grayson said. "Let's start there and check it out, okay?"

"Sure." Savannah felt a bit embarrassed taking Grayson to her ex-husband's bedroom, although she hadn't been there for ages, and the last time she was there was probably well before Zane and she unofficially split up.

But that might make it a perfect place for him to hide something, right? Not that it would have mattered after she moved out. He could even have hidden the recorder in the room she had last used inside this house, the master bedroom.

She showed Grayson where Zane had slept while staying far away from her at night. They went up the wide wooden stairway, turned left at the end of the upstairs hallway and walked along the hall that was covered with imported Persian carpets laid end to end.

It felt so odd to Savannah to be here, seeing some of the things she still loved about this place. Her emotions roiled, but she ignored them. She was here to think, not to feel.

The white wooden door was closed but not locked. Inside, the place looked as Savannah remembered it, with a king-size bed beneath a woven, imported coverlet embroidered in gold and silver threads. Zane had a very tall and wide chest of drawers on one side and an ornate, full-length mirror beside it. He always liked to admire how he looked.

The place still smelled like him—not that "dead" Zane was likely to have visited recently. But he had used an aftershave with a lime citrus scent, and that aroma remained in the air.

The large dresser had two sides, each with separate drawers, with a bottom cabinet area with two separate doors. Savannah began searching through the drawers on the right side. Not that she appreciated thumbing through Zane's expensive underwear, but she had to find that recorder—unless Grayson did.

Nothing in the first drawer, and as she turned she noticed that Grayson was on his side on the floor, looking under the bed. Then he rose a little and began prodding the area between the mattress and the box spring.

Savannah turned back and closed the top right drawer, opening the next one—and almost gagged. It contained mostly socks of different styles and colors, no big deal there. But it also held a moderate-sized box with a colorful exterior that was labeled with a manufacturer's name and the word "Condoms" written decoratively in the middle.

She knew full well how much Zane engaged in sex with other women, and this suggested he had continued to have a lot of fun in that way before his "death." Before their divorce? She'd known he had but never found a good way to prove it.

She started slamming the drawer shut, too—but before she could, Grayson's arm reached out to stop her, startling Savannah. "Just a sec," he said.

Why? Did he want to take some of those condoms

along with him? Even having him see them in Zane's drawer embarrassed Savannah. She had wanted out of that horrible relationship, but this could give the impression not only that her ex was a sex fiend, but that Savannah hadn't satisfied him in that department.

Sure enough, Grayson pulled that box out of the drawer. Feeling mortified, justifiably or not, Savannah started to walk away. But then Grayson opened the box and crowed, "Here we are! I figured that might be a place to hide something without nosy people getting into it—except for us."

He pulled a black technological gadget out of the box. It was not very large but had a screen in front with buttons below and auxiliary ports. It was maybe an inch thick at the widest spot but tapered toward the bottom. With it were a couple of long wires with plugs at both ends.

"What is it?" Savannah asked in a hushed voice.

"Not my area of expertise, but I'd guess it's a landline phone call recorder. I just hope the memory card has lots of helpful recordings on it. Now we can continue looking for something else, too, but—"

A loud noise sounded from downstairs. "Police!" yelled a loud voice. "Is anyone here?" Savannah noticed what looked like some bright lights through the door from that direction. It was late morning, but even so maybe the cops were using inside searchlights before barging inside.

"Damn!" Grayson muttered softly. "Could the alarm have gone off after all?"

"Zane might have modified it," Savannah said nervously. He had talked about hiring a security company to improve the system someday, but he hadn't done that while she was living here.

"Anywhere we can hide?" Grayson whispered.

She felt her face light up, if only a little. "Yes. Zane was always secretive." She, too, kept her voice low. Raising a finger, she beckoned Grayson to follow her. She hurried as quietly as she could back to the same dresser, where she pulled open the wooden door on the bottom left. The open area there was surprisingly vast and even extended into the wall. Savannah had wondered what Zane planned to hide there someday. Cash stolen from his job? She wouldn't have been surprised—but if he had, he'd fortunately taken the money with him. That left an area large enough to hide both Grayson and her.

They both got down on the floor and crawled inside, and Grayson, holding the recorder, pulled the door closed behind them.

They waited. Savannah felt terrified, but it helped that Grayson snuggled against her as they both sat on the base of the cabinet and bent forward at the waist. He even put an arm around her. He was warm and comforting—and Savannah hoped that the cops didn't find them here and now.

It apparently took a while for the police to conduct their search of the place, and eventually Savannah heard footsteps in the hallway, then voices as the cops came inside Zane's bedroom. She glanced at Grayson, who was hardly visible in the darkness of the cabinet. He hugged her slightly harder as if in reassurance, then eased up. And stared at the cabinet door as if ready to leap out and attack the intruders.

But it didn't sound as if they would remain there long. They seemed to be grumbling about being there, talking about how the damned wind might have blown a door open and set off the alarm at the security company, which had notified the police station. From what Savannah could tell, they just walked through Zane's bedroom, circling it for maybe a minute as they talked, then started out again—or so she hoped.

Savannah was a bit startled when Grayson pushed the door open just a little and looked out.

And appeared a bit startled, too. He closed it quietly and quickly, then held Savannah's arm to keep her motionless for a short while that felt like forever.

He seemed to be listening. Concentrating.

And in a while he whispered to her, "Let's go."

Chapter 19

Grayson extracted himself from the bottom of the cabinet first and stood. He stretched, listening, and heard nothing. No one.

Not even his cousin Spencer.

Grayson had thought he recognized Spencer's voice when the cops were in the room talking. That was why he had carefully peeked out. And confirmed who it was. And fortunately hadn't been noticed.

If the other cops hadn't been there too, would Grayson have let Spencer know of his presence and Savannah's?

No. He couldn't do that to either Savannah or Spencer. Spencer would have had to arrest fugitive Savannah, even if Grayson made a good case for her innocence.

Which he certainly believed he could.

Even so, to do his job right, Spencer would probably have felt compelled to take Grayson into custody for abetting her.

Maybe even Grayson's brother Rafe's fiancée, Detective Kerry Wilder, would feel the same way.

Grayson hadn't thought he would have to hide anything from his family members, but that was before Savannah.

Grayson waited another few minutes in case he heard more from the cops, then said quietly to Savannah, "Okay, I think they've left. Time for us to get out of here."

He helped her to her feet, noticing the pinkness to her face beneath her makeup. That jacket had to be making her feel awfully warm. But it did help in her disguise, so he didn't suggest she take it off, at least not yet.

In fact, in case someone saw them, he handed her the recorder and its wires, and asked her to hide them beneath the jacket, since it wouldn't fit in her small purse nor in his pockets. The base of the jacket was secured by a cord belt, so the recorder should easily remain there.

"Okay," she said. "Do you think it's all right for us to go out the same way we came in?"

"Better than the front," Grayson responded. "And I gathered that the neighbors at that side don't use that entrance to their place, or so I figured from the amount of cactus around their gate. They probably won't notice us. So, yes."

Grayson insisted on preceding Savannah slowly along the hallway and down the stairs to the kitchen, continuing to remain alert the entire way. But fortunately, he still believed he was correct in assuming the police had left.

Finally, they reached the door they had come in. Again, he insisted on going first and opened the door just a little to ensure he didn't see or hear anyone outside before they exited.

In a few minutes, they had gone out that door and through the gate. He held Savannah's hand as they inched their way along the fence to the alley.

Soon, they were making their way along that alley. A breeze was still blowing, but it didn't affect them now. In fact, Grayson was glad for that wind. It had sounded like the cops had accepted it as the reason the house's front door had opened and set off the remote.

Did anyone look this way from their homes backing onto this alley or otherwise? Grayson didn't think so, or at least he hoped not. They walked quickly to his car and got inside.

Grayson felt relieved. "Let's listen to those recordings back at the bunker," he told Savannah as soon as he drove away in that direction.

"Fine with me," she said, "although do you have enough batteries to power the recorder along with the lights? We may be listening to it for a while and using up its juice."

"I've got something better," he told her. "A generator. As I mentioned, I used to spend a lot of time at my bunker."

He hoped, though, that they'd be able to work things out so Savannah didn't have to spend much time there. It was partially underground, after all, an even more stressful place for her to hang out than the fishing cabin, or so he believed. Still, although it was a former mine, since he'd closed off the shafts years ago he didn't consider it dangerous.

Besides, now that they'd begun testing her disguise,

maybe she would be able to get out and about, at least a little.

Better yet, prepare to move somewhere else altogether and let Grayson ultimately figure out how to clear her name around here. But his ability to do that might depend on what was on that recorder that was now on the center console between them.

"That bunker of yours is amazing," Savannah said. "You've got the place furnished quite nicely for what is pretty much a cave. You must have really liked it while you were growing up."

"I did," he said, "though now I have even better ways of staying away from my family when I choose to. And I never let them control my life."

"You're fortunate," Savannah said, surprising him a little. "My dad's gone now, but I married Zane largely because of his urging me to. I miss my father, but I certainly don't miss his pushiness."

Interesting. "My dad's on the pushy side, too," he said. "Or he was, before." He knew Savannah was aware of how Payne Colton had been shot and remained in a coma. Even though he still resented some of his father's attempts to control him in the past, Grayson felt awful about what had happened.

Another thought struck him about his family, something he really ought to let Savannah know about. "By the way, I should tell you one of the reasons I acted a bit stupid while we were hidden and peered out toward the cops. I thought I recognized a voice, and I was right. My cousin Spencer Colton was one of them."

He heard Savannah draw in her breath. "Oh, that could have been terrible. If he'd found you, I mean. I'm so sorry that I've been putting you into that kind of position, where even your family members might turn against you."

"Oh, I doubt that would be the case with Spencer." Grayson tried to keep his tone light, though he appreciated that this woman was smart enough to recognize problems like that without his suggesting them.

And it wasn't only Savannah's intelligence that he appreciated about her. He enjoyed her company, her warmth and caring, her body, and, well, nearly everything about her. Would there be any possibility of their developing a relationship after Savannah was cleared? He was beginning to hope so. A lot.

But none of that mattered now, while he still had to figure out how best to help her. Hopefully, that would get resolved when they listened to the recordings.

And the things he admired about her might not matter after this was all over.

They might wind up going their own ways…

But he certainly hoped not.

Meanwhile, now, he continued to drive around town as he had become used to doing, avoiding potholes and ruts still there after the earthquake, looking in the rearview mirror often to see what vehicles might be behind them, turning off onto smaller streets to ensure they weren't being followed, then veering off again to keep checking all was well.

He knew the cops were smart, too, especially Spencer. It was possible his cousin had seen him in Zane's house, or saw him after they left the house, and was now stealthily following them.

He had to be sure that wasn't the case before they finally headed to his bunker. It was not someplace he had ever told Spencer—or anyone—about.

It was still late morning, so no chance of hiding easily if anyone happened to be following them. But Grayson was being careful. He pulled into the parking lot of a small chain grocery store. "We need some supplies for tonight," he said. "And probably tomorrow, too."

Like breakfast, he thought. Would he stay the night again?

Quite possibly. If he could.

"Wait here," he told her, but she got out of the car at the same time he did. She drew closer to him on the sidewalk in front of the entrance. There were other people around, so he didn't want to scold her.

Especially when she got close enough to kiss him on the cheek—just pretending they were an item, he figured. She also used the opportunity to whisper to him, "Just checking my disguise again."

"Be careful," he instructed, and shook his head as she stuck out her tongue and preceded him inside.

He looked around the parking lot but didn't see anything that made him suspicious, so he followed.

The stuff they picked up after quickly strolling the narrow aisles of the store was the usual—a few sandwiches, more water, some chips and dip, and sweet rolls for the morning. Not a lot of the latter, but enough that they both would have an adequate amount if he did wind up staying the night, and Grayson was sure Savannah recognized that. But neither of them mentioned it.

He paid, of course. The young woman at the cash register didn't pay much attention to them, a good thing. Then, with Grayson holding the paper bag, they returned to the car and he began driving again.

On the route back, he did a few more twists and turns just in case but still saw no indication of anyone following or otherwise showing any interest in them. He finally headed his SUV toward his bunker.

"So everything's okay?" Savannah asked from beside him. Of course she would have noticed his weaving around local roads even after their small shopping expedition and understood why—smart lady that she was.

He aimed a smile at her before turning onto the street that would take him to the dirt road toward the bunker. "Yep, but we can't be too careful, can we?"

"No," she said, then added, "I'm learning so much from you, Grayson. And I'll never be able to thank you enough for all you're doing for me."

"Sure you can," he said teasingly. "I'll always be glad to hear it. First responders always are."

Once more he glanced at her—and wished he could just pull over and put his arms around the woman who was smiling so sadly at him. A pretty woman despite her disguise, including those silly glasses.

A sexy woman—and he definitely knew that about her, thanks to experience. Not that he dared to anticipate much more, if any.

But he had to keep his eyes on the semblance of a road through the forest beyond his family ranch, so he turned back to look out the windshield. Soon, they got to the area where he always parked and he put his car in its secluded spot.

She waited for him to go first as they approached the opening to the former mineshaft, though. Inside the cave, he again used the light from his phone to illuminate their path, and they quickly reached the rear part and entered the bunker area.

He lit the lanterns, then walked quickly to where he had stored the generator in an area off to the side and picked up the large container of gasoline he always left there, poured it into the machine, then turned it on.

Savannah had apparently been watching. "That's so cool," she said. "This place could turn into quite a home if you ever wanted to live here."

"That was the point," Grayson responded.

He couldn't resist. The last time they were there, the previous night, he hadn't been able to keep his hands off her, and he wanted to touch her now. Which he did. But he limited himself to giving her a quick kiss. For now. And was delighted that she returned it.

Then he plugged the recorder into the generator while Savannah went into the bathroom to change back to looking like Savannah. They soon sat down on two folding chairs in the middle of the room and used a third to hold the recorder. Grayson looked the machine over, then pushed the buttons he thought would get the audio started, hopefully from the beginning.

It took a little more effort, though, since what they heard at first included some static and telephone sounds like a busy signal. But soon Grayson had it working just fine.

And from what he could tell, they were initially listening to telephone conversations Zane Oliver had had some time ago, maybe a few months. Most seemed to be with business associates, though not all of them.

Grayson was sometimes captivated, sometimes amused, by the conversations they heard, though nothing was particularly helpful when Zane talked with, chided, and even threatened people who apparently were mostly customers of his. Grayson was disappointed that he heard nothing from Zane admitting anything incriminating. Even the threats were fairly inconsequential.

Grayson only hoped there would be some other, more helpful conversations to come.

It felt so weird to Savannah to be listening to these phone conversations. Listening to Zane being Zane, encouraging business associates to invest lots and lots of money in his bank.

Before sitting down, she had removed her disguise. That felt better, but it also felt good to know her trick had worked.

The folding chairs Grayson had in this attractively decorated cave were surprisingly comfortable, with cushioning on the seats and back, a good thing because Grayson and she might be there for quite a while hearing the recorded conversations. Grayson had given Savannah yet another pad of paper to write on, this time so she could make notes about whose voices they heard, if she recognized them or figured out who they were from what they or Zane said.

Savannah was able to identify quite a few people, even those who didn't live in Mustang Valley. Zane had had a lot of contacts all over; at parties and other occasions many people attempted to get to know him better, impress him, so he would not only do business with them but would also provide information and support for them and their companies.

Some of the names she heard included Rex Affler, owner of a local brewery, and Miranda Borden, from a national clothing manufacturer. All businesspeople who

undoubtedly had appreciated having a contact at a successful investment bank like Zane's.

All people who apparently wanted something from
him.

Which Zane clearly knew, sometimes stringing them
along, sometimes telling them to call back the next day
when he was at work. Sometimes insulting them. Sometimes insinuating threats if they didn't invest money
through his bank's services. And sometimes even telling
them he was sorry, but he couldn't help them.

But Savannah knew Zane and his voice well enough
to be sure he wasn't sorry at all, at least in most cases.

Plus, after some of those calls, the next conversations
would be with one or another of his own employees at
the bank, with Zane often making fun of those business
associates he'd just spoken with.

At least none of them were with his lovers, thank
heavens. Not then, at least.

Grayson and she listened for an hour without hearing
anything that could be helpful to her.

No, what she wanted was to reach out and grab Zane
by the throat—not to kill him as she allegedly had, but
demand when he would actually say something helpful.

Assuming he ever would.

"Are you okay?" Grayson asked. She must have made
some kind of movement or otherwise indicated her frustration, since he was looking directly at her.

"Fine," she grumped, then repeated "Fine" in a tone
that she hoped was closer to sounding fine.

"Hey, I'm going to bring our lunch over here," Grayson said.

"Good idea." But Savannah didn't let him do it on his
own. She rose and began helping him—and when their

arms touched, she looked up at him…and she wanted so much to drag him over to that bed.

Not then, though. The recording was still droning on, and it was vital that they heard all of it as quickly as possible.

Surely sometime, it would contain the voices of at least Ian Wright and Schuyler Wells—along with Zane.

And when it did, would they be conspiring to frame her for Zane's eventual imaginary death?

Now, though, Zane held a conversation with one of his employees. How did he ever decide which calls, or other work, to take care of at home rather than at his office? Savannah had no idea.

Grayson and she each chose a sandwich. They turned to sit back down and bumped into each other.

"Sorry," she said.

"I'm not." Still holding his own sandwich, roast beef, Grayson bent down to kiss Savannah right on the mouth. "Mmmm," he said. "Potato chips and dip. I can't wait to taste you again after you've eaten your sandwich."

Savannah laughed, and the thought of dragging him over to the cot once more permeated her mind.

Not going to happen, but her windows of opportunity to get him to bed again were dwindling.

But after another hour of listening and nibbling on their sandwiches, they still had nothing useful.

Savannah was beginning to give up hope.

"What should we do if there's nothing here?" she finally asked Grayson. At that moment, Zane was talking to someone whose name or voice Savannah didn't recognize. From the conversation she had learned that the other speaker was apparently not only a female executive of a local consumer electronics company, but someone he'd slept with—or was trying to seduce.

Not a surprise, but Savannah was disgusted anyway. She was happy when that call ended.

And the next one? Hearing the second voice caused her to stand up in excitement.

Zane was talking to Ian Wright! So he had known the attorney, as she'd come to believe.

"Hey," Grayson said softly. "That's good news." Then he put one long finger over his own mouth as if to shush himself and listen.

Savannah kind of wished it was her finger there—but instead concentrated on the conversation.

Ian was apparently returning a call from Zane about possible representation on a legal matter for the investment bank.

Nothing about Savannah. Nothing conspiratorial about framing her for Zane's murder.

But at least this proved they'd known one another.

And it gave Savannah hope there would be more later on. And ended at least some of her frustration at all the unhelpful calls before.

She couldn't rely on what she heard now between Zane and Ian being of much use, though. She needed the reality of more conversations, discussions that finally made it clear that those two had done more than discuss banking and legal issues.

With Schuyler, too.

Grayson had also finished his sandwich. He must have seen the conflicting encouragement and discouragement on Savannah's face that she felt inside. He moved his chair closer and put his arm around her as they continued to listen.

For another hour. Savannah, who put her head down on Grayson's shoulder, appreciated his nearness, even if they wouldn't, couldn't, do anything about it.

She appreciated him. Still. More.

Realized she had come to hope for a future that included him.

But—

She closed her eyes, figuring it wouldn't hurt to go to sleep—and then, there it was.

Zane was not only talking to Ian, but to Schuyler, too. Was it a three-way phone conversation? Were Ian and Schuyler together?

No matter. The main thing was what they were saying.

"So, Schuyler," Zane said. "You know my divorce is final, but unfortunately that's not the end of things. Did Ian explain what I want both of you to help with?"

"Hey, yeah," said Schuyler Wells. Savannah recognized his voice. Of course. Wasn't she supposed to have been having an affair with him at the time of this conversation?

She would have laughed—but she needed to be completely quiet to hear this.

"I gather," Schuyler said, "that you're about to be murdered, right? By your wonderful ex—and I'm going to get to know her better. Way better. You'll disappear, and the cops will just happen to find some damning evidence against dear Savannah. But without your body around—well, there should be arguments that you're okay, that your ex is innocent. And our buddy Ian there is going to take her case to prove it."

"Or not," Ian said, and all three men laughed.

The conversation continued a little longer. Savannah

was staring straight at Grayson, knowing her eyes were wide and she was smiling. She had proof now. She didn't kill Zane, and the world—and the authorities—would know it. She would be exonerated in court at last. She wanted to shout, to hug Grayson, to laugh and laugh and engage in nice, celebratory kisses with him.

And when those men hung up, Grayson said, "We've got it!"

Chapter 20

And that call wasn't the last of it. Grayson chortled as, still sitting there with his arm around an excited Savannah, they heard a couple more conversations—and the final one on this subject contained verbal confirmation of everything they would need to demonstrate to the police that Zane was still alive, and Savannah was not guilty of killing him.

It should also let the authorities know there were a couple of better suspects in the murder of Ian Wright—one of his coconspirators in framing Savannah.

"This is so amazing," Savannah said, looking at him with a huge grin after one of those calls finished. "I don't know why my ex was stupid enough to record those calls, since they're proof of so much against him. But I'm so glad he did!"

"He might have wanted some kind of reminder of

what was said in case he needed to use it against his coconspirators," Grayson told her. "Or maybe he just wanted to save them as proof that he hadn't been alone in this, if the truth ever did come out. As it will now."

One of those last calls was certainly the best. In it, the men had all agreed to do what was needed to frame Savannah as Zane's revenge against her. He promised to be generous in his payments to the others, and the amounts he mentioned seemed a lot more than that.

And the very last call? It described how Zane would cut himself with the knife and hide the bloody thing in her closet. He would disappear then.

Too bad he didn't mention where he would disappear to.

Grayson's mind began spinning. What should they do next? But his thoughts were interrupted when Savannah rose and pulled him up to stand, too. In moments, they were kissing, sweetly and happily at first, and then more heatedly.

Grayson felt his body reacting. He wanted more, much more, as part of their celebration. But this definitely wasn't the time. They had to act on this and get Savannah cleared before anything else.

And after? Well, maybe they could get together again, to celebrate or whatever. And determine if that would be their happy ending, or if there could be more...

There had to be more. He hadn't planned on it, but he had fallen hard for this vulnerable, yet smart and sexy, woman. She had stood up in the face of adversity and was about to win. They had to have a future together.

But this wasn't the time to think about that.

He finally broke away from Savannah, as much as he hated to. He looked down at her ecstatic face.

"Here's what I want to do now. I intend to take this recording to the police, of course, but first I want to get a copy of it. I know enough cops I can trust, including Spencer and my brother Rafe's fiancée, Kerry. But I want to make sure this doesn't get misplaced, intentionally or otherwise."

"Great idea," Savannah said, still smiling but a bit less so. "Where will you get it copied? Do you have any equipment that'll do it in your office, or do you know someone you trust enough to do it?"

He nodded. "I may not adore all my family members, but most of us do care enough to help each other whenever possible. My brother Callum is a bodyguard, and you wouldn't think someone like him would have technological equipment as part of his profession, but Callum does. I'll call him from my car and head to his office. I don't know if he's working at the moment, but unless there's something going on right now, he'll meet me there and we'll get this copied right away."

"Sounds good." But Savannah's tone didn't sound as enthused as before.

"It is," he said. "I want you to stay here, where it will be safer. Even if you get your disguise on, I don't want the cops to see you until I turn the recording over to them and they have a chance to listen to it. I'll come get you then, okay?"

"Sure." Savannah looked up at him again. "But make it fast. Please. I can't wait till I'm cleared and this is all behind me."

"Me, too." Grayson unplugged the recorder.

He took Savannah into his arms then and gave her a long, deep, celebratory kiss.

"Hey, girl," he said when the kiss ended and he had

stepped back just a little, looking down into her gorgeous green eyes. "In case you can't guess, I've fallen for you. Hard. See you soon."

"And I've fallen for you, too," she said, making him smile.

Then he left.

Savannah paced the inside of the bunker after Grayson left. She wanted to clap, to cheer, to run outside and restart her life. With Grayson in it. Forever.

But she knew it was too soon.

After Grayson got everything handled, took a copy of the recording to the police and made sure they listened to the right part, he would return here for her. He'd promised.

In the meantime, she simply had to wait.

Not so simply, though. She at last had more than hope. This horrible time would soon be over.

For now, she just needed to be patient.

Right.

Grayson hadn't been gone long, and Savannah needed to occupy her mind as she waited. She spent a few minutes sitting on one of those folding chairs and checking things on her burner phone but nothing captured her interest. She put the phone down on the chair beside her.

Work on Grayson's first responder website idea? She wouldn't be able to concentrate.

She wasn't hungry, so she didn't try eating another of those sandwiches.

Looking around, she spotted the tall, thick bookcase that didn't look as it if belonged out here in this former mineshaft. The shelving looked potentially unstable and likely to collapse on this uneven floor and spew the many kinds of books on it onto the vinyl tiles. It seemed surprising that it hadn't toppled in the earthquake a few days ago, but maybe the shaking hadn't been too bad right here.

Who knew when Grayson had brought the bookcase to this bunker? It had probably been when he was a kid, and she gathered that it hadn't fallen over yet. Or at least he hadn't mentioned it, and she saw no damaged parts.

In any case, she approached it for the first time and looked more closely at the books on it. They ranged from thrillers to biographies and travel guides to all sorts of countries.

To her own surprise, she picked out a fiction book that was apparently about a first responder. She was fascinated not only by Grayson himself, but also what he did.

She would need a new life after this was all over. Would she be able to become a first responder and have him hire her?

After all, she enjoyed helping people. Had learned a bit from Grayson about all that first responders do. Enjoyed the idea of becoming one herself.

And that way, they would definitely remain in each other's lives—even if only professionally.

As she sat there starting to thumb through the book, she realized she hoped they would remain in each other's lives for additional reasons, too.

It might be too soon for her to embark on a real relationship with another man. But if she ever did, Grayson was one man she was certain she could trust.

And love.

Unlike that horrible former husband of hers, who had tried so hard to ruin her life.

A noise sounded from the entryway. This was much

too soon for Grayson to return after having a copy of the recording made and taking it to the police. He'd hardly left. Did he forget something?

She stood and put the book down on the chair. Surely it could only have been Grayson she'd heard, though—right?

Unless some animal also called this bunker home sometimes.

Or—

Oh no!

"Hello, Savannah," Zane Oliver said with a smirk, walking through the opening.

He was a man of moderate height, with dark hair but a receding hairline. He was a few years older than Savannah's thirty-one, but his sagging jawline made him look a lot older. He'd been relatively good-looking when they had met, but not any longer. Or maybe that was just because Savannah had come to despise him.

How had he found her here? This place was Grayson's. It pained Savannah even to see this miserable person in a location she had come to value so much, thanks to the wonderful man who had brought her here.

Like her, Zane was wearing a completely casual outfit—a light yellow T-shirt and black shorts—that wasn't at all like his usually professional attire.

"Hello, Zane," she said back, forcing her tone to remain calm, even though she wanted to scream and race out of there.

She couldn't, though. Zane, blocking the exit, held a gun in his hand and was pointing it toward her. "Interesting refuge you've got here. I'd never have thought someone like you would wind up living in a former mine. On the other hand, I never thought someone like you would wind up escaping from the cops and eluding them for so long."

"How…how did you find me?"

"Oh, that wonderful phone recorder I rely on so much has other functions, too. There's a GPS transmitter on it. I followed it, and here I am."

Savannah felt herself shaking. But something about that didn't make sense. "It's not here," she told him. Grayson had it with him wherever he'd driven to, but she wasn't going to say anything to her horrible ex about that.

"I know that. Your new buddy—he's a first responder guy, right? Anyway, we saw him drive off a little while ago, and the dot showing the location of my recorder went in that direction. But we could see he was the only one in the car, so I followed what the dot showed before, and here I am." His smile seemed to grow even more evil, if that was possible.

"Who's *we*?" Savannah had to ask.

"None of your business, but I want to take care of both of you and get my recorder back."

Which meant Grayson could be in danger, too. But at the moment, there was nothing Savannah could do about it. She had to save her own life first, before she could try calling Grayson.

Under the circumstances, she had to assume that the other person was Schuyler Wells. There could be others she didn't know about, of course. But right now it didn't matter who it was.

"Okay, Zane, let's talk about this." Savannah spoke in as reasonable a tone as she could. "I'm a bit surprised to see you in this area. Don't you think someone will recognize you?"

"Like someone recognized you? Hey, I'm not going into town. This is far enough out that I'm not too worried. But I do have one concern."

He paused, so Savannah did as she figured she was supposed to and asked, "What's that?" She was still standing near her chair, from which she'd risen before. Zane, however, was walking around the room, glancing around as if looking for something.

"I'm debating whether just to shoot you here or take you somewhere else. This isn't a bad place, since when your buddy is gone I gather not many people, if anyone, would think of looking for you here."

Then they were planning on killing her, and maybe Grayson, too. She had to warn him somehow.

"The thing is," Zane continued, "I want this to look like a suicide. After all, you did murder me and your lawyer. It's only natural you'd feel some sense of guilt." Another of those evil smiles.

That was enough. He wanted her to be afraid. And she was. But after everything she had gone through, she wasn't simply going to submit to whatever he intended to do with her.

Thinking quickly, she said, "Oh, I do. I feel terribly guilty that I didn't dump you sooner. And I'm sure you're the one who killed your friend Ian."

He didn't deny it. "Could be," he said, still smiling.

"But why did you do all this?" she couldn't help asking. "Why pretend to be dead and frame me? Are you low on money and needing to hide? Or do you just hate me enough to want to ruin my life? Or—"

"All of the above," he said with a laugh. "It was so nice to have you around as a scapegoat, dear wifey, though I'm sure I'll be able to pop back eventually from where I recovered after you 'killed' me and bring my business back from its current mediocre status to its former huge success. I'll just tell everyone you scared me enough when you tried to kill me that I pretended at first to be dead. When I survived, I couldn't bring myself to return for a long while, so I hid in another town. But hell, you divorced me. That was the best reason for me to do all this. I'm in charge. I always was. And when you did something I didn't choose so you could change my life, I had to do something to pay you back. And now, when you're found dead, I'll pretend to give a damn. Pretend."

That was enough. Savannah a bit scared but even more determined, turned briefly and grabbed the chair, using it as a shield as she approached Zane.

Would she survive to see Grayson again? She had to.

Zane shot at her, but she darted sideways, still holding the chair. Zane went the same way, keeping his aim steady as she dashed to one side of the room.

She leaped forward and hit him with the chair, hoping she'd knock him out or at least distract him enough that she could run away.

That didn't happen. Instead, Zane moved sideways again, not aiming at her for the moment as he regained his equilibrium—

That was when Savannah got the idea of how to stop him.

Not looking to her side, she nevertheless moved that way, dropping the chair and grabbing that tall, unstable bookcase she'd been examining before and yanking it sideways so it toppled. Onto Zane.

Knocking him to the floor. One of the large, thick wooden side panels hit him in the head, as books tumbled all around him.

Knocking him out.

Savannah grabbed his gun, smiled as evilly as she could at the unconscious body of the man she hated, snatched her phone from the chair that had been beside her—

And fled the bunker.

As soon as she got to the opening and figured she would have a good signal, she called Grayson.

He answered right away. "What's up, Savannah? I haven't gotten very far, and—"

"It's Zane! He found me. I knocked him out and I'm running away, but he said someone is after you in your car, too. Watch out, Grayson. Please be careful."

She didn't hear another word from him.

But she did hear what sounded like a car crash.

"No!" she screamed and began running along the dirt road.

Damn. His head had hit the side window before the airbags deployed. And now it hurt like crazy.

But at least Grayson was still awake. And mad at himself. Never mind he was here in the middle of nowhere. He should have remained careful, watching around him.

Seeing that car that hit him before it could run him off the road.

And now?

Pain shot through his head. But he knew better than to move.

Zane was with Savannah? Damn. Grayson should be there with her, protecting her. But he wasn't. Although it sounded like she'd handled the situation well, at least for now.

She was okay. She had to be. He wanted to grab her and shield her and care for her forever.

But they both had to survive for a forever to happen. What about him?

Well, if Zane was with Savannah, someone else had run Grayson off the road. Chances were that it was Schuyler Wells. But who it was didn't matter, at least not much.

How Grayson handled this did. He had to get back to the bunker fast. To Savannah.

He heard a nearby car door slam shut. If whoever it was thought Grayson was unconscious, all the better. Grayson allowed himself to continue slumping against the inside of his door.

Sure enough, that door was pulled open. Not a great thing, but Grayson allowed himself to slide out onto the ground, fortunately hitting his shoulder before his head came to rest on the forest floor. Pain nevertheless shot through him yet again, but at least he remained conscious.

"Okay, first responder guy," he heard a voice say and recognized it as Schuyler's. He didn't dare open his eyes yet. "Where's that damned recorder? Zane should have known better. I didn't know he was taping his conversations. He just told me about it."

The guy was talking as if he was holding a conversation with Grayson, but since he didn't do anything to hurt Grayson further he had to believe his target here was unconscious. Good.

Feeling a movement against his side, Grayson fought not to moan or move. But he did open his right eye just a little, in time to see one leg hoisted over him as Schuyler—yes, it was the man he'd seen on those real estate websites—stepped partway into the car, apparently trying to find the recorder.

Also good. Grayson remained lying there for another few seconds until Schuyler bent forward even more. Then Grayson roared to life, pulling the guy from between his legs and onto the ground, pummeling him in the face.

Schuyler screamed and attempted to fend Grayson off—unsuccessfully. Ignoring his own pain, Grayson rolled the other man over till his face was on the ground and pulled his arms behind him. Too bad he didn't have cuffs with him. Holding Schuyler down by kneeling on his back and arms, Grayson pulled his fortunately long-sleeved T-shirt over his head and rolled it until it became rope-like. He used it to tie Schuyler's arms together.

"Hold still, jerk," Grayson said to the man squirming beneath him. "It's over."

Only it wasn't. Not completely.

Grayson was worried about Savannah, where she was—and how long Zane would stay immobilized.

He felt a little chilly in the shade of the forest without his shirt, but at least it was springtime in Arizona.

He stepped over Schuyler and leaned into the car, extracting the oh-so valuable recorder from the floor on the passenger's side and tucking it into his belt. He also found his phone on the floor and retrieved it. Then he opened the glove compartment, extracting a small but definitely lethal gun. Backing out again, he pointed the gun at Schuyler.

"Okay," he said. "Here's how it's going to be. Your buddy Zane has been subdued, too, but we're going back to the bunker and make sure both of you are sufficiently secured. Stay there a sec, then you'll stand up."

First, though, Grayson wanted to call Savannah. He took a few steps backward, still facing Schuyler, still pointing the gun at him. He didn't particularly want Wells to hear his conversation, but he wasn't going far enough away from his captive to ensure he didn't.

He pushed the button on his phone to call Savannah. She answered immediately.

"Grayson? Are you okay? What happened?"

"I'm fine, and I'll explain it all in a few minutes, when I see you. I'm not far away. But are you outside the bunker?"

"Yes, but I'm near it, hiding behind some bushes, watching the opening to make sure Zane doesn't come out."

"Perfect! Stay there. If he does come out, try to figure out his direction but don't get close, okay?"

"Okay." She paused, then added, "I'm so glad you're okay, Grayson. I was so worried."

That sent a zing of pleasure through him that he had to ignore for now.

"Don't worry," he said. "And I think this'll all be over with very soon."

Chapter 21

Savannah continued to crouch on the dirt behind the bushes. The best part was that they were thick and concealing. There were uneven rows of them in this area. A good place to hide.

She was so glad Grayson was okay. The sounds she had heard after calling him had been scary. Had the person who'd been after him, presumably Schuyler, hit his car?

She wished he had told her more, but he'd promised to do so soon. And she had come to believe Grayson's promises. She would see him in a little while. He'd said so.

And she couldn't wait. Wisely or not, she had come to really care for him.

To love him.

It was late in the day now, but fortunately there was still enough light for her to see the bunker's opening.

She had certainly intended to hurt Zane, and the fact she had knocked him out was a good thing, even though she couldn't have been certain of that outcome. She just hoped she hadn't killed him. Wouldn't that be ironic under the circumstances?

The good thing was that she would have proof he had remained alive, at least until now. And that he had conspired to frame her for his murder.

Time seemed to pass so slowly as she waited there. No indication that Zane was leaving, at least, unless he had found some exit she didn't know about. Through the mine somehow? And what direction would Grayson come from?

How long would it take him to get here—

There! She saw movement from the edges of the dirt road. Two people, walking.

Fortunately, one of them—the one walking behind—was Grayson, not wearing a shirt. Savannah couldn't help staring at his sexy body, even in these stressful circumstances. But she quickly brought herself back to reality.

The man in front was Schuyler Wells, the guy who'd claimed to be Savannah's lover as part of the attempt to frame her. As she'd believed, he must have been the one who'd gone after Grayson and the recorder.

The one who'd apparently caused Grayson to be in an accident. At least Grayson appeared okay. He walked normally, and she saw no blood on him.

She just observed his gorgeous, carved chest...

And Schuyler appeared to have his hands tied behind his back as he moved slowly forward, prodded by Grayson.

She wanted to scream out in happiness and relief and

run toward them, but she didn't. She would wait until they had entered the bunker, keeping watch out here in case Zane had somehow escaped another way, but then join them inside.

And so she waited—and good thing that she did. Sure enough, Zane appeared at the opening to the bunker. As far as she knew, she had his only weapon.

Grayson apparently saw him too, and stopped. "Hey, Zane. Good to see you," he called.

"Not good to see you," Zane called back. His voice sounded a bit fuzzy, and he wasn't moving fast, either— possibly as a result of his injuries from the bookcase.

Or, possibly, he was faking it to put Grayson off guard as he approached.

In case it was the latter, Savannah moved away from her hiding place and out into the open—holding Zane's gun and aiming it at him.

"Hi, Grayson," Savannah said, glancing in his direction but looking back immediately. "Should we go inside the bunker now, or somewhere else?"

"The bunker will do. I've got some rope there and you can help me tie both these guys up. I've got Schuyler secured, but that would work better."

"Damn you," Zane cried. "I'm not going back in there. And you're not going to tie me up like some stupid animal you've captured."

"Oh, is that what you are?" Savannah couldn't help asking. She basked for a few seconds in Grayson's smile. "Anyway, that's exactly what I'm going to do. And if Grayson wants you inside the bunker, that's where we'll go."

"Actually," Grayson said, "we can hang out in the entry area." He had his gun in his hand, and now he aimed it at Zane, too. "Looks like our buddy Zane is the bigger flight risk at the moment, and I've got control over Schuyler. Let's go into the entryway, then I'll tell you when to go inside for the rope, Savannah, and where it is."

Which made her feel wonderful. She'd started to fear that maybe things weren't over after all.

But now she had reason again to believe they were. Or could be.

And she could only hope that the future became as wonderful for her, with Grayson, as she now desired to have.

Oh, yes. She desired it. And him.

They were sitting on the stone floor of the entry cave to the bunker—Zane and Schuyler, both secured with good ropes, and Grayson certainly knew how to bind them well. But just in case, he still held his gun and encouraged Savannah to hold hers, as well.

Savannah. She looked so happy now, so radiant.

And he loved her smile.

He also loved the fact that she would soon be cleared of all wrongdoing, particularly of murdering her ex.

Would she want to put it all behind her now, including him?

If so, he would have to convince her otherwise. And not just on a cot in a bunker.

Grayson had put his shirt back on. Now, his phone rang. He looked at the caller ID and smiled. Sergeant Spencer Colton of the Mustang Valley PD.

His cousin. The cop he had called after he and Savannah had tied up the two men. He'd given Spencer a fairly detailed explanation of what had occurred in as few words as possible, and told him where he could come to pick up the criminals in this situation. His cousin had said yes, he and some colleagues would come to take the real bad guys into custody.

This time, Grayson would be glad to see him. "Hi, cuz," he said, answering the phone.

"Okay, we're here. Give me better directions. Where the hell are you?"

Talking to him a bit more, Grayson learned that Spencer had passed the area of his car wreck and continued down the dirt road. "You're probably right outside," he said. "I'll send Savannah out to greet you when you get here."

Fortunately, although it was getting later, there was still some daylight left, so Spencer and his fellow cops should be able to see her fairly easily.

"You okay with that?" he asked Savannah.

"If the other choice is staying here with those two—" she gestured with her gun hand in their direction "—then I'm definitely okay with it."

She looked so good that way. So natural. Would she have any interest in becoming a first responder, too? That would be one way they could work together, though he wouldn't want that to be the only way.

"Good."

She exited through the opening.

"Look, Colton," Zane said. "You really don't have to do this. I may be 'dead.' To most of the world, but I still have resources. Financial resources even you wouldn't believe. If you just work with me, tell your cronies that everything was set up by Schuyler, here, I can pay you—"

Grayson laughed. "Oh, you're really a hoot, aren't

you, Oliver? Even if I needed your money, assuming you still have any after disappearing that way, no way would I take it."

And on the ground near Zane, Schuyler was shouting, "You SOB," and clearly attempting to get closer to him by edging along on the stone base.

Grayson didn't need to stop him. Three cops were suddenly at the entrance to the bunker, followed by Savannah. None of them appeared to be taking her into custody, fortunately.

As the two other uniformed officers, probably the same ones Grayson had glimpsed at Zane's house, took Zane and Schuyler into custody, cuffing them and reciting their rights, Spencer came over to Grayson, who now stood near one of the rough stone walls.

Spencer looked a lot younger than he really was— but he had a good reputation as a cop. He had sandy blond hair and blue eyes, and usually had a keen sense of humor—although he looked awfully serious right now. "Okay, cuz. Why didn't you tell me before what was going on? You were helping a wanted fugitive all this time, and you now have recorded proof of her innocence? I should arrest all four of you, then figure this all out."

"You know I won't run away, so if you learn something different from what I told you—which you won't— you can arrest me then. And I believe that Savannah feels the same way."

She had approached them, and now nodded. "I'm innocent. I said so all along, and you finally have proof. You're taking the man I allegedly murdered into custody, Sergeant Colton. I've already handed Zane's gun to you. And I won't run away again. I don't think I have to. In fact, I suspect I'll need to go to the police station now, right? But you don't have to cuff me or anything."

Grayson couldn't help it. He drew near Savannah and put his arm around her, smiling triumphantly at his cousin. "Thanks to this wonderful lady, you're going to be the primary cop to solve this situation," Grayson told him. "You'll get recognition for it. I think you'll be thanking me soon."

"Don't count on it," Spencer said—but then he smiled. "I gather the two of you are more than first responder and rescued soul."

"Count on that," Grayson said, giving Savannah a kiss.

It finally appeared really to be over. Savannah felt overjoyed.

Oh, she did accompany Grayson to the police station, as his cousin, the police sergeant, insisted. But no one took her into custody then, either, although she did have to make an official statement.

Sergeant Spencer Colton apparently called an EMT, not one of Grayson's employees, to check his cousin out after the car accident. Fortunately, except for some bruising, especially on his head, he apparently was fine.

Afterward, standing in the station's reception area, Savannah was told by the police chief that the situation remained under investigation and she was not to leave town.

"Tell us where we'll be able to find you," said the tall and mostly bald Chief Al Barco.

"I—" Savannah tried to answer, but she didn't know what to say. She would prefer not to return to the bunker or the cabin, and certainly not Zane's guesthouse, which she'd been staying in.

"For now, she'll be staying with me, at the Triple R," Grayson broke in and gave the address. "And here's her current phone number." He provided the burner phone's number to the cop.

His family home? That sounded wonderful to Savannah. But was it a good idea?

"Sounds good," the chief said. He had been regarding her sternly, but now he smiled. "I've got a feeling we're going to have no further official interest in you, but stay tuned. We'll have to let you know."

"Of course," Savannah said. She wished he'd been more positive, but at least there was reason for hope now. A lot of reasons.

"I think you've got some investigating to do," Grayson added. "You have a couple of killers in custody, and one of them's allegedly a dead guy."

Chief Barco laughed. "Let's see how that all works out," he said.

"Yes," said Grayson. "Let's see." He took Savannah's hand and began leading her out of the station.

Sergeant Colton came over to them. "I haven't completely forgiven you," he said to Grayson, but he looked at Savannah and winked.

A cop winked at her! For some reason, that made Savannah feel a whole lot better. She was free now, hopefully forever.

"What'll it take for you to forgive me?" Grayson said.

"Keep me better informed next time, for one thing."

"I just hope there's no next time, at least not like this," Grayson said, and Savannah could only smile and nod her concurrence.

They left the station. But now what? It was dark outside. And Savannah knew her ultimate goal that night was Grayson's home.

Bad idea? Oh, she loved the idea of being with him longer. He had done all he had promised, and it appeared that she was exonerated from the charges that had disrupted her life so horribly.

She really liked the guy. More than that. She had certainly come to care for him, a lot. Probably too much. But in some ways there was no reason for them to stay close together any longer.

Even though she knew she would really like that.

But she had vowed not to get involved with any other men after her ugly divorce —and she wasn't sure she could so easily trust another guy so deeply, after what Zane had done.

Did she dare get even more involved with Grayson now?

They did stop for dinner at a nice restaurant on their way home, an Italian place. And for once Savannah was hungry.

She wished she could pay. She should be able to soon, since she would be able to get access to her bank account and other assets.

But for now—well, Grayson said he would pay, and she let him.

This time.

And next time? There had to be a next time. This simply could not be the end of his being in her life.

She hoped.

But she wasn't certain. And she felt tears fill her eyes as they headed back to Grayson's car.

Chapter 22

Grayson knew his home would never feel the same again.

Savannah and he had stopped for dinner last night after leaving the police station. Savannah had seemed quite happy that her food was warm and fresh for a change, and the restaurant was filled with people—although apparently no one who knew her. At least no one said hi, or pointed at her.

He'd driven them to the ranch after that in an SUV he'd rented temporarily while his car was being fixed.

Savannah and he had walked to his portion of the house and he'd shown her into a guest room.

But she hadn't stayed there. No, they'd celebrated the recent happenings by spending the night in bed together, in the most enjoyable way possible.

He loved it. He loved her. And this simply couldn't be the last night they spent together.

In the morning, they had gone out to a fast-food place for breakfast, and Grayson told Savannah he was taking her back to his office for now.

"I've got something I need to do at the ranch," he said as they finished eating.

"I understand," she said. "Are you going to check with your brothers and sisters and stepmom about how your father is doing?"

"That, too, maybe. But—well, like my siblings, as you know, that wing in the main house where we stayed last night is my own. You are welcome to stay in the guest-room there as long as you want."

"Oh." Her expression, as she looked down at her empty plate, appeared downcast. "You don't need to do that. I'll find another place very soon."

"No," he said firmly and fast, not wanting to even ask where she had in mind—and assuming she didn't yet. "You won't. And that doesn't mean we won't see each other. It simply means we'll each have our own space, so we can decide how much time we will spend together."

Like forever? That was the thought that rolled through his mind. Damn it, he had fallen for Savannah.

Did he want to spend the rest of his life with her? Well, maybe. He certainly felt more for her than he had for any other woman. But she'd just gotten a divorce—was she ready to trust again?

Could he trust that she would stay with him forever if she seemed ready to make a commitment?

He walked her back to his office building and made sure his staff had started to arrive. He was amused at how Winchell demanded Savannah's attention, which she gave without reservation, kneeling on the floor and hugging the smart and skilled search and rescue dog.

He had not been able to bring Savannah here before, not while she was a fugitive, so the people on his staff didn't yet know her. After introducing Savannah to them, he told them her current status: unofficially exonerated from committing a murder.

Of course all of them, Norah in particular, became highly excited for Savannah and demanded to hear how that had happened.

"Go ahead and tell them," Grayson said to her. "I've got to get on my way. See you all soon."

He drove back to the ranch, half wishing he could have stayed to hear how they all discussed what had happened yesterday—and also get a sense for where Savannah's mind was now, what she thought her future might contain. He would make sure she had a place to stay and anything else she needed, of course, whether or not it was at the ranch. But he had come to know her well enough to feel certain she would make plans for what came next, then implement them.

With his involvement? If so, how much?

He now hoped they would stay in each other's lives, at least a little. Maybe a lot.

He soon drove back through the gate at the Rattlesnake Ridge Ranch and parked in an empty spot near the car he recognized as Asher's. He assumed his other siblings weren't around just then, which was fine.

In fact, his younger half brother was a good one to talk to about how things were going with the family. Asher was actually the ranch foreman.

Of course Asher might be in the stable or out on the grounds, but Grayson entered the main ranch house, planning to go up to his wing on the second floor. But hearing a noise from the kitchen, he figured he had better stop in and say hi to whoever was there, Asher or staff or someone else, rather than startling someone with his presence. He walked through the living room, with its luxurious, floor to ceiling walls and exposed beam ceiling of the open living room. He also passed the dining room, as always taking in how nice this place was, with its wooden floors and lots of trim and expensive decorations.

"Hi, bro. It's a surprise to see you wandering around here at this hour." Asher had just exited the kitchen, a mug of coffee in his hand. "You just picking something up, or—"

"I'll be hanging around here more now," Grayson told him. "And you'll probably be hearing in the news the reason why."

"Yeah? Tell me." They first went back into the kitchen where Grayson, too, got a mug of coffee, then headed into the living room and sat facing one another.

Asher looked like a perfect foreman, Grayson thought, not for the first time. His younger brother certainly looked like a cowboy, with longish dark brown hair, a slight brush of facial hair that included a dark goatee, and a casual denim shirt and slacks that appeared entirely appropriate for horseback riding. All he needed was a cowboy hat, but since they were inside, that wasn't likely at the moment.

Even better, Asher was dedicated to the ranch and to making certain everything went well there—especially important now, with their father in a coma.

"So what's going on?" Asher asked right away.

Grayson told him, keeping the story brief but starting from finding the dead van driver, then Savannah hiding in a fishing cabin, and ending with her exoneration yesterday. "And till she figures out where to go and what to do, I'm letting her stay in my guest room. And—"

The doorbell rang. One of their staff hurried to open it, but Asher headed that way, and so did Grayson, partly out of curiosity.

A man stood there, and he looked vaguely familiar. He immediately looked toward the two brothers while the maid left the entry. "Hi," he said. "I'm Jace Smith and—well, I think I'm your brother, the real Ace Colton. Can I come in? I'd like to talk to you."

Grayson felt as if he'd been hit over the head. Really? He didn't spend a lot of time around here with family, but he certainly tried to keep up with the news about Ace. Sure, they'd been told Ace wasn't their brother by blood.

But it seemed a shock to have someone come in like that and claim to be that real sibling.

"Sure, come in," said Asher, beside him, and they all stepped aside.

Grayson studied the man some more. No weapons— or malice—apparent. If he truly was the real Ace, then they'd have shared a mother, Tessa, along with sister Ainsley. He did have dark hair and blue eyes like they did.

Tons of questions immediately began forming in Grayson's mind. This stranger was his brother? Really? Could he prove it?

The maid returned to the kitchen when Asher asked and Jace said he'd like some coffee, too. Soon, they were all seated in the living room looking at one another—although Grayson noticed that Jace was also glancing at the high-quality decorations around the room.

"So tell us more," Grayson said, taking a sip of his

own coffee, forcing his hands not to tremble. This was
strange timing, that he happened to be here when this
guy arrived. Was Jace for real? Or was he just some guy
off the street who had heard about the family issue and
decided to take advantage of it?

"Well, I'd been told a little while ago that I might be
the real Ace Colton," Jace responded, "and the earthquake made me realize I'd better check it out sooner
rather than waiting any longer, before I lose any opportunity to find out." He said he had heard from a friend
who was a nurse that there was a switch of newborn babies at Mustang Valley General Hospital on Christmas
Day forty years ago—his birthday.

"My mother is Luella Smith," he said, which made
both Grayson and Asher sit up straighter. Jace explained
that he hadn't spoken to Luella in many years and didn't
know where to find her to ask questions, but from what
that he'd heard, and what he knew about his own early
life, he truly thought he could have been switched at
birth. "I'd be glad to take a DNA test," he finished. "I've
always felt there was something more to my childhood,
and I've been looking for where I belong for as long as
I can remember."

Could it be true? Well, they certainly needed to find
out.

What would Ace think about this? About this Jace
showing up and making his claims. To Grayson, Ace
was still his brother.

"Let's get everyone together here for dinner tonight,"
Asher said, "and we can see what our other siblings
think about this. Oh, and Grayson, I think it's time we
also met your lady friend that you saved from prison."

"I didn't exactly save her," he said, but he did agree

to bring Savannah to join them for a meal here that night as long as she was okay with it.

He didn't mind seeing how she fit in with his family. Not that he was ready to ask her to join it…yet. Would that time come?

And these circumstances certainly weren't the best for her to meet everyone.

Savannah had had quite a morning. There apparently hadn't been any emergencies, so she had gotten to talk with Grayson's first responder employees—Chad, with his dog Winch, Pedro and Norah. They had each told her about their specialties, pasts and how they enjoyed helping other people.

Savannah loved it! She had already been growing somewhat bored with her life, just holding events to collect contributions for the poor and needy. It was too distant and impersonal. What about doing something even more worthwhile, which could directly help people survive? Could she complete what she anticipated to be grueling physical training to become a first responder?

Or was there some way for her to just help Grayson's first responders as they helped other people?

She'd intended to discuss it more with Grayson, and he'd called her to invite her to dinner with his family tonight at their ranch.

That discussion would have to wait.

He had picked her up early at her request so she could buy a nicer outfit to feel more comfortable meeting his family.

She made a mental note of the cost and added it to the amount she'd been keeping track of to repay Grayson when she got access to her own assets.

Now they were nearly at the ranch. Grayson had told her he had related her story to one of his brothers, so he figured the rest of his siblings were now aware of it.

"Plus," he said, "that possible brother of ours is going to be there, too." Grayson had described the situation to her, including the likelihood that the man known as Ace Colton, their oldest brother, was not related to them by blood at all, and that the mysterious Jace Smith now claimed to be the real Ace.

"Do you think, then, that this is the real guy?"

"I guess we'll find out," Grayson said as he pulled in through the gate and pulled into a parking spot. near the entry to the main house. "He's agreed to a DNA test."

Would she ever want to live here? Staying overnight in Grayson's suite was okay, but more? That thought came to her as he strode beside her up the wide walkway to the front door. He didn't knock but opened it.

She was glad she had chosen a dress and heels that appeared elegant enough for this venue, a slate blue dress decorated with white flowers, short sleeved and of a flowing fabric—dressy, yet far from formal. And except for the length of her hair, she knew she looked like herself once more.

Grayson showed her through the living room to the dining room, where most of the seats were occupied. He introduced her to a lot of people, all Coltons—except the guy who was Jace Smith and still, possibly, a Colton.

Some of them had spouses or significant others there, too. Savannah was happy when she sat at Grayson's right side, and to her right were his brother Callum, with whom she understood Grayson was very close, plus his fiancée, Hazel Hart, and Hazel's adorable daughter, Evie, a five-year-old who had long brown hair and a fun, out-going personality.

The kind of daughter Savannah might wish for some-day.

And that thought caused her to look toward her left, where Grayson sat.

At that moment, he was looking in her direction, too—though not directly at her. He appeared to be ob-serving little Evie, as well.

Was he interested in having kids, too? Savannah had never asked him that.

Could she, would she, like an ongoing relationship with Grayson, including a marriage and kids? At that moment, with his family around, and with her own life a whole lot better than it had been, Savannah had to be-lieve she would, in fact, like it.

But would Grayson?

"So what do you think of my family?" Grayson whis-pered into her ear.

"They seem like nice people," she said noncommit-tally. "This is certainly different from how I was brought up. My family's a lot smaller."

"Well, maybe you need a larger one," Grayson mur-mured, then appeared to realize what he had said and took a swig of beer from the stein on the table at the far side of his salad bowl. "Or you should have had one to help you through the mess you just went through a lot better than I could help you."

Savannah was amused at his attempt to back down from what he had said—even as she began to ponder how she really would get along with his family...if.

"No one could have done better than you," was all she said.

She didn't have an opportunity to discuss what he meant any further, since it seemed his family members wanted to get to know the strangers in their midst a bit more. From Ace to attorney sister Ainsley, Rafe, twins Callum and Marlowe, and ranch foreman Asher, they all started asking her questions. Savannah concentrated on their names, wanting to remember them even if she didn't know who else they had brought to this dinner. Her mood was high, thanks to her exoneration—and she had something to announce that she hadn't yet told Grayson, either. This seemed like a good enough time to let him know.

"And it's now official," she said, looking at him. "I received a call from Police Chief Al Barco before. All charges against me have been dropped."

"I knew that," Grayson chimed in. "Barco let me know he'd told you, and it's in the media today, too."

And Savannah could only laugh as the others in the room congratulated her.

They next held a detailed conversation with Jace, who told them about a really awful childhood, where his mother was hardly present. But his attitude, at least, was good.

That led to their last major discussion of the evening—about Payne Colton, who remained in a coma. Savannah felt so sorry for him, and for all his children. She wished she could do something to help.

And maybe she could—at least a little. She would encourage Grayson to go see his dad tomorrow.

So when the time came for Grayson to bid her goodnight, she invited him into his own guestroom for a nightcap.

And more. A lot more.

* * *

What a night.

It had been enjoyable to spend time with his siblings and their significant others—and that cute little Evie.

Grayson liked kids. Did he want them someday? Yeah, quite possibly—if he ever got married.

And at the moment, after spending the night again with Savannah and having incredible, though protected, sex...

Well, marriage wasn't out of the question. He cared for her. Probably loved her.

But he recognized that, thanks to her particularly ugly divorce and what happened after that, she probably would never want to marry again.

When he left the ranch, he dropped Savannah at his office. She'd said she intended to go talk to his first responder staff again soon. Seemed like she might actually be interested in becoming a first responder, and working for him. Being with her every day like that sounded great. And maybe being with her every night, too?

The thought had definitely crossed his mind. And not just once.

But for now, he was on his way to the hospital. Savannah had urged him, after that wonderful family dinner at which his dad couldn't be present, to go visit Payne.

He'd promised to do so. And now, he was walking through the medical facility's front door again.

He had noticed the Affirmation Alliance Group's table across the street again and ignored it.

But when he ran into Selina in the lobby this time, too, he wanted to turn around and leave again. Instead, he confronted her. "Well, hello again," he said to his former stepmother. "I hope you're just leaving, since I'm coming in."

"Oh, I think you're just leaving, too," she said with a sadistic grin and started to rail at him about being a miserable son and worse—so Grayson turned his back on her and, yes, left.

But this time he didn't go to his car. Instead, he walked around the hospital till he reached another door. He went inside and hurried through the sparkling, crowded hallways, past nurses and doctors in their respective scrubs, to his father's room.

It was a private room, and the door was being watched by a private security guard hired by one of Grayson's siblings. Grayson showed his ID and was allowed in.

It was hard to look at the powerful, egocentric Payne Colton that way, lying unconscious in the hospital bed, hooked up to IVs and monitors.

"Hi, Dad," Grayson said, then sat down carefully at the edge of the bed. His father's skin was pale, his eyes closed, but at least he appeared to be breathing—with help. "Sorry I haven't spent more time here, but I've been busy." Which was true, though not much of an excuse. He talked for a while about the earthquake and helping a woman unjustly accused of a murder and more. Did his father hear any of it? He doubted it.

But Grayson found that the subject he talked most about was Savannah, how she had been framed and how her ex-husband had been at fault—and was actually a murderer himself, or at least an accessory.

The longer Grayson stayed there, the more he wanted his father to regain consciousness and talk to him. Advise him? Probably not, since they had never really agreed on much when Payne was well. But still—

Being in Payne's presence this way underscored the realization that life was too short.

Better to do everything to live it well right now.

Better to do what Grayson knew he really wanted.

He had a goal when he left.

"Bye, Dad. See you again soon."

And he meant it.

Savannah had just had another delightful time talking about First Hand First Responders with Grayson's employees. They were going on a training mission together later that afternoon, which happened often when they weren't on assignment, since they needed to remain fit and smart and skilled.

It sounded enticing to Savannah. Would she be able to undertake initial training and join them soon?

She hoped so. And if she didn't have the stamina to become a first responder like them, she was still determined to help in some way, maybe raising money for his agency so it could grow and help more people.

But at the moment she was waiting for Grayson to come back to his office and pick her up. He'd called and said he wanted to show her something early that afternoon, and she had of course agreed.

She was watching for him, though, through the window in the lobby of his office building—and saw Norah's amusement as she watched Savannah keeping an eye out for Grayson.

And then, there he was, with his car parked right in front of the building. Savannah didn't wait for him to come in. She rushed out the door and got into the passenger seat of Grayson's rental SUV. "So will you tell me now where we're going?" she asked.

"Nope. You'll see." Grayson shot her a particularly sexy grin, which made Savannah's body react, but her mind was stewing. What was this man up to?

He drove out of town and into the familiar forest. They even passed the site of the destroyed van from days earlier—though it felt like weeks ago.

"Are we going to the fishing cabin?" Savannah finally asked.

"Good guess."

"Why?" was her next question.

"You'll see," was the frustrating answer.

They soon arrived. Savannah got out of the car, as did Grayson. They entered through the window since they had locked the door when they'd left before. There was still no sign of whoever the owner was, so they had the place to themselves.

"Please sit here," Grayson said, moving Savannah's favorite chair out from under the table and taking her hand to help her into it.

Strange. She didn't need assistance, and he surely was aware of that. But she appreciated what seemed like a caring gesture.

She appreciated what came next even more.

"Savannah," Grayson said, sitting down on a chair beside her. "I would never have thought that I'd help to save a woman from being unjustly accused of murder, let alone that it would change my life so much." He was looking straight at her with his emotional blue eyes, and Savannah felt her own tear up. "But it did. And I'm glad I can help. I'm glad I met you. And I want you to stay in my life."

"Oh, Grayson." Savannah's voice choked up, so she moved forward till she stood in front of him. He rose, too, and held her tightly against him.

"You've met my family now," he continued, and she felt his chest vibrate with his words. "And though I try not to get together with them a lot, they are part of my life. They would be…well, I'm hoping you are okay with them, and will remain part of my life, too. Savannah, I love you."

He took a step back. Again he looked down at her, and she responded, "I love you, too, Grayson, Colton family ties and all. And I enjoy families. I want kids someday. Your kids."

Grayson laughed. "And I want yours, too. But, after all you went through, are you willing to trust another man?"

"Yes," she responded vehemently. "If that man is you." She tried to move even closer again, to kiss him.

But Grayson pulled away, making Savannah feel bereft. Only temporarily, though.

Grayson got down on one knee and pulled a small box from his pocket. Savannah heard herself gasp. "Is that—"

"Savannah Murphy Oliver," Grayson said, "Like I said, I love you. Will you marry me?"

Savannah nearly screamed her answer, even though, if she'd asked herself before, she'd have hesitated or worried or—

"Yes," she cried. In moments, after he placed the ring on her finger, she was in the arms of the man who had cared for her, believed in her, saved her life and her future—and now wanted to share his future with her.

"Yes, Grayson," she repeated to the man she loved. "I love you, too."

"Now that's the kind of first response I like to hear," he said, and placed his lips on hers once more.

* * * * *

Don't miss the previous volumes in
Coltons of Mustang Valley series,

Colton Family Bodyguard *by Jennifer Morey*
Colton's Lethal Reunion *by Tara Taylor Quinn*
Colton Baby Conspiracy *by Marie Ferrarella,*

Available now from Harlequin Romantic Suspense!

Next month,
check out Book 5—
In Colton's Custody *by Dana Nussio*
*and Book 6—*Colton Manhunt *by Jane Godman—*
both available in March 2020!

SPECIAL EXCERPT FROM

ⓗ HARLEQUIN

ROMANTIC SUSPENSE

*After a suspicious death on her team, environmentalist
Emma Copley knows someone needs to investigate.
When the authorities won't, she decides to do it herself,
despite Beau Kingston's warnings. He may have a
financial incentive to stop her investigation, but he
certainly doesn't want her hurt. Can they trust each
other long enough to find the real culprit?*

Read on for a sneak preview of
Deadly Texas Summer,
the latest thrilling romance from Colleen Thompson.

She looked up at him, her expression stricken. "You don't
believe me either, do you? You don't think I can prove
that Russell was on to something real."

"I'm reserving judgment," he said, keeping his words
as steady as he could, "until I see more evidence. And
you might want to consider holding back on any more
accusations until you've recovered from this shock—and
you have that proof in hand."

"Oh, I'll find the proof. I have a good idea where, too.
All I have to do is get back to the turbines as soon as
possible and find the—"

"No way," he said sharply. "You're not going out
there. You saw the email, right? About Green Horizons'
safety review?"

She gave me a disgusted look. "Of course they want to
keep everyone away. If they're somehow involved in all

this, they'll drag out their review forever. And leave any evidence cleaned and sanitized for their own protection."

"Or they're trying to keep from being on the hook for any further accidents. Either way, I said no, Emma. I don't want you or your students taking any unnecessary chances."

"I'd never involve them. Never. After Russell, there's no way I would chance that." She shook her head, tears filling her eyes. "I was—I was the one to call Russell's parents. I insisted on it. It nearly killed me, breaking that news to them."

"Then you'll understand how I feel," Beau said, "when I tell you I'm not making that call to your folks, your boss or anyone else when you go getting yourself hurt again. Or worse."

She made a scoffing sound. "You've helped me out a couple times, sure. That doesn't make me your responsibility."

"That's where you're wrong, Dr. Copley. I take everyone who lives on, works on or sets foot on my spread as my responsibility," he said, sincerity ringing in his every word, "which is why, from this point forward, I'm barring you from Kingston property."

Don't miss
Deadly Texas Summer
by Colleen Thompson

Available March 2020 wherever
Harlequin Romantic Suspense
books and ebooks are sold.

Harlequin.com

Love Harlequin romance?

DISCOVER.

Be the first to find out about promotions, news and exclusive content!

f Facebook.com/HarlequinBooks

y Twitter.com/HarlequinBooks

◉ Instagram.com/HarlequinBooks

℗ Pinterest.com/HarlequinBooks

ReaderService.com

EXPLORE.

Sign up for the Harlequin e-newsletter and download a free book from any series at **TryHarlequin.com**

CONNECT.

Join our Harlequin community to share your thoughts and connect with other romance readers!
Facebook.com/groups/HarlequinConnection

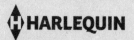

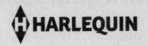
HARLEQUIN

Heartfelt or suspenseful, inspiring or passionate, Harlequin has your happily-ever-after.

With new books published every month, you are sure to find the satisfying escape you know you deserve.

HNEWS2020